SHADOWS

Further Titles by Stella Cameron from Severn House

ALL SMILES
NO STRANGER
SECOND TO NONE
SHADOWS

SHADOWS

Stella Cameron

This first world edition published 2011
in Great Britain and the USA by
SEVERN HOUSE PUBLISHERS LTD of
9–15 High Street, Sutton, Surrey, England, SM1 1DF,
by arrangement with Harlequin Books.
First published 1986 in the USA in mass market format only.

British Library Cataloguing in Publication Data

Cameron, Stella.
  Shadows.
  1. Love stories.
  I. Title
  813.5'4-dc22

  ISBN-13: 978-0-7278-8001-7 (cased)

For Jerry, with love.

The truly generous is the truly wise:
And he who loves not others,
Lives unblest. Horace

All Severn House titles are printed on acid-free paper.

Severn House Publishers support The Forest Stewardship Council [FSC],
the leading international forest certification organisation. All our titles that
are printed on Greenpeace-approved FSC-certified paper carry the FSC logo.

MIX
Paper from
responsible sources
FSC® C018575

Printed and bound in Great Britain by the
MPG Books Group, Bodmin, Cornwall.

Chapter One

Leah. Guy Hamilton concentrated on the white wine he swirled in his glass and tried the woman's name in his mind once more. Then he studied her again. Leah suited her—soft, feminine, yet not easy to forget. She would never be easy to forget.

She leaned and spoke to her husband. "Would you like something else, Charles, dear?" Her voice was low and clear. "A little more of the burnt creme, perhaps?" The man's impatient shake of the head barely acknowledged his wife's question before he returned his attention to a red-faced woman littered with diamonds.

Guy shifted uncomfortably. Leah Cornish was too far away for him to give her an unobtrusive word of comfort and help her over the awkwardness she must feel in front of those observant enough to notice the rejection.

Fortunately, most guests were too absorbed in their own conversations, but a slight flush had risen on Leah's cheeks, and there was an unnatural brightness about her intensely blue eyes. She seemed to be an island—a gorgeous, slightly overdressed island—at one end of the immense dining table. He suppressed an urge

to go to her on some pretext. As a total stranger, it
wasn't his place to interfere.

"And you come from Phoenix, Mr., ah—"

The deep, masculine voice to Guy's right startled him.

"Hamilton," he said quickly. "Guy Hamilton. Yes,
that's right. I'm visiting Wichita Falls from Phoenix."
He remembered this man from the initial introduc-
tions. A local congressman. Tall, almost as tall as himself, but thickset and swarthy. Joe Malley, or Marley.

"And the general is your brother, I understand. A
fine man. You must be very proud of him," the congressman said effusively.

Guy glanced down the table at his brother, Clark, re-
splendent in air force dress uniform. "Yes," he agreed
genuinely. "Very proud. And glad to have a chance to
spend a few days with him. Doesn't happen often." He
flexed his own shoulders uncomfortably inside the dinner jacket he'd borrowed from Clark. Too narrow
across the back, too much fabric at the waist. It would
be a blessing when this evening was over.

"What do you think of Texas?" his companion
asked.

"I like it," Guy said. "I like it very much. But I
didn't expect it to be this hot in March. Or at least not
this humid."

There was more inconsequential prattle that Guy only
half heard. He made generic noises to punctuate every
short silence. But his attention returned to Leah Cornish. At first he'd thought she was Cornish's daughter
rather than his wife. She had to be twenty-five, maybe
thirty years younger than her husband, who was an impressive, silver-haired man in a custom-tailored white
silk suit.

Charles Cornish clearly gravitated to the flashy, which probably accounted for Leah's too-frilly chiffon dress and sparkling earrings. No doubt the single huge sapphire that hovered provocatively in overly displayed cleavage was also Cornish's taste. She constantly deferred to the man, and the habit was likely to go beyond the dining room. Guy would lay a bet that Cornish chose what she wore. Fortunately, no man could alter the luster of her dark, shoulder-length hair, gently waved about an oval face, or the healthy glow of her olive skin, the perfectly bowed mouth. He blew into a clenched fist. She would feel silken—

He gritted his teeth and forced himself to face the congressman. "I'm sorry. What did you say?" Admiring a beautiful woman could be a harmless occupation but potentially dangerous when she was married. And he was hardly in a position to allow his imagination free rein on a woman—any woman.

"I was remarking on how handsome our hostess is," the man said lightly, as if reading Guy's thoughts. "Charles is a lucky devil. She adores him. I'm told she was only nineteen when he married her, and she's never looked at anyone but him."

"How old is she now?" The question was out before Guy could stop it.

"Twenty-nine, thirty, maybe. And Charles must be close to sixty. I've known them both for some years." The reply was unperturbed. "Leah seems like a bright woman from what little she says. Between you and me—" the deep voice grew more hushed "—I think Charles prefers to keep her in the background as much as possible. He's definitely a bit possessive—the age difference and so on, you know?"

He knew he shouldn't pursue the issue, but Guy couldn't help himself. "She looks even younger. Do they have children?"

"No." The man's suggestive laugh chilled Guy. "But then, maybe good old Charles gets all his kicks from looking. Imagine what that must be like, hmm?"

Guy glanced around uncomfortably, but no one appeared to have overheard the comment. He looked at Leah briefly, and the pit of his stomach tightened. The creep beside him had a point.

"Let's go out on the terrace for coffee and liqueurs, everyone," Charles Cornish boomed abruptly. "Leah, sweet, tell Martin to attend to things."

Dinner had been pronounced over. Guests pushed chairs back over glistening oak floors and began to drift outside. The congressman joined Cornish and the diamond lady, leaving Guy alone, still seated at the table. Clark, laughing at something his wife said, had clearly forgotten him. Guy checked for Leah, but she had already left.

The room was incredible—vast gilt-edged mirrors, dark oils, velvet drapes tied back with gold tassels. It was all too heavy and oppressive for the north Texas climate. He looked at an armoire, fussily inlaid with colored lacquer and gold, then allowed his attention to wander over porcelains crowded on every highly polished surface. One large wall displayed a magnificent Aubusson hanging in shades of rose and magenta. The place was a museum—everything that could be easily recognized as worth a lot was gathered together in one place to impress.

He stood up and headed outside via the hall and the front door rather than the French doors leading to the terrace. A walk by himself would give him the strength to face it all again. He wouldn't be here if he weren't Clark's visiting brother. For Clark's sake and for Miriam's, his charming wife, he'd put on a good face— after a solitary breather.

Extensive grounds surrounded the Spanish-style home. Stucco walls enclosed all that antique European splendor. Guy shook his head and grimaced. The stucco reminded him of Phoenix and his own home, but any similarity ended there. Laughter came to him in muted bursts from the other side of the house, and he set off purposefully in the direction of a shadowy grove of trees.

He passed the edge of the stand and went deeper, enjoying the evening coolness that whispered through swaying branches. Ahead he spotted a faint bluish glow. Guy stopped, squinting, then went on more slowly, noting how the eerie light intensified as he got closer. To his left, something rustled, and he stopped again, close to a tree trunk.

Someone was there, walking in the same direction but much faster and more surefootedly than he. The indistinct figure threaded a path, and Guy followed slowly, unable to overcome his curiosity.

The trees thinned abruptly, cut off in a tidy circle around a large lighted swimming pool. Incongruous. Why would the Cornishes choose to build their pool so far from the house? White chaise longues and several umbrella tables were scattered around. There was a low building, probably for showering and changing, fronted by a wet bar. The layout was traditional, if expensive, but in a very untraditional location.

Then he saw who had preceded him to the clearing. Leah Cornish stood at the pool's edge with her back to him, staring down into the water. A breeze whipped her hair into a darkly flying cloud and plastered her filmy dress to her body. Back lighting turned her curvaceous figure and long legs into a shadowy statue. She might have been nude but for the occasional billow of thin fabric.

Guy's skin turned clammy. He should go back and not intrude. She would be shocked, and probably embarrassed, if he approached her out of the darkness. He closed his eyes for an instant. At least she'd never be aware of the man she'd unknowingly aroused merely by her presence, her aura, to a level he'd chosen to suppress for years.

He stepped back, sensing her need to be alone. All this hubbub, this grandiose posturing, was suffocating her as much as it did him. He felt a sudden, intense sympathy. Unlike himself, she couldn't walk away once the party was over.

A lizard ran over his foot, and he automatically exclaimed, then held still, scarcely breathing.

Too late.

"Who's there?" Leah swung around, one hand at her throat. "Who's there? Charles, is that you? Martin?"

Guy expelled a long breath and moved into the light. "Don't be alarmed, Mrs. Cornish. Just another wanderer from the party. I didn't mean to frighten you." All he could do was approach casually until he stood a few feet away.

"Oh, yes," she said softly when he was close enough to see clearly. "Mr. Hamilton. General Hamilton's brother. I'm sorry I shouted like that." Even in shifting shadow he could tell she had paled.

"You didn't shout. But I shocked you. Sit down a minute." He indicated a chair by one of the umbrella tables. After a fractional hesitation, she did as he suggested and waved Guy down beside her.

"I saw the trees," he continued, "and couldn't resist exploring. I must admit I didn't expect to find a swimming pool. Not so far from the house."

"It's secluded," she said. "And Charles prefers me..." The sentence trailed off, and she made much of smoothing chiffon over her knees.

Guy wondered what to say next. Charles prefers her to what? he wondered. Not to be seen in a swimsuit by anyone else, probably. Or maybe Charles *preferred* her to swim nude; then the necessity for privacy would be even greater. Guy swallowed hard, vaguely shamed by his own sensual musing. Sensual and...jealous? Insanity. The muggy heat of the day must have unhinged him.

"You don't live in Wichita Falls, Mr. Hamilton?"

Strangely, her trying to carry on an exchange surprised Guy. He took a second to recover. "No, ah, no. My brother, Clark, is at Sheppard Air Force Base for a few weeks, as you know. It's the closest he's been to Phoenix, where I live, for years. I decided to make the effort to see him."

Her blue eyes met his squarely for the first time, and his belly contracted. "Do you and the general have other family?" she asked, and immediately shifted in her chair, presenting her profile. "That's not my business. I'm sorry."

"A perfectly normal question." Why was she so timid? "Our parents died some years ago. There's just Clark and me. I'm the baby who wasn't anticipated," he said, smiling. "Clark was an only child for nineteen years. And even though I've reached the ripe old age of thirty-two, he still seems to regard me as wet behind the ears."

"I know how that feels." She laughed, an unaffected, husky sound. "Charles is all I have. I'm thirty, but he definitely thinks I haven't grown up enough to make my own decisions." She pressed her lips together, then went on. "It's good to be cared about, though, isn't it?"

"Yes," Guy replied, cluing in to her need to feel right about her situation. "Of course it is."

She pulled a strand of hair from the corner of her mouth. "This is my favorite place—to hide." A mischievous glimmer took some of the guilelessness from her expression. "Unfortunately, they know where to find me. But if I can get a head start, it takes someone a while to reach me. I don't usually come here at night," she added.

"You like to be alone sometimes?"

Her lengthy indrawn breath was audible. "Frequently."

"Me, too." Guy looked sideways at her. She'd relaxed slightly and was staring at the sky, its velvety blackness pricked by a scattering of distant stars. The color of the dress, azure, suited her, and he began to wish that he, rather than the gentle breeze, could move the scalloped frills at her shoulders and neck.

"How long have you been married?" He could figure out the answer to that one but wanted to keep her talking.

"Eleven years."

"Were you born here, in Wichita Falls?"

One long, pink fingernail made absentminded patterns on the table. "Mmm."

"Your family moved away?" He was asking too many questions. Any minute now she'd replace the protective shield.

"I never had any brothers and sisters—as far as I know." She paused. "My daddy moved on someplace before I ever knew him. Mother worked in a restaurant when I was growing up. She didn't have to after Charles married me. With his help she went South then, just like she'd wanted for so long. Charles has always been so good. My mother had a chance to make a fresh start, and she took it."

Did that mean Charles Cornish paid her mother to get out of the area? "You keep in touch, though?"

"What?" She started and faced him. "Oh, with my mother? No, no. I think maybe she remarried and went to Mexico. I—we haven't corresponded since then."

"I see." But he didn't really.

Leah couldn't take her eyes from his—green eyes that glinted in the lights around the pool, depthless and looking at her as if no one else existed. Charles would wonder where she was. He'd need her to help with their guests. She ought to go.

"Do you work, Mrs. Cornish—Leah? May I call you Leah?"

The stirring inside her was wrong. She shouldn't be here.

"Leah?" he repeated.

"Please," she said. "Yes. Do call me Leah. I've never worked since I was a teenager. That's when I got married, Mr. Hamilton, and since then my husband and home have been my work. I'm not trained, you see. I can't do anything but what I do here except be a waitress. When Charles met me, I was a waitress, like my mother. I didn't even finish high school. I'm—" She

stopped, horrified. She'd almost said she was nothing.
This had been a difficult, tiring evening. Her defenses
were down. She'd already said far too much—all the
things Charles insisted she shouldn't discuss with anyone else. What was it about this man that made her
want to tell him everything?

He rested his chin on his hands. His face was only
inches away. "Everyone can do something, Leah. Particularly someone as bright and special as you."

She felt color rush to her cheeks but wouldn't drop
her head. "You don't know me, Mr. Hamilton. I assure you I'm neither very bright nor special. Just
lucky."

"Guy," he said. "If you're comfortable using my
first name, call me Guy. And you are special. I can feel
it. I would say Charles Cornish is the lucky one to have
found such a charming woman to spend his life with.
Now tell me, what did you *want* to do? Don't you ever
dream of something else? This is all very beautiful." He
made a wide gesture with one hand. "The house. The
grounds. Spectacular, in fact. But you're restless here,
incomplete."

"No, Mr. Hamilton—Guy. I have everything a
woman could want. I don't dream of anything different, and I'm not restless." She was rushing, too em-
phatic. "Not restless at all," she said more slowly. "I
really don't remember thinking about what I'd do when
I was young. There wasn't much choice. Not everyone
has a choice, and you have to accept that. What a dull
place the world would be if we were all sophisticated
and educated, don't you think?"

He was quiet for a long time. Even sitting, he towered over her. A very tall, slender man, with slightly

curly blond hair and angular features. Handsome. Too handsome to be wasting time on a married woman.

"I think it would be a shame if you were sophisticated, Leah. You're lovely the way you are. But I don't think I believe you when you say you never dream. You may think you don't, although I doubt that, too. But I wouldn't be surprised if you were *quite* a dreamer." He dropped one large-boned hand to the table, letting his fingertips rest a fraction of an inch from hers.

Leah twitched. A current seemed to jump from Guy Hamilton's body to her own. For a crazy instant she wanted to twine their fingers together.

"Well," she said at last, hating the slight tremor in her voice, "I guess I always thought I might be good at organizing things. But that sounds like a silly dream."

"No, it doesn't. Go on."

"I used to imagine being some sort of administrator. I'm good with figures and at planning things. Maybe— well, I have thought about it sometimes. Maybe I'd be useful organizing a charity or something—if Charles approved, of course. But even for that I'd have to get some more schooling."

"How old were you when you went to work?" Guy asked levelly.

She hesitated. "Seventeen—almost."

"I see. And now you run this very complicated household, with all these intimidating parties?"

"Yes."

"I suppose you have to plan menus and keep the household accounts—without having had any more education than you'd had by the time you were sixteen. Or does Charles do that, too?"

She must have imagined a sarcastic note in his voice. "No, I do it. I enjoy it—the planning part, I mean. And the accounts." Then she added, "I hate the parties," and without meaning to, laughed self-consciously.

Guy laughed, too, tipping his head, his white teeth glinting, a reflective glow almost turning his pale hair to strawberry blond. His brows were darker, arched; his nose was straight and his mouth wide and mobile.

Suddenly, he stopped laughing and looked at her. "I hate parties, too. My life is pretty quiet, thank God," he said fervently.

"What do you do?" she asked as she checked his left hand for a wedding band and found none. Her nostrils flared with irritation at herself. It wasn't her business. Nothing about him was her business.

Guy didn't answer immediately, and when he did, he seemed slightly awkward. "My work isn't very glamorous, I'm afraid. I'm in public service."

"Oh." Leah didn't know what that meant but couldn't bring herself to pry further. She noted the way his dinner jacket pulled across the shoulders. Probably a loaner from his brother. The cuffs and the collar of his immaculately white shirt were a little worn, too. Intuition told her he was unconscious of his dress rather than too poor to spend more on clothes. This wasn't a man who cared much about impressing people. Unlike Charles. She squashed the disloyal notion at once.

The wind picked up, whisking her skirt high off her thighs. She fought with the dress, loathing its little-girl flounces even more now than when Charles had brought it home and insisted she wear it tonight. A glance at Guy confirmed what she'd suddenly felt—he was looking appreciatively at her legs. The flash of exhilaration that seared her was out of line, but she reveled in the satisfaction it brought.

She shivered, from excitement rather than the unexpectedly chill air, and stood. "Duty calls," she said, pleased with her steady tone. "I must get back."

"I'll come with you," Guy said, immediately at her side. "You're shivering. Here, put my jacket on. I'm always too hot, and the thing doesn't fit, anyway."

"Thank you." Without a second thought, she let him drape the jacket around her shoulders. He made no attempt to prolong the contact beyond what was absolutely necessary. "Thank you," she repeated, and looked up into those limpid green eyes—gentle but fantastically sexy.

"You're very welcome." He was slightly behind her, his head inclined. She saw the way his lips parted a fraction and felt her own do the same.

"Ah, there you are, Leah. What the hell—"

Charles Cornish, plainly out of breath, broke into the clearing and spoke to Leah, apparently before noticing Guy behind her.

She moved quickly to her husband's side. "I needed a little break, Charles, dear. You know how I get with all those people sometimes. You shouldn't have worried. I was just coming back."

"Yes," he said slowly. "So I see. I'm glad you had company for your *little break*. Mr. Hamilton, isn't it?"

Guy strode confidently in front of the man. "Guy Hamilton, sir. Clark's brother. Your wife was kind enough to allow me to share her oasis for a few minutes." He noted a fine film of sweat on the older man's skin. Pale blue eyes flicked over every inch of him, then darted to the dinner jacket around Leah's shoulders.

"Leah is a perfect hostess. She learned well," he said unctuously. "Cold, my love? Let's get you back to the house for a wrap. Here." He tossed the jacket to Guy. "Thank you for your concern."

In a gesture that was too studied not to be deliberate, he put an arm across Leah's back and under her arm, pulling her to him in such a strong, possessive move that the shaded valley at the neck of her dress deepened.

Guy met Leah's eyes and saw the distress there. Her husband was laying claim to what was his, making sure there could be no misunderstanding. The emotion that shook Guy came as an unfamiliar and totally unexpected jolt—hate. He hated Charles Cornish. For the first time in his adult life he longed to smash a fist into another human being's face.

Their progress back to the terrace was leisurely. Cornish kept his grip on Leah and talked about things of little interest to Guy. Oil, investments, tips on the market—only topics related to money and its accumulation. Guy answered as intelligently as he could and tried not to glance at the woman walking between them.

The rest of the evening passed in an uncomfortable blur. He watched Leah confer often with a white-coated waiter carrying a silver tray who threaded skillfully between groups of guests and artfully placed potted plantings on the red-brick terrace. She moved from one cluster of chairs to another, leaning to ask if her guests were comfortable but never making conversation— more like a waiter herself than the hostess. She avoided Guy. Once or twice their eyes met and held; then she lowered her lids or turned away. She must be exhausted, he thought, and afraid of what that man would say or do later. He ached for her, and the constant inner reminder that he hardly knew Leah Cornish did not help.

"General, Mrs. Hamilton?"

The sound of Leah's husky Southern voice startled him. He was sitting with Clark and Miriam, and Leah had come to stand solicitously at his brother's elbow. "Are you comfortable?" she asked, not looking at Guy. "Can I get you something? Mrs. Hamilton, would you like a wrap?"

Miriam declined, but as Leah turned away, Guy saw how the skin stretched tight around her mouth, the fatigue in every feature.

Disregarding her attempt to pull away, he clasped her wrist and brought her ear to his lips. "We probably won't meet again, little one. But I'll think of you—and your dream. If you ever decide you want to try your hand at some of that organizing you talked about, you can come and organize me. I could sure use it." He let her go, but she didn't move immediately. "Don't lose yourself completely. You *are* special," he added.

Without a word, she straightened and walked away.

Chapter Two

The clock on Leah's bedside table read six o'clock when she awoke. She rolled to squint through open drapes at a silvery sky streaked with early-morning wisps of lemon and pink. It would be another beautiful May Saturday—too hot for comfort by noon but cool enough now, and cooler again once the sun went down.

Briskly, she climbed from bed and selected aqua shorts and a matching sleeveless polo shirt from her closet. Barefoot, she entered her plant-strewn bathroom with its glass bubble dome open to the sky.

Often, she luxuriated in the circular sunken tub and stared up at the shifting clouds by day or the stars at night. A quick shower would fill her needs now. She intended to spend time in the greenhouse among her orchids before lunching with Charles. Dear Charles. He'd given her all this, and she'd always be grateful.

Deliberately, she chose to keep the shower water invigoratingly tepid. It beat on her upturned face, her shoulders and breasts, making her skin tingle. She soaped vigorously and rinsed, then washed her hair quickly. Only when she twisted off the faucets did she linger. Again, as it had every day for weeks, sometimes many times a day, Guy Hamilton's face came to her mind—and his odd little invitation the night they had met: "...you can come and organize me..."

He'd been joking, and she was a fool. An ungrateful, dreamy fool, old enough to know better. He'd said she was a dreamer. Damn. Sex, or the lack of it, shouldn't be enough to turn a sensible woman into a preoccupied romantic.

But it wasn't a desire for sex that made her long to see those green eyes. Oh, yes, the thought of that tall, hard body wrapped around hers in the great lonely bed no man entered anymore was appealing. But more than that, Leah yearned to have Guy look at her again, ask questions, listen—just talk to her again. For a while, by the pool, in the soft blue light that paled into a dark sky, she'd felt as if their minds touched. *Forget it,* she ordered herself fiercely.

When she flapped downstairs in her thongs, Leah heard the familiar sounds of Jewel clanging about in the kitchen. The smell of freshly brewed coffee and home-baked cinnamon rolls wafted along the hall.

Leah batted open the swinging kitchen doors. "Morning, Jewel," she said brightly, and went to bend over the dark-haired cook, who worked at the sink. Sun from the high windows shot blue highlights into her long braids.

"Good morning, Mrs. Cornish."

Leah made a face behind the woman's back. The banging pots should have alerted her. Jewel was in a formal mood today. Probably had a fight with her hot-tempered husband, Sam. Leah only became "Mrs. Cornish" to Jewel when the cook was in a sour mood.

Surrounded by brilliant blue-and-green mosaic tiles and light oak cabinets, Leah felt the usual warm glow that inevitably came in this, her favorite room in the house. With satisfaction, she surveyed her hanging plants and the little troughs of cacti along the window-sill. Her green thumb was legendary among the staff. Even Charles seemed to take pride in her ability to grow just about anything.

She returned her attention to Jewel. "The cinnamon rolls smell fantastic, as usual," she tried.

A "Hmmph" was her reward.

"Coffee, too. Join me for a cup?"

Unable to ignore her mistress after a direct question, Jewel withdrew her plump arms from mountains of suds and wiped them on a towel. "I guess," she said flatly. "But I'd better lay off the rolls."

Leah lifted one eyebrow as she filled two brown pottery mugs to their brims with coffee. "On a diet? Not you, Jewel. I didn't think you believed in skinny women." Her own lack of what Jewel termed "extra meat" was a constant battle between them. Even more so in the past few weeks, when Leah had become thinner.

Jewel was Indian, short, well-built, with classic features. Now her high cheekbones flamed. "That Sam. One of these days I'm going to turn *him* in on a new model."

"Meaning?" Leah swallowed a laugh.

"He told me I was dumpy. *Dumpy.* Said I was too young for middle-aged spread but I'd already spread too far to go back. He said if I didn't watch it, he'd find himself some slim young thing instead."

"And?" She was going to laugh. "And what did you say to him, Jewel? *Before* he told you off?"

Jewel dropped into a bentwood chair. "Nothing."

"Jewel—"

"Well, I told him the beer was giving him a belly and no woman finds it sexy to go to bed with a man whose belly hangs over his belt."

Leah sat down with a thump in a peacock-backed rattan chair and drew up her knees. "You're something," she said through tears of laughter. "You tell that tall, handsome husband of yours he's not attractive, then get mad when he strikes back."

"It's not funny," the cook said icily.

"It certainly is. He wouldn't change you for the world. You go home tonight with a flower behind your ear and a smile on your face and tell him how much he turns you on. And that's an order."

"Miss Leah! I'm old enough to be your mother, and we shouldn't be talking about these things."

Leah got up and threw her arms around the woman's neck, wishing for an instant that this warm soul were her mother. "I always come to you, Jewel, and you give me advice. Why can't I give you some? Particularly when I'm right?" She held up a palm to stop the woman's retort. "I am right, aren't I?"

"I guess so," Jewel said reluctantly. "As usual. But just let that—"

The sound of the doorbell cut off the rest of the sentence. A wire tapped into a box in the kitchen carried the muted ring.

Leah glanced at the clock beside the window. Seven-fifteen. "Who would come to the front door at this hour, Jewel? Are you expecting a delivery?"

"No, miss. And it would be to the back door, anyway. You stay here and I'll get it."

"*You* stay here. It's probably someone with car trouble or something," she finished lamely.

As Leah crossed the wide hall, she glanced upstairs. Charles would still be asleep in the room across the corridor from her own. He always slept late after a night on the town, and there had been more and more of those in the last two years, since he'd been unable—She shunned finishing the thought and reached the door. At least she knew her rivals were cards and booze, not other women, she acknowledged wryly.

She peered through the small peephole and saw two men in uniform—blue-gray with a stripe down each well-creased pant leg. Gold badges glinted. Police.

Carefully, she unbolted the door, leaving the chain in place, and pulled it open a crack. "What do you want?" she asked, an odd knot in her stomach. Could it be something to do with her mother?

"Mrs. Cornish?" one man asked politely. She nodded, and he flashed an identification badge at her. "Officers Landon and Garth. State patrol. May we have a few words with you?"

Leah studied the card until the words ran together.

"Miss Leah, what is it?" Jewel came beside her, peered out at the two men, then slid off the chain and opened the door wide. "Is there trouble?" she said, putting an arm around a trembling Leah. When there was no reply, she stepped back, waving the officers inside.

"I'm Officer Garth," the taller man said, taking off his hat. "Is there someplace private we could talk to Mrs. Cornish? A place where she could sit down?"

Jewel nodded toward the stairs. "Miss Leah, maybe I should get—"

"No!" Leah said, suddenly very alert. "Follow me, please. We'll talk in the kitchen, if you don't mind. There's less chance of being interrupted out there." She was already wondering where the police car was parked and if Charles would see it from his window. He hated scenes. "Jewel, will you come with me?"

She half expected the policemen to protest about an audience, but they followed Jewel without a word.

Once in the kitchen, the other officer took charge. "Landon, ma'am." He smoothed thinning red hair with a flattened palm. "When was the last time you spoke with your husband?"

"Spoke with Charles?" Leah said, puzzled. "I—I'm not sure. What are you saying? Please don't drag this out. Just get to the point."

"I will." He remained polite. "But would you sit down, please."

"I'd rather stand."

Landon opened his mouth, but Officer Garth silenced him with a shake of the head. "Very well, Mrs. Cornish," Landon continued. "Do you know where your husband was last night?"

Leah gaped at Jewel, who turned pale under her bronze skin. "Well—I. He was out. But that's not unusual. I can't tell you his exact location. I'm sure he'll be glad to give you that." What had happened? Had Charles gotten drunk again and into some sort of trouble this time? Maybe he'd quibbled with the wrong person over one of his gambling things. Leah knew nothing about gambling.

The policemen were staring at each other, clearly nonplussed. Landon cleared his throat. "I take it you aren't in the habit of waiting up for your husband.

Immediately, Leah felt defensive. *Until four or five or eight in the morning?* she wanted to retort. Loyalty made her study her painted toenails and mumble, "No."

"Does he sometimes not arrive home until after—say, after this time?" Landon checked his watch. "It's almost seven-thirty, ma'am."

"That's not unusual," Leah managed.

Jewel rubbed her back. "Shouldn't I get Mr. Cornish?"

"Mrs. Cornish," Officer Landon interrupted. "I wish I could soften this for you, but I can't. Your husband's car went off the road just outside town sometime last night or early this morning. He drove straight into a river. His body was found around five, facedown in two feet of water. There'll have to be an autopsy, of course, and I shouldn't say this, but I think you deserve to know. There was an open whiskey bottle in the car. It looks pretty obvious he was too drunk to walk to shore and couldn't get up once he fell over. From on-the-spot observation I'd say he probably hit his head trying and that's what killed him."

Leah slid slowly into a chair. "Charles is upstairs—in bed."

She heard Jewel crying, saw the blur of pale blue, the flash of gold and faces bobbing around her. Then, shaking free of hands that tried to restrain her, she leaped from the chair and dashed through the house, up the stairs, along the corridor, and burst into Charles's room. He must be there. He was always there. Charles had been there for her since she was a lost kid, living from hand to mouth with a mother who brought home and slept with every man who had a few dollars in his jeans.

"Charles," she shouted, and ran to his smoothly made bed. "Charles, where are you?" Leah sank to her knees and buried her face in the nubby weave of the spread. "Where are you, damn it?" He'd promised to guard her forever, to keep the past away.

When the sobbing started, she screwed her eyes shut and crawled into a tight ball on the bed. She never remembered how long it took for the blackness to come.

STUCCO WALLS GLISTENED warmly in the midday sun. Leah parked in the driveway and walked around to let herself into the house through the kitchen. There was already a lockbox on the front door.

Several inches of cold coffee still stood in the pot. She poured it into a mug and set it in the microwave to heat. Was it really a month since Charles died? She looked around the kitchen, and her eyes filled with tears. How different this day was from the one she'd begun right here, with Jewel, a few weeks ago.

Jewel was gone. So were the cascading plants—and the glow of life in a prosperous home. Jewel had easily found work in another house on the far side of Wichita Falls. Martin, the butler, too. The plants had died. After her final interview with Charles's lawyers this morning, Leah felt Jewel and Martin were the only ones around here who weren't beyond hope on this baking June day.

In the rosewood-paneled chambers of Lapwood and Enders, her sentence had been delivered by a man who had once played golf with Charles. Her lips had quivered slightly as Max Enders explained her reduced circumstances. He finished, in a voice that broke with mock emotion, by saying how very sorry he was.

The buzzer on the microwave sounded, and Leah straightened. Damn it. She wouldn't give up. So Charles had steadily squandered a huge fortune. So she couldn't even expect more than a very meager inheritance after the sale of the house. So what if Charles had already used his life insurance as collateral against loans. She was Leah Bennett Cornish, survivor. And she *would* survive.

With coffee in hand, she marched into the living room and shoved aside a white sheet to make a space to set down the mug on a shiny black table.

The wall hangings and the paintings were gone. She'd never liked them, anyway. What was left of the furniture had been shrouded. Still. All still. The faint musty odor of disuse sickened her.

Dust motes danced in a shaft of light from the French windows. Leah walked to peer outside. The white iron furniture was stacked around pots of drooping plants. She could have watered those.

For an instant she thought she heard laughter. Closing her eyes, she imagined the groups of animated guests—Martin, in his white jacket, balancing a silver tray, and Charles, immaculately impressive, holding court.

He'd been a good man—most of the time. A laugh bubbled up in her throat. For years he'd been this town's leading light. Most of the fine people of Wichita Falls never knew until after his death that he'd become one of the wildest drinkers and gamblers this side of the county line. They would never know he'd also been impotent for the last two years of his life. Leah would preserve that final dignity for the man who had never once brought up her own shaky beginnings.

Although possessive—sometimes suspicious and jealous—he had loved her. And she would always believe it had been his impotence that finally broke him.

She'd spent her last night in this house. Her own pile of bags and boxes stood in the hall. When she'd finished the coffee, she would pack her possessions into the Porsche, which must be traded for something cheaper, and head for the room she'd rented downtown.

Tomorrow she'd start looking for work. And there would be no point expecting help from any of the many people who had enjoyed her own and her husband's hospitality or Charles's business influence. They'd disappeared with the discovery that Charles had been on the verge of bankruptcy when he died. A penniless widow was of no interest. She wouldn't even look good on some magnanimous soul's charity record. Leah laughed mirthlessly.

She fumbled in her purse for the keys to her car, and her fingers closed on a stiff envelope. Her scalp prickled as she withdrew the note. "Leah Cornish." Without looking, she visualized the simple script on the envelope—her name and address. She knew by heart the words on the card inside: "I'm so sorry, Leah. I hardly know what else to write. All the stuff in the newspapers shocked and hurt me—for you. But don't let it take everything away from what your husband was. We can all slide off the tracks—too easily. In time he'd have found his way back. If I can help in any way, let me know. Guy Hamilton."

Leah slid out the card and sank slowly onto a covered couch to read it for the hundredth time. A cloud of dust rose around her, tickling her nose. Guy Hamilton, a man who, unlike many, owed Charles nothing, gave him the kindest eulogy. He would help her, too. She was sure of it without knowing why. If only he weren't in another state. He wouldn't pass her by on the street as if she were a stranger, as others had in the past few weeks. And these were the people she'd have to go to for a job.

There were no friends for her in this town, no prospects, nothing. And nothing was what she could easily end up with—again. When Charles died, Leah had also lost the respect his wealth and power had bought. Very few of their acquaintances were unaware of her rocky beginnings. The whispering had already begun. Men looked at her speculatively, women with suspicious contempt. They saw her as an opportunist who married a man many years her senior for his money alone. Now they expected her to hunt for a replacement. A pool of nausea formed in her stomach. Despite his weaknesses, Charles *had* been a good and special man. His memory shouldn't be distorted.

A light crack sounded against the window, and she glanced up, only to see a single locust hover at a pane. Its fat tan body and transparent wings trembled as the creature recovered from the blow; then it flew away.

Leah sighed and stuffed Guy's card back in her bag. She was trembling, too, deep inside and trying to recover. It might be more difficult for her than for the locust.

The bags and boxes filled the trunk and back seat of the Porsche. Leah was sweating, her palms raw, by the time she'd finished hauling everything through the back door and out to the driveway. Eleven years of being Mrs. Charles Cornish, waited on in everything, had made her soft. Those days were over, and she'd have to toughen up once more.

When the last piece of luggage had been stowed, she carefully locked the kitchen and replaced the key under the mat, smiling at how some things never changed. Jewel, Martin, herself—and how many others knew that key was always there?

She hesitated beside her car and shaded her eyes to gaze across an open expanse of flat, sandy ground to the west, where a sullen band of yellow haze hovered above the land. Since her marriage, this had been the view from her bedroom window, and she'd miss its comforting familiarity. Her two-room apartment would overlook a supermarket from the front and a brick wall from the back. She took a last look at the house, feeling for the first time totally separated from its security.

A rhythmic clacking in the scrubby grass nearby sent her scurrying inside the car. A rattlesnake had come out to bask in the pitiless sun its kind loved so much.

She started the powerful engine and swung onto the highway, but only went a few hundred yards before stopping again. "If you ever decide you want to try your hand at some of that organizing..." Had he meant it? Did she dare call his bluff and find out?

Her chest expanded slowly, then she allowed air to hiss through her pursed lips. An almost-breathless sense of daring filled her. She was about to do something she'd never done before, to take an enormous risk on the basis of her own intuition. Too bad the deposit she'd paid on the apartment would be forfeited. She couldn't afford to waste money, but she didn't want to stay in Wichita Falls anymore.

After a swift U-turn, she headed west. Phoenix was almost due west; she knew that much. Organizing was exactly what she felt like. That and some new faces—and a familiar one.

Get there. Check into a motel and call Guy. He'd help her find a job and get started. He'd talked about being in public service—whatever that meant. Maybe there was something in his operation for her. Regardless, she felt deep inside that he wouldn't turn her away flat.

The little car ate miles. Charles had always made sure
it was kept in perfect condition, and this was its first
really long run. She loved the vehicle. Wistfully, she remembered how Charles had given it to her, making an
issue of its being totally hers, her possession, her toy.

Leah drove straight through the rest of the day and
into the night, stopping occasionally for large cups of
black coffee. Once she pulled into a rest area and dozed
for an hour before setting off again.

Sunday's first hour had slid past as she punished the
now filthy white Porsche across the state line from New
Mexico into Arizona and zeroed in on her destination.

She reached Phoenix at 7:00 A.M.—too early to call
anyone, least of all a man who wasn't expecting her.

Too tired and too dirty to search for more than a
clean and adequate motel, Leah settled for the Salt
River Stopover. She showered, set her travel alarm for
ten and crawled gratefully into bed. The chances of
catching Guy at home on Sunday should be good. His
telephone number had been scribbled on the top of his
card. As if he really had hoped she'd contact him, she
thought comfortably, when she began to drift.

THE PHONE RANG twelve times. Leah hung up and
paced the shabby little room. She'd tried Guy's number twice without success, but it was only eleven-ten.
This time she'd force herself to wait longer.

A few minutes after twelve, she dialed again. One,
two, three... He wasn't going to be there. For the first
time since she left Texas, she felt vague panic. What on
earth had made her drive all those miles on nothing
more concrete than a chance invitation—probably
meant as a joke—and a sympathy card?

"Hello."

At the sound of his voice, she almost dropped the phone. Her mouth dried out completely.

"Hello," he repeated in the same low, soft tone.

Leah cleared her throat. "Guy?" she said in a whisper. "It's me." Immediately, she flushed. She was acting like a silly kid. How was he supposed to know who "me" was?

"Leah?" There was a pause, and she heard him expel a breath. "Leah Cornish, is that you?"

Her heart made a slow roll. He'd remembered her voice. "Yes, Guy," she said breathlessly. "Leah. I'm here in Phoenix. I drove all night. Remember how you said I could come and help you if I wanted to— Well, I need a job, and I know you probably don't have one for me, but I thought maybe—"

"Whoa." He stopped her headlong rush of words. "Back up and start again. No, on second thought, don't. I heard you. Give me time to absorb it all."

Leah felt sick. Sick enough to throw up. He wasn't just surprised to hear her; he was shocked. This was a terrible mistake.

"I shouldn't have done this," she started.

"No—yes," he cut in. "Of course you should. Where are you? I'll come and get you."

"It was a silly thing to do. I just didn't know what I was going to— There wasn't anyone—" Her voice cracked. She mustn't start crying, but she was so tired and alone. "Forget I contacted you, please, Guy. It was good to hear you again. Good—"

"*Don't* hang up," he ordered, suddenly commanding, as if he felt her confusion. "Give me your address and I'll be right over."

Quietly, Leah told him where she was staying and listened while he calculated that it would take him about twenty minutes to get there.

They both hung up, and for several seconds she sat numb, watching the wall. What would he think of her? What would any man think of a woman who came so obviously chasing after him? How could he possibly understand that she simply needed someone, anyone, who would offer a hand in friendship?

Twenty minutes! In a sudden wild frenzy, Leah went into action. She dragged out a gauzy cotton sundress that didn't show packing wrinkles and slipped it on. The light peach color accentuated her deep tan and the smoothness of her skin. She found matching flat sandals and then turned her attention to a face that showed definite signs of exhaustion.

Makeup helped disguise dark areas of fatigue beneath her eyes. Brighter than usual lip gloss drew attention to her mouth—and, she hoped, away from lines of tiredness. She was brushing her hair, glad of its shimmering quality, when a knock came at the door.

Her heart stopped, and to play for a few more seconds, she rummaged for perfume and sprayed her wrists and throat.

There was another knock, a little louder this time.

With her pulse thundering in her ears, Leah approached the door. "Guy?" she asked, already knowing the answer.

"The same," he replied, and she heard that wonderful hint of laughter in his voice.

She flung open the door and stepped back to let him in.

He came hesitantly, his green eyes, flecked in the daylight with brown, searching her face. "How are you,

Leah?'' Long, tanned fingers touched her jaw fleetingly.

All she could do was stare.

Guy Hamilton wore black—short-sleeved black shirt and black pants. And at his neck was a stiff white clerical collar.

Chapter Three

He closed the door behind him and grasped her shoulders tightly. "Oh, Leah," he said quietly. "This must all have been such a nightmare for you. Let's sit down."

She couldn't move. A priest. Guy Hamilton, the man she now silently admitted to fantasizing about all these weeks, was a priest. A swell of bemused shame mushroomed in her.

"What is it?" he said when she failed to answer. He held her chin between finger and thumb to stop her from turning away.

"Nothing," she lied, avoiding his eyes. "Nothing." Inside she was slowly crumbling.

"I don't believe you. You're tired—exhausted, obviously. And you've been through too much. But there's something else, isn't there? Something I don't know. Are you ill?"

She looked at him squarely, pressing her lips together, and let her gaze travel over his garb. "I'm not ill. I'm fine. What do I call you? Father Hamilton or just plain Father? I guess I should have given more thought to what 'public service' meant."

Guy's brows came together fractionally; then his expression cleared, and he began to laugh. He draped an arm around her shoulders and walked her to the room's only chair before perching himself on the side of the rumpled bed.

As he continued to watch her and laugh, Leah felt a spark of irritation pierce her tired confusion.

"Feel like sharing the joke?" she said at last, running out of patience.

He sobered with visible effort. "It's you." He chuckled, then ran a forefinger around the collar. "And this. You saw the collar, and it immediately spelled priest—Catholic priest. Right?"

"Right," she agreed.

"Well, I'm not."

She stared at him disbelievingly. "You mean you're masquerading as a priest? That's awful."

He threw himself flat on the bed and roared. "No, you naive woman. I'm not masquerading as anything. You happened to catch me in my Sunday best. I'm a minister. Just not Catholic. Is *that* okay? And would it matter to you if I was, anyway?"

With the last question he turned serious eyes on her and waited. Leah felt a dull flush creep up her neck to her cheeks. She could pretend all she liked, but they'd both felt a spark of something more than platonic interest pass between them. In Texas and today.

She sighed deeply. "Of course it's okay. And it shouldn't matter if you were, I suppose. It's just that they seem to have an aura that says, 'Stay away,' and I suddenly felt foolish, as though I'd been too familiar." An insistent pain had begun to nag at both temples. She'd taken about as many shocks as she could handle.

"So. Now that that's out of the way, we can be friends again?" he asked with disarming frankness.

"Friends," Leah said, and immediately wondered why he should want an albatross like her for a 'friend. He ought to wish her as far away from him as possible.

He sat up and eyed her critically. "You're beat, friend."

"It shows, huh?" She massaged her temples. "I should never have come bolting in on you like this, Guy. It was just a crazy, spur-of-the-moment urge. I'll have to stick around a day or two to get my wind back. Then I guess I'll head for—" She stopped and frowned.

"You were going to say home?" Guy suggested. "Only you aren't sure where that is anymore, are you?"

The truth hurt. "Texas is home—Wichita Falls. Where else?" Tears stung her eyes, and she tipped her head to stop them from falling.

"No," Guy said softly. "For people like you and me, people with no close family, home is wherever you can make it feel right. Preferably a place where there's a friend or two, or even just a reason to be there—because you're needed, maybe."

She was going to cry, damn it. "And people need you here, Guy. That's why it's your place." She sniffed. Even blinking rapidly wasn't helping.

"And I need you." He was on his knees, pressing her head into his hard shoulder. "Once I said I needed organizing, and boy is it true. You wouldn't believe what a mess I can make of a ledger in no time flat. No one I hire to help stays more than a day or two. They throw up their hands and march off, wild-eyed and muttering. Maybe you're the one who can do the job. Think so?" Leaning away, he glanced at her tear-drenched cheeks before holding her face against his neck. "Cry as much as you need to. Then we'll start sorting things out."

Reluctantly, willing her senses not to riot at the feel, the clean smell of him, Leah eased from his embrace and found a tissue in her bag. "You're just being kind. It's all you know how to be."

"No way." He held up one hand. "Scout's honor, lady. If you hadn't showed up, I'd have had to put an ad in the local paper for a clerical assistant who doubles as a part-time housekeeper and sifted through another raft of applicants. And it would probably be hopeless in the end, just like it always is. Keeping me straight is more than anyone's managed so far."

She tried to smile, then winced. "I've got to get some aspirin." Another search in her voluminous shoulder bag produced a small tin. Guy had brought a glass of water from the bathroom before she'd finished wrestling open the container of pills.

"Just the thought of working for me gives you a headache," he said, smiling ruefully. "I don't blame you. But remember, you'll be free to quit, just like the rest, if I drive you mad."

A tiny shaft of hope began to live in Leah. "You really think I'd be able to help? I can't even type. And I already told you how little schooling I've had."

"You can hunt and peck at the typewriter—you'll soon learn. And if you could run that enormous house and give intimidating parties like—" He stopped. "I'm sorry," he said solicitously. "Bad choice of subjects."

"It's all right. I've got to get used to talking about all that. Just not yet, I guess."

"You need to rest." Suddenly, he was all business. "But not here. We have to find you a place to live—somewhere convenient to the church—and after you've had a long sleep, I'll help you get settled in. My people are nice—good people, you'll see. They'll help you as

best they can. They may even help more than you want
sometimes.''

He half turned away but faced her again, abruptly. ''I
know exactly where you can live. Wally Timmons has
an upstairs apartment in his house. Converted it after
his wife died. He rents it out, and it's empty right now.
Wally's retired, but he does odd jobs for me. Great old
guy. Needs a bit of company more than the money—
just to feel someone else is coming and going. That'd be
perfect, if you like the place.'' His expression became
dubious. ''It's not what you're used to, though. Very
small and a bit spartan.''

Leah got up on wobbly legs. ''I like small,'' she insisted. ''And I love spartan. Does it have a bed?''

Guy nodded, smiling faintly, and eased her back into
the chair. ''We'll go right over. I don't need to call; he's
always around somewhere. If it's okay, even for a while,
you can do what you've got in mind. Sleep the clock
around.''

Through drooping eyelids, she watched his tall frame
bend to heft her suitcase onto the bed. He opened it,
toured the room to gather her possessions and tucked
them inside. He glanced around. ''Did I get everything?'' When she nodded, he closed the case and offered her his hand.

Outside, he settled her in the passenger seat of the
Porsche. His own vehicle was a battered jeep parked in
front of the office. He would come back for it, he insisted. He also insisted on settling her bill so she
wouldn't have to move again, assuring her, when she
argued, that she could repay him later.

Leah took little notice of the sprawling modern city
they crossed or the mountain Guy pointed out in the
distance as Camelback, because it resembled a reclin-

ing, blue-gray camel against the cloudless sky. The land was flat, seeming more so as they entered another suburb. Beyond houses that snaked along the road lay sandy plains dotted with pinkish rock outcroppings and plants she couldn't quite make out. Mostly cacti, Guy informed her—interesting but not as spectacular now as they would be when the desert bloomed in early spring.

Bougainvillea, iridescent purple and white, spilled over a nearby wall. Leah sat straighter. Perhaps there'd be a chance to raise unusual plants again. On a corner stood a giant saguaro, its fat arms raised like upturned hooks on a coat stand. She liked Arizona, Leah decided, then slumped back in her seat. What difference did it make whether or not she liked it? She probably wouldn't stay long.

Wally Timmons was at home and delighted at the prospect of a new tenant. A thin, grizzled old man, Wally accepted without comment Guy's explanation that Leah was a good friend, soon to be his own new assistant.

The tiny apartment could be entered via a winding metal staircase at the side of the house and consisted of one large room with a couch that made into a bed, a kitchenette behind folding doors and a turquoise-and-lavender tiled bathroom. Leah instantly loved almost every cramped corner on sight, particularly the jutting bay window and sharply apexed ceiling. She tried not to look too hard at the garish bathroom tile.

They agreed on a rent that seemed ridiculously low to Leah, but at Guy's warning shake of the head, she stopped arguing with Wally. She and Guy hadn't discussed salary yet, but it wasn't likely to be much. She could turn out to be worth nothing as far as either of them knew; then she'd have to find other work. There were restaurants in every town, and she knew she could manage in one of those. Meanwhile, her skimpy funds might have to stretch a long way. In the next few days she'd contact Max Enders with her new address. He'd promised at least a small sum when all Charles's debts were settled. As soon as possible, she must trade the Porsche.

When Wally Timmons had left them alone, Guy carried up all Leah's luggage and stacked it tidily inside the door. He opened the couch, found linen in a closet and started making up the bed.

"I can do that," Leah protested.

Guy waved a dismissive hand. "No, you can't. Sit down. I'll get my pound of flesh out of you later."

"I feel like an absolute pest," Leah said, and yawned. "Absolute pest."

"Right," Guy said in a soothing voice. "A sleepy absolute pest." He finished and checked the air-conditioning thermostat. Apparently satisfied, he pulled out the suitcase she'd taken into the motel. "Can you manage if I open this and leave you?"

A little snuffle made him glance around. She was asleep and gradually sliding sideways in an upright chair. He crossed swiftly to gather her in his arms and deposit her on the sofa bed. The sundress was light enough; it wouldn't hurt if she slept in it. He slipped off her sandals and lifted her head a few inches to settle it more comfortably on the pillow. She sighed but didn't stir.

Guy sat beside her and smoothed damp tendrils of dark hair away from her face. Immediately, he remembered how the breeze had fanned it as he'd watched her beside the pool in Wichita Falls. Since that night, he'd visualized her again and again and made love to her in his mind— He covered his face. Not now. There would probably never be a right time for that. She was a grieving widow who'd come to him for solace, nothing more. Leah had no family, no friends; she'd made that clear. It was up to him to be both if he could.

She moved, rolling over on one side, and pulled up her knees. Guy smiled. She probably always slept like that. His smile slowly faded. Behind her knees, smoothly tanned skin curved over firm muscle. There was something so fascinating about that little area at the back of a beautiful woman's thigh. His gut tightened painfully. If she slept in his arms, she would curl against him that way, their bodies molded together, his hand over her breast.

With more force than he intended, he stood and moved away. This was don't-touch time. It would probably always be that. In her grief and loneliness it was possible she might come to him for physical comfort, but that would be wrong—and out of the question, anyway. It was his responsibility to make sure nothing happened between them.

He studied her carefully. She'd lost weight. She'd been through some tough times. There was an almost-childlike quality to her form, a defenselessness, that made him want to take care of her. But that wasn't what she was going to need. After too many years of suffocating care, Leah Cornish needed to become self-sufficient. If he could help her do that, he'd have been successful. Maybe then there would be a time to think about a different relationship.

Careful not to let the door slam, Guy let himself out. As usual, it was hot as hell in this almost-seasonless city he'd made his home. He liked it. Fortunately, Leah must like the heat, too—another plus. He grinned in self-derision. Regardless of his fine principles, he wasn't going to find it easy to keep his distance from her.

TWO WEEKS. Leah pushed the creaky old chair away from her desk and surveyed her new domain. She'd already been installed as the new clerical assistant at St. Mark's for two weeks. Unbelievable. And everyone had been so friendly and helpful, just as Guy had predicted.

She stood and stretched. Since eight that morning she'd only left the desk to go to the bathroom. It was four in the afternoon, and she hadn't even had lunch.

Leah didn't care whether or not she'd eaten. A satisfied glow swept over her. In two weeks she'd managed to transform this bulging little room from total confusion into some sort of ordered chaos. Another week or so and it would be totally habitable. Peeling green paint and rickety blinds would have to go eventually. But that would take longer.

Fortunately, Guy worked in a small wing on the far side of the sprawling rambler, and apart from willingly answering her many questions, left her alone to cope. He also lived and slept there, keeping three central rooms free, one for counseling church members and two always ready for anyone who needed a temporary place to stay. Like Leah's office, a big kitchen faced the front of the house.

On her first day at work, Leah had wondered briefly why Guy hadn't immediately suggested she use one of the guest rooms as an interim haven. She blushed at the thought now and pressed her palms to her cheeks. The answer to that question should have been obvious to her. He was unfailingly kind and helpful, clearly grateful for her efforts, no matter how inept, but he kept their contacts to a minimum. The last thing his image needed was a single woman installed in his home.

Guy was determined to maintain a professional basis for their relationship. He had even seemed awkward on the several occasions when she'd noticed how long he'd been shut away working and taken him coffee and a sandwich. When they were in the same room, the air between them was instantly electric.

Absently, Leah started pulling books from a shelf and piling them on the floor. She'd dust each one and re-place them in alphabetical order according to author. Every volume was huge and filled with intimidating subject matter. Had Guy read all these? she wondered. He was so intelligent, constantly writing and reading between dealing with the hundreds of small and large problems his parishioners heaped upon him. And he seemed to love his job, to thrive on pressure without sign of strain. He had a kind word and a gentle squeeze of the shoulder for everyone who came to the house.

Was she one more of his good works? Leah sup-posed so and squelched a spear of disappointment. The important thing was to become useful here and make a place for herself.

The books could wait. With a weary moan, she slumped back into her chair and pulled the dreaded ledger toward her. It was every bit as confusing as Guy had promised. All the small congregation's finances for the year were contained in this miserable black tome filled with chicken-scratch numbers.

She opened the ledger to the last page she'd worked on at the same time as she heard the familiar sound of the jeep's powerful engine roar to a stop outside. It was Guy, back from visiting a hospitalized church member. After a second, she buried her head in her work—at

least the calculator he had produced was a help, and so
was the natural flair she had for figures. That still surprised her.

"Hi, there."

Leah glanced up to see Guy's head protruding around
the door. She smiled a little wanly. "Hi. How was Mrs.
Krause?"

"Better." He gave a satisfied nod. "She's recovering
nicely from her surgery, and I think a few days in the
hospital will do her a world of good, anyway."

"What do you mean?" Leah rested her chin on the
heel of a hand.

Guy chuckled. "If you had six children and a husband who rarely worked, you'd be ready for a rest, too.
Anywhere, including a hospital after having a hysterectomy."

Leah smiled and swallowed hard at the same time. "I
guess you're right." He cared so much about people and
had so much empathy.

Earlier she'd seen him working in the garden, surrounded by several small, laughing children from the
church nursery. He'd stopped to give each one a pig-
gyback ride, and the sight had warmed her heart. He
ought to have a family of his own, and she wondered,
yet again, why he didn't.

He was watching her closely. "Are you overdoing it
here?" he asked. "You've done wonders, but I don't
want *you* laid up with exhaustion." He checked his
watch. "You were here early, and it's after four-thirty.
Why don't you knock it off for the day and go home?"

To what, she thought, *four walls and a few plants?* "I
will when I get a bit farther along with this ledger," she
said, hoping her tone didn't betray the emptiness she
felt.

"Ah, the beast." Guy came all the way into the room and picked up the ledger. He sat on the edge of the desk and leafed through pages. His strong, tanned throat above an open-necked blue shirt intrigued her. So did his muscular thigh, encased in worn denim, and the long, sensitive fingers. He turned another page and kept reading. The sun was lower now, sending a shaft through the window to turn his hair to molten honey and shade a high cheekbone and the slight cleft in his chin. Guy Hamilton was the most attractive man she'd ever met, and the nicest.

"You're something," he said finally, laying the book back in front of her. "Methodical. It's even starting to make sense to me, and I detest figures. Can I answer any questions for you?"

"No," she said regretfully, wishing she could think of some excuse to keep him with her a while longer.

He stood. "Then I'd better get to my own work. I'm trying to think of something inspiring to say on Sunday. Unfortunately, there are days when I don't feel very inspired."

His dear, wry grimace remained imprinted on her mind long after he'd left the room. An inner glow emanated from Guy. The result of his faith, she supposed.

Leah braced her chin on one fist. She remembered how, as a child, she'd seen other families going to church on Sundays. *Normal* families, she had tagged them. Often she'd wished she were trotting along as part of a normal family, laughing, secure. Leafing through a battered old bible beneath the covers of her bed had been the closest she got to church. The flyleaf of the tattered volume bore the inscription "For Jack, with love from Grandma." Leah had never dared ask her mother who Jack was, but she liked to believe he was her father. She'd never know now. Shaking her head, she picked up a pen.

The next time Leah looked at her watch, she was shocked. She was also elated. It was ten o'clock and dark outside, but she'd done it—actually done it. Up to this very day the ledger was in order, and it balanced. Her methods were homegrown, and without the calculator she would undoubtedly have taken twice as long, but the wretched black book was in order. She must show Guy.

Without thinking, she snatched up her treasure and ran along the hall. When she turned the corner, a sliver of light showed under his study door.

"Guy!" She knocked and rushed into the cluttered room without waiting for an answer. "Guy, I made the thing balance. I did it—" She halted halfway to his desk, feeling goose bumps dart over her skin. "I'm sorry," she stammered. "I shouldn't interrupt that way."

Guy didn't answer. He was leaning back in the chair, his bare feet crossed on a desk littered with mountains of papers. He wore only a pair of frayed cutoffs and balanced a brandy glass on his flat stomach. But it was the haunted expression in his eyes, and his hair, pushed into a tousled mess, that had made Leah recoil.

"I'm sorry," she repeated falteringly. "I seem to have a habit of barging in when you don't expect or want me. This—" She waved the book. "I was so excited. It made me feel like I was worth something."

"Leah," he mumbled, moving slowly, swinging his feet to the floor. He slid the glass among the papers and stood. "Got to do something about the air conditioning in this house. It's too hot in here."

Leah watched, biting her lip and clutching the ledger to her chest. Guy seemed distant and deeply troubled. He fumbled for a shirt and shrugged it on. His fingers hovered over the buttons as if he couldn't decide how or whether to fasten them. She fought an urge to help him, touch him, smooth the frown line between his arched brows. She did nothing. Guy hadn't looked at her since she first entered the room.

"I'll show you this tomorrow," she said quietly, and took a backward step toward the door.

"No! No." Guy faced her, every feature sharply drawn. "I was surprised to see you, that's all. I thought you'd gone home hours ago." His voice cracked, and he dropped his head to rake at his hair again.

Something was wrong. "Guy..."

He lowered his hand and knocked a stack of notebooks to the floor. "Hell." His gesture was wide, helpless. "I'm so damn disorganized and clumsy."

Immediately, Leah knelt to gather the books together with one hand. The lump in her throat grew larger with each second. She wanted to share whatever was upsetting him, but how could she when she dare not ask? He probably wouldn't dream of discussing anything personal with her.

"Stop, please. I'll do it." He was beside her, one thigh almost touching her hip. "You don't have to clean up after me. Or anyone. You're becoming a whole person now, Leah. You're on your way to a new life you've decided to make for yourself."

He'd covered her hand and stilled it with his own strong fingers. "Yes" was the only word she could form. Surely he must feel her tremble.

"And you were wrong when you came in and said I didn't want you. You'll never know how much I want you. And you're worth so much—to me and yourself."

The joy Leah felt was tentative at first. She was afraid to believe he'd really said what she thought he had. All she seemed capable of was to stare up into his face.

He stood, pulling her with him. "You ought to go, Leah." Even as he said the words, he stroked her hair. "Please go."

A small jab of defiance gained strength with the depth of her longing. "I don't want to." She stretched to take the glass from his desk and swallowed some of the smooth liquor. "I want you to kiss me." The glass wobbled when she set it down. This was madness, and she'd probably regret it. She could ruin everything, and afterward they'd both have to pay the price.

Guy uttered a low, incoherent sound and slowly bent his head to nuzzle her neck with his lips. His jaw was slightly rough, and the sensation it caused made Leah close her eyes. Millimeter by millimeter, his mouth approached hers, touching, feeling every hollow and contour of her face on the way until his lips closed over hers, cool and incredibly sweet, tasting faintly of brandy.

Except to hold her hand, he hadn't touched her, but now he took the ledger, reached blindly behind her to drop it on a chair and held her tightly against his broad chest.

The kiss deepened, and Leah felt the almost-forgotten, heavy heat in her womb. She ran her fingers beneath his shirt and through soft, golden chest hair, smoothed his wide shoulders and locked her wrists behind his neck. His firm hands at her waist heated her flesh and lifted her almost from the ground.

For an instant, he drew back, searching her face before kissing her again, more urgently, his tongue searching for and finding hers as they strained more fiercely against each other.

"Guy," Leah whispered when they paused for breath. "Oh, Guy—" There seemed nothing else to say, but his thumbs went to the soft sides of her breasts. They ached inside her cotton dress, and she yearned to feel her skin naked on his.

He kissed her again, with enough force to rock her head, as he covered each breast and tucked his fingers under her neckline. Her flesh throbbed.

"Leah, Leah," Guy said brokenly. "I knew I shouldn't touch you. That I wouldn't want to stop if I did."

Don't stop. "Kiss me again, Guy." Her lips sought his while he ran his hands over her shoulders and down her back. At her waist he hesitated, then crossed his arms around her, spreading his fingers wide over her ribs.

"Sweetheart," he muttered, and the thrust of his hips into her belly proved he was fully aroused.

Bright, searing desire burst free in Leah. She wanted this man, and he wanted her. Everything was right. Her eyes fluttered shut, and when she opened them again, Guy's were closed, his features darkened with passion. They needed each other.

He pressed hard little kisses along her jaw and down her neck, then stopped to scan her face. "You are so beautiful," he said. "So perfect. Inside as well as out. I can feel it."

Leah rested her cheek on his shoulder. Somewhere in her brain came the small thought that she'd never known a young man's powerful, stimulating body,

never known the exquisite desire that filled her now. For
two years she'd scarcely felt a man's touch at all. She
shut off her brain. This moment was all that mattered.

"Make love to me," she said quietly, holding his gaze
but taking a backward step toward his bedroom. "Take
me to bed. I want to lie in your arms."

As she watched, his expression changed. Pure, raw
pain slowly replaced passion. He shook his head, his
fingers passing fleetingly over her hair, her brow, along
the outline of her mouth. His last contact was a brushing, almost-reverent cupping of her chin. Then he
turned away.

Leah struggled for composure. When she gripped his
arm, he stiffened, making a sound that was a choking
groan.

"What have I done?" she asked. "Please, look at me
and tell me what's wrong."

His head dropped forward, and he braced his weight
on the edge of the desk. "You didn't do anything except be wonderful. And I want you—Lord, how I want
you."

"Then what is it?" She was crying now.

"I can't allow myself to make love to you." Guy
swung around, his chest heaving. "I'm married."

Chapter Four

Guy ground his back teeth together, willing his heart to slow down. What had he done? What had possessed him? He'd hurt and shamed her—and cut wide open his own torment.

"Leah, listen." He took a deep breath. "Oh, God. Don't look at me like that. I—"

Her face had paled beneath its smooth tan. Every rounded feature seemed drawn and sharp. The blue eyes were huge and dark, tears welling to spill, unchecked, down her cheeks. She pressed her lips together in a trembling line.

"Sit down. I'll pour us both a drink," he said, pleading.

Leah recoiled from his outstretched hand. "No, thank you. I don't want anything. I'm—I'm sorry I pushed myself on you. There was—" She cleared her throat and scrubbed at her damp face. "I never guessed. You didn't say anything. No one did. I—I need a Kleenex."

He took her elbow and guided her into a chair. "Sit there, please. I'll find some tissues."

What a lousy mess. And it was all his fault. He preached, actually preached about honor and truth, to

people who stared back at him with self-guilt in their
eyes. If only they knew. *Guy Hamilton, minister and
fraud.* He slammed through the door to his bedroom
and strode into the bathroom. No Kleenex, damn it.
Toilet tissue would have to do. He unwound a wad and
retraced his steps rapidly, terrified Leah might bolt before he could get there. Why hadn't he explained his
situation to her as soon as she showed up in Phoenix?
Fear? Yes, fear of losing a woman he had no right to in
the first place.

His throat closed when he reentered his office. For
seconds he couldn't move. Her body was scrunched in
the chair, knees drawn up and tightly wrapped in her
full skirt. She was retreating with the wounds he'd in-
flicted. Small sniffing sounds came irregularly, jerking
her body.

Guy pounded one fist against the other palm. He felt
absolutely useless to put right the misery he'd caused
this woman who'd come to mean so much to him. He'd
known she was attracted to him from the outset. Her
arrival in Phoenix had proved that. And he'd also been
acutely aware of their mutual and growing attachment.
If he'd told her...

"Leah." He smoothed her hair until she raised her
face. "This was all my fault." With light strokes, he
wiped her tears. "Please, don't feel bad or hurt or embarrassed. I'm the one who should feel those things. I
gave all the signals—signals I was wrong to give."

She made a visible effort at control, pushing her hair
back, taking the tissue to wipe her eyes and nose. "It
isn't important. Just a silly reaction. I was excited about
the work, I guess, and got carried away. It's late." She
glanced at her watch and made a move to stand. "Time

I got out of your hair and let you get back to whatever you were doing.''

I was thinking about you, sweet lady. All he could do anymore was think about Leah Bennett Cornish. "Don't go, Leah. Not yet, not like this. Let me explain.''

Her fingers made mangled shreds of the tissue. "No need." But she stayed in the chair. "You don't owe me anything, Guy. Least of all the personal details of your life. And you've already given me so much. It was probably natural for me to start dreaming of being closer to you. I've been too alone for too long. You were a convenient outlet for the loneliness, that's all. What happened..." Her voice trailed off, and her next breath shook the length of her body. "It wasn't anything.''

"Yes, it was. And we're going to talk about it." Guy dragged another chair close until he could sit immediately in front of Leah. "Will you let me hold your hands?" he asked softly. "I feel like I need to hold on to a friend right now.''

Tentatively, she extended shaky fingers, and he grasped them. Her gaze, direct at first, slid away as bright color stained her cheeks. He had embarrassed her deeply.

"I was married while I was still in college," he started. Why did everything he said sound ridiculous? "In California. I was majoring in business—international business. Susan..."

Leah's grip tightened. Guy massaged her cold fingers.

"She was so special. We met at the wrong time and married at the wrong time and for the wrong reasons. Thinking you know where you're going and knowing for sure are very different states. At twenty I only thought I knew what my future held. And boy, was I wrong."

Soft flesh at the neck of Leah's sundress rose and fell rapidly. Guy tried not to notice nor to acknowledge he'd managed to add to the heap of insecurity her life must have been for months. She made no attempt to answer—or draw away. Inertia seemed to be slowly replacing the emotional riptide of the past half hour.

Sweat stung the corner of his eye, and he blinked. He couldn't risk releasing her hands. "Susan's a psychiatrist," he said. "A very successful one."

"Here?" Leah's voice was a hoarse whisper.

He slid his fingers to her wrists. "No. Oh, no. Still in California."

"But you see her? You get together?"

Guy closed his eyes fractionally. "No, Leah. I haven't seen Susan in six years, since we separated. By the time I graduated, I knew how I had to spend my life. We stayed together through my three years in theological college. She tried, really tried, but she never understood, and I don't blame her—anymore. She married one man, and he turned into someone different. My first posting was to a small California church. For a year Susan commuted to school every day, and every day she came home to a husband too involved in everyone else's problems to be the kind of partner, and lover, she needed."

"She left you?" The effort each question cost Leah was clearly etched in her pinched expression.

"I received an offer of a post here. Susan hadn't finished school."

"You mean you left *her*?"

Guy stood with enough force to topple his chair. He stared at it for a moment, rubbing a hand across the base of his neck. "We decided the time had come for a fresh start for both of us. The decision to part was mutual."

His muscles felt leaden when he bent to right the chair. What he'd just said was yet another lie albeit a half-truth. He hadn't wanted to give up on his marriage. Love died slowly—he'd always believe that. If Susan had asked him to stay in California, even permanently, he'd have done it, because he had loved her. But she didn't ask. In the years when he'd been so preoccupied with his calling, while he'd taken his wife for granted, she'd gone through the process of feeling her love for him die. By the time he realized what had happened, it was too late.

"Why?" The rustle of cotton told him Leah had left the chair. "Why didn't you get a divorce? Six years is a long time to be alone. Maybe you don't accept divorce, or would it be bad for—for Susan in her work? I don't know much about these things."

Again, she was feeling inadequate, overshadowed by what she saw as the shortcomings in her own experience. His fault. "It's complicated," he said. So complicated he wasn't sure he understood himself anymore. Susan had supposedly filed for divorce—at last—but now wasn't the time to discuss his possible freedom with Leah. She'd misunderstand, think he was excusing his earlier behavior, perhaps wonder why he'd rejected her since he was technically almost free.

"What I'm going to ask you is just for me, okay, Guy? I want to understand all this if I can."

The unnaturally tight quality of her voice made him stare at her. Her shoulders were pulled back, rigid, her chin tilted. He nodded, swallowing his apprehension.

"You've been separated from your wife for six years." It was a statement, and he knew he must only listen. "Do you expect me to believe you've lived like a monk—sorry if I'm too personal—for all that time?" She was gaining momentum. A brittle spark lit her eyes. "I find that hard to believe. So why was it hands off with me? Am I so repulsive?"

The ground felt suddenly insubstantial beneath his feet.

"Guy?"

"Repulsive? Leah, you're beautiful."

"Are you still in love with your wife?"

"No!" he shot back emphatically. "It took a while, but I don't feel anything for her now—except a hope she'll be happy."

"But you don't want me," Leah stated flatly.

"Don't. You'll never know how much I want you at this moment. It would be so easy to be with you, so wonderful. But I told you, I'm still married." Let her leave it at that. He didn't want to say what he knew should be said or get any closer to his own pain of the past years.

"You're married, but you've been alone for a long time," she persisted. "You say you feel nothing for your wife now, but you won't make love with another woman, although you want to. I guess I don't understand any of this."

He touched her cheek, her shoulder, then dropped his hand. Her skin was maddeningly soft. "Adultery isn't acceptable to me." There, he'd said it, and she was bound to think him pious and judgmental. Whatever she thought, there was no way to soften the truth.

The words hung between them. Leah said nothing, but he felt her mind withdrawing, turning inward. She had to believe he'd indicted her with his own values.

Leah opened her mouth but couldn't get enough air. Somehow she must get out of this room, this house, without breaking down again. She'd taken the initiative, asked him to kiss her in a way he'd obviously found brazen. He *had* kissed her—but no one could blame a man who must suffer daily because of his own dedication to fidelity.

"I'm sorry, Guy." The instant she voiced the apology, a shard of anger started its slow burn. He'd taken his own good time to put her off. And he hadn't bothered to tell her the truth about himself when there'd been dozens of opportunities.

A fine film of sweat shone on his brow and upper lip. "I'm the one who should be sorry," he insisted. "The only one. And I am."

She bit back the urge to agree. "Don't work too late." Graceful exits must be one of the few social graces Charles had failed to teach her.

"I won't be able to work tonight, Leah. Surely you know that."

All she knew was that he'd learned almost everything about her and had evidently gained some sort of satisfaction out of playing the crusader. He hadn't considered that sharing his own problems might make her feel more worthwhile or that in doing so, any misunderstandings would have been avoided.

"Forget it, Guy. I intend to." She sounded convincing. "Excuse me." The distance to the door seemed miles.

"Leah—please, don't go like this."

At least he hadn't tried to touch her again. The briefest contact could send her into his arms, reaching, seeking comfort. Then the fire would spark between them again, and if he gave in to it, as he might now—out of guilt—she'd always know it had been for no other reason.

The doorknob slipped in her damp palm, and the door slammed behind her. The noise echoed dull and throbbing in her ears while she quickly traveled the hallway back to her office. She hesitated on the threshold. This wasn't *her* office anymore. It couldn't be after what had happened tonight.

She'd left the light on. At first she moved sluggishly, turning confused circles, from scattered books on the floor to the disorganized desk and a chair where she'd piled the overflow of papers. Clean up and get out was her immediate and desperate instinct. Yet her fingers fumbled at drawers and knocked stacks of correspondence into confused jumbles.

Leah left the desk and tried to concentrate on the bookshelves. She must at least replace the volumes she'd heaped all over the room. Titles blurred, and author names ran together. All that mattered now was to get everything back in some sort of order and leave.

She picked up the publications, one, two, three, at a time, depending on their weight and thickness, and knelt to stuff them into their shelves. Her hands shook uncontrollably. *Charles.* The old, familiar stab of longing, the yearning for his comforting protection, returned, and she sat on her heels.

Yes, the people who said Charles had filled the place her father should have taken were right in a way. Yes, he'd made her feel safe and wanted and important after she'd grown up feeling like nothing. Was that so wrong?

He'd also loved her very much as a wife—until the drink took over. And she had loved him and would never forget that love, or the gratitude that went with it, as long as she lived.

The tears started again, and she swiped at her nose with the back of one hand. Wretched books. She jammed them away as fast as she could. It hadn't been Charles's fault alcohol made him impotent. Maybe if she could have fulfilled more of his needs, he would never have turned to booze. Maybe he had sensed when she'd started to pine for a young man to fill her life, her arms—her bed.

No! She shoved the thoughts away. He could never have known. Only now did she acknowledge the truth herself. She *had* wanted the excitement and sexual gratification of a lover closer to her own age. But how could Charles have known it when she herself remained unaware at a surface level?

"Leah."

Guy. She couldn't face him again. Not now. Maybe never again. Yet she'd known he'd come—hoped, without forming the wish, that he would.

He took the three books she held. "Please, stop this. You must be exhausted. I am."

"I'm terrific," she lied. "Absolutely terrific. I just wanted to clean up a bit before I left."

Their eyes met, total comprehension of her meaning passing between them, before Leah took the books back and slid them onto a shelf.

"It is time you went home," he said levelly but without conviction. "How's the Bug running?" he asked, referring to the old yellow Volkswagen that had taken the place of her sleek Porsche.

Making conversation, she thought. He was as un-comfortable as she. "Fine. Not the same as my other car, but that wouldn't be possible. Charles always kept it in first-class condition. He worried about me when-ever I drove." She swallowed, hating herself for trying to inflict some sort of injury but incapable of resisting the urge to strike back out of her own hurt and debase-ment.

"He was a good man," Guy said very quietly. "I'm glad he was there when you needed him."

Leah felt the tears prick at her eyes again. Damn. The man would have to be gentle and kind even when she was deliberately spiteful. "Yes," she said, and gulped. "Charles was always there. He was— I still miss him."

"That's natural," Guy replied tonelessly.

"Maybe," she began, tipping her head to breathe. "Maybe if he hadn't had to worry about my loyalty, he'd be alive today."

Nothing could have prepared her for Guy's reaction. He grabbed her shoulders and pulled her upright, shaking hard until she gripped his shirt, gasping. His eyes burned into hers.

"Garbage," he rasped. "What are you saying? I saw the two of you together, remember? You were a perfect wife, irreproachable. Even the crumby papers said so." His grip hurt.

Leah breathed deeply through her mouth. She felt sick. "The crumby papers said a lot of things. What did they know?"

"If you want to punish yourself, fine." Guy held a trembling bottom lip in his teeth before going on. "If that's what it takes to make you feel better, fine. But I don't have to listen to the drivel. Charles was good to you, and I'm glad. I only wish I could have been the one there when he was showing up to play Sir Galahad. Must have been a real penance. Leah, I'd have been glad to pay that penance for you, sweet lady.'' He averted his face, but not before she saw the moist glitter in his eyes.

She covered his hands for an instant, then carefully disentangled his fingers from her arms. She reached to touch the sharp angle of his jaw but changed her mind and tapped his shoulder lightly instead. "Thank you for being so good to me, Guy. So very kind.'' Not that he'd know how to be anything else, she thought. "You look tired. Please, don't worry about me. Like you said, I must be tired, too. Sometimes I say things I don't mean when I'm worn out. Get some sleep now. I'll lock up as I go.''

He blocked her path to the desk, and for the first time she noticed he held the ledger. "You left this in my office,'' he said, keeping his head down as he flipped through the pages. She saw his neck jerk. "And you did do it. You made it balance.'' His sudden glance unnerved her. "How did you manage it?''

Leah turned her back. She'd never learned how to play games—particularly this one of emotional tension, point for point for a prize of what? Ultimate pain and frustration?

"It wasn't so hard,'' she muttered. "One step at a time. Checks and balances—ordinary stuff by an ordinary brain.''

"You aren't ordinary.''

If only he would stop making this so difficult. "Guy.'' She swung to face him. He might be able to handle the stress; she couldn't. "This was a mistake.'' Her legs shook.

He'd moved between her and the door now. "What was a mistake, Leah?''

"My coming here. I was too impulsive. It's too much for you. Unfair to you. You have enough to cope with without my neurotic inadequacies."

"I want you." He took a step toward her, and she retreated. "I want you right here, and you aren't neurotic. You needed someone, and so did I. The timing wasn't perfect, but it rarely is. Can't we be patient?"

What was he saying? That if she waited, he'd eventually—possibly—be prepared to return some of the passion she'd already displayed so eloquently. Humiliation reddened her face.

Guy set the ledger on the closest chair. "Can't we?"

"What?" Her mind blanked.

He came closer until he could run a knuckle along her chin. "Be patient, Leah. I don't want to lose you. You're needed here. By the people—and by me."

"Thank you," she said stiffly. "But I'm sure a lot of employees could fill the bill if you look carefully enough." If all he needed was a bookkeeper who could also wield a mean duster, he could look elsewhere.

He stuffed both hands in his pockets, and she saw his nostrils flare. "Why do you choose to misunderstand?" His mouth came together in a hard line. "You know perfectly well what I mean."

She didn't. How could she after his earlier turnoff? "I've been a real pain to you, Guy." Her voice automatically softened. "You tried to keep your distance—to make sure our relationship was professional. I was the one who misread your signals. I pushed things over the edge for us. There's nothing I can do to change that now—except to remove the irritation."

"Meaning?" His tone was steady, still.

Leah avoided his eyes and went to yank open desk drawers. "I can't believe how much crud one person can collect in a short space of time."

"I can hardly remember when you weren't here," he said, not moving.

She cast around for her purse and opened it on top of the desk. "Look at the rubbish in this drawer. Pens, most of them useless. Old notes, pencil shavings. Disgusting." Without pausing for breath, she dragged the trash can from the corner and scooped grubby debris into it with her fingernails. The broken pens she dropped into the purse, without knowing why.

Finally, she dumped the drawer upside down over the garbage container. "There," she said with hollow triumph, refusing to meet Guy's gaze. His steady regard was a laser on her face.

"Finished?" he asked, too softly.

She moved to the bookcases once more. "Almost." If only he would leave so she could escape without any more fuss.

Rapidly, Leah slid volume after volume back onto the shelves, no longer bothering about alphabetizing. *Keep busy. Don't think for as long as it takes to get out of here* were the only lucid ideas her mind could form. And they meant she must continue working and stay in control, at least until Guy gave up and went away.

"Stop it!"

He almost shouted, and she jumped before continuing her task.

"Stop it, I said. Or I'll stop you. You're overreacting. We both suffered back in that room, but we can get over it and carry on."

Her movements became frenzied. Dim recollections of a man whose face she didn't remember returned, a series of men—and her mother leading them through the house, shouting, "You stop it, Leah. Stop your crying and go to sleep." And her mother's bedroom door would close before the laughter came. Leah never saw her mother's visitors clearly. By morning they were always gone.

That had been long ago, and it had nothing to do with what was happening to Leah now, unless...unless...no, she bore no resemblance to her mother. This was different, and she'd never been drawn to a man purely for sex or money.

Charles had spent eleven years convincing her she was special—her own person, untouched by what her mother had been. "Never allow anyone to make you think you're less than you are," he'd said so often. "We don't know all it took to turn your mother into what she became. She was worth something; remember that. She had you." And he'd smile, softening his cool blue eyes in a way Leah knew only she ever saw. While Charles was with her, it had been easy to believe she wasn't trash. But he was gone now.

The past weeks had been too much. It was time to find a quiet place and regroup—alone. Much as she wanted to be with Guy Hamilton, he had no place for her. He'd made that so very clear.

She squeezed her eyes shut and whispered, "Let me go, Guy."

The sudden, biting grip of his hands on her shoulders, jerking her around and pulling her close, made her stomach plummet. She opened her mouth, but no sound came. His face bent a few inches above her own, every handsome feature dark with fury.

"Will you stop? Will you listen to me? Or do I have to make you? You're hysterical, overreacting—totally out of line."

Something snapped inside Leah. "Maybe," she said with deathly calm. "But whose fault is that? And no one calls me hysterical or out of line anymore. I'm not a kid. You've been good to me, but I earned my way around here." She poked at the ledger. "This mess is straight now, thanks to me. And I thank you for allowing me to find out I *can* do something. Otherwise, I owe you nothing more."

He lessened his grip, smoothing her arms from shoulder to elbow and back. "You're right. And I'm sorry for coming on so strong. I can hardly wait to see what else you can do to help set me straight."

Leah shrugged away, forcing a bright smile. "Thank you, Guy, but forget it. If there's one thing you don't need, it's me. These past weeks have been good—probably for both of us. But I've had enough of Phoenix. It's too hot here, and I don't like the work." Leah whisked her purse straps over her shoulder and made it halfway around the desk before Guy shut the door.

He thrust both hands deep in his pockets and tried a smile that didn't quite come off. "You grew up in Wichita Falls. The weather's just as hot there, and humid to boot."

"That's different," she said, and took another step toward him.

Blond hair glimmered as he bent to study his bare feet. "Worse, you mean. Awful. You do like it here, and you like the work. I've seen the thrill in your eyes when you accomplish something. And you like the people—I know you do. You're great with the old folks and wonderful with children. This is a perfect job for you—your slot. Whether you knew it or not, this is where you were always intended to be eventually."

Leah chewed the corner of her mouth while she decided what to say next.

"You agree, right?" Guy leaned against the door. "You wouldn't be happy anywhere else?"

"No wonder you decided to become a minister," she said wearily. "Gives you the perfect excuse to tell other people what to do with their lives. You have a natural flair for being pushy. The bigger the challenge, the pushier you get. I'm not a little lost sheep, Guy. Someone you have to gather up and save. I'm all gathered up together now—by me—and I've got enough sense to figure out when it's time to quit and move on."

"Leah—"

"No—" She cut him off, one palm raised to reject his next protest. "You can't buffalo me into sticking around until your conscience heals. I mean... Damn, that's not what I meant."

He crossed his ankles, watching her face intently. "I think it's exactly what you meant. You think I'm only trying to get you to stay because I made a mess of things tonight. You're wrong, Leah. Totally, completely wrong. I *do* believe this is the place for you. And I'm very sure no one else will come along to fill your shoes here as well as you do."

"I'm going to take this slowly, point by point," Leah said patiently. "I wasn't suggesting you had a reason to feel guilty about anything that happened between us. What I said simply came out wrong. I intended to explain that I see you as feeling responsible for everyone, including me, and you're trying to make sure you've done all you can before I strike out on my own again.

You're a natural caretaker, a collector of lame ducks.''
She paused for breath.

"But I—"

"Guy, I haven't finished." She would have her say
before he could muddle her up yet again. "Second,
there is no *one* place in the world for a person. And if
there was, you certainly wouldn't be granted some sort
of privileged insight into the location." She didn't allow the narrowing of his eyes to deter her. "Finally, I'm
flattered to hear how useful I am around here. But I
think, if you'll only face it, that neither of us will work
as well together from here on. So it's best that I go—
without any more fuss." A vague smugness warmed her.
She'd finally learned how to take charge of her own life.

His only response was to cross his arms.

Leah approached steadily until one more step would
bring her closer than she wanted to get. Desperation
mingled with helplessness. Guy Hamilton was mule
headed. He'd stop at nothing, including putting his
quarry on the defensive, to get his own way. She ran her
fingers agitatedly up and down the straps of her purse.
"After all," she muttered, "it's not as if I'm leaving you
in the lurch. You didn't have someone here before I arrived. You'll get by."

"Don't go."

For several seconds, she watched his mouth as if
she'd see the words repeated. Then she met his irresist-
ible eyes. Sticking to a decision was never going to be
more difficult than now. "Guy, I'll always be grateful
for what you've done for me. You gave me a fresh start
and a chance to get my head straight. But I can't stay,"
she said.

"You can if you want to," he suggested persuasively. "Please want to."

"Guy." She spun away and threw her purse back on the desk. "You can be the most exasperating man. And you take advantage..." *Good grief.*

His laugh was a mellow rumble. "You do have a way with words sometimes, my girl."

"Okay, okay." Leah felt her resolution crumble. He would get his way, at least for now, but she'd be on her guard in future. "I'll continue to work for you until you can find someone to replace me."

"I'm going to be very selective." The laughter was still in his voice. "You're going to be a hard act to follow."

She looked at him over her shoulder, then turned resignedly to slump on the desk. "We'll just have to make sure we advertise in the right places, won't we? And of course I'll be only too happy to weed out unsuitable applicants."

Guy's expression sobered. "We won't find it tough working together—any more than we have until now. I promise you that, Leah. We both know where we stand, and we're both mature. How can we go wrong?"

Leah lowered her eyes, afraid he'd read in them the answer to his question. Guy, the optimist, was forgetting—or choosing to avoid—the obvious. They were healthy members of opposite sexes, and their attraction for each other went beyond a level they'd be able to ignore for very long. He slouched there, rationalizing, while she tried to close out the remembered sensation of his arms around her, his fingers in her hair, her own hands smoothing the broad, hard chest. Her pulse pounded in her ears.

"Leah," he persisted, "we'll be able to do very well, won't we?"

She balled her fists. He wanted her, and not just as a bookkeeper-housekeeper. This man, so determined to fight his natural urges, willed her not to leave because he'd fallen as hard as she. Leah stood and met his inquiring gaze. "Sure, Guy," she said at last. "We'll do just fine—until someone else can take over my job. It's late." She checked her watch and moaned. "If I don't get home, Wally will send out a search party. I'm surprised he hasn't called already."

Guy raised expressive brows. "Wally keeps tabs on you?"

Leah couldn't stop a sheepish grimace. "Not exactly," she stalled.

"What does that mean?"

Guy had never allowed any other subject to be glossed over. She might have known he'd pick up on this one. "I'm supposed to thump on the floor when I get home for the night, that's all. Just so he knows I'm safe. He's a neat old guy."

"Mmm." Guy blew into a fist and moved away from the door. "He's neat, all right. And I can't remember him really giving a damn about another human being since his wife died. He needed someone to care about. Everyone does. I told you you had a way with old folks."

"See you in the morning." She swept past, skirt swishing, sandals clicking on terrazzo floors in the hall.

Guy listened for the grumble of the Volkswagen's engine, the scrunch of gravel spewing behind rubber, then strained to hear the last possible noise from the little car.

The faint breeze she'd let into the house smelled pungently of fallen oranges—and Leah. Roses and sandalwood, something subtle but hauntingly exotic.

He went to sit in her chair and rubbed his fingers over its arms and the worn edge of the desk.

He'd managed to pull it off; he'd bought a little time after what had almost turned into an immediate fiasco. He leaned to rest his forehead on folded arms.

What was he supposed to do? What was right? Sometimes hanging on to old convictions took more *strength* than a man could be expected to have. Strength. Guy laughed bitterly and rolled his head slowly from side to side. He felt weak and insecure— and desperately lonely. After years of believing he'd made peace with his solitary state, he was sickeningly, hopelessly empty.

While he'd prattled on, throwing platitudes and assurances at her, doubt had shone in Leah's blue eyes. He was supposed to be the wise one, the one who had it all together. Laughable. She was honest and true and didn't know how to deceive. And she was gaining confidence with every day. No wonder Charles Cornish had fallen so quickly and completely in love with her—even when she was little more than a child. He must have seen beyond the lovely girl to the beautiful, accomplished woman she was capable of becoming. Too bad Cornish made one fatal mistake—not allowing her to fulfill her potential.

Guy's next thought shook to the core his belief in his own goodness. He was glad Cornish hadn't finished what he started with Leah. Glad because she was still malleable and ripe to succeed completely—with Guy.

He pushed wearily to his feet and left the house, hardly noticing rough, still-warm concrete beneath his bare feet.

The church was cool inside; one small light flickered yellow over whitewashed walls behind the pulpit. Guy hesitated beside the first pew he reached, then walked on. He wasn't ready to pray.

In a storage cupboard where extra hymnals were stored, he fumbled to locate his battered guitar and headed through a side door into the darkened grounds. Leah had never entered the church or shown any interest in what went on there. He wanted to share everything that mattered to him with her, but he mustn't push. At every service, he played his guitar and sang with the congregation. He loved his people and relished the times he felt the little community fuse. Now he wished he could sing for Leah—to Leah.

Crickets sent up a raucous accompaniment to his first gentle chords. Overhead, palm fronds clicked. She was alone, too, and vulnerable. Without meaning to, she'd let slip how little money she had and confessed she didn't even know where her mother was anymore. She had no one—but him. The thought first thrilled, then unnerved him.

Leah might be making strides toward independence, but she wasn't there yet. Even if he could face letting her go, he'd never rest if she did. Experience was the element she lacked most—worldliness. He slid down a tree trunk to sit on a sandy hummock. Worldliness was something he wished she never had to gain.

Guy closed his eyes and ran his fingertips across the guitar strings. He wouldn't let her leave. Somehow he'd keep her with him until he was free to admit his growing attachment—and to accept hers. And she *was* beginning to care for him. She'd tried to explain away her sweet advances as an excited overreaction. A lousy excuse. Leah wasn't the kind of woman who offered herself lightly to a man like some sort of party favor.

God, let him play the cards right, in the right order, perfectly timed. He rested his head on ringed bark, breathed deeply of the night's scents, then listened to the clear, poignant chords he played. Each note came far more from his heart than the guitar.

Chapter Five

Leah parked in the church lot and walked around the building, its little belfry topped by a simple cross. The red-tiled roof stood out in sharp relief against white stone walls and the pallid early-morning sky.

Sleep had been a fitful waste of time. At five, she'd given up and started assessing and discarding one outfit after another. She hesitated, looking down at the demure navy linen dress and jacket she'd settled upon. Definitely businesslike with its white piping trim and the matching plain navy pumps. From here on, business would be the order of the day, every day. Leah wrinkled her nose. The only drawback was likely to be that she'd probably disintegrate from the heat by midmorning. At least the French braided chignon she'd labored over should help keep her neck cool.

Farther along Fan Lane, the bell on a Catholic church rang out seven dolorous chimes. With any luck, Guy would still be asleep, and she could make a start without having to face him. By the time he put in an appearance, she'd be involved in the task she'd set for herself during the hours of tossing and turning. Then she'd find it easier to appear casual.

The church was separated from Guy's house by a
broad expanse of palm-studded grounds. Fan palms—
the same kind that lined the street named after them—
and in between, some taller, more majestic, date palms.
Guy had filled huge beds on each side of the driveway
with multicolored dahlias, in full bloom now. A neat
oleander hedge screened the front of the house, and
every day brought a fresh crop of pink-and-white blossoms. Leah approached the front door, fishing for her
key while she longingly took in every detail. She missed
her yard and garden—and most of all, the orchids.

St. Mark's had an extensive vegetable patch behind
and beside the house, and she'd considered asking Guy
if she could help with its cultivation. That was out of the
question now. So was suggesting he fill the pool in the
cool courtyard sheltered by his wing. Day after day
she'd ogled the blue leaf-strewn pit and tried not to
think of her own tree-shaded grotto in Texas. Someone
else would be swimming there by now.

An hour later, already sweating, Leah was deeply involved in her self-appointed project for the day cleaning and organizing the kitchen. She'd found a floral
wraparound apron in a drawer and donned it without
removing her jacket.

The place was passable on the surface. Closer exam-
ination revealed grubby corners, a stove that hadn't
been cleaned for ages and the most jumbled cupboards
Leah had ever encountered.

Leah was adding to a pile of bowls, pots and utensils
on the mosaic-tiled table in the middle of the room
when she saw the cockroaches. The inch-long monsters
chugged contentedly along the baseboard with all the
confidence of permanent and very satisfied boarders.

"*That* does it," Leah muttered, poking at strands of escaping hair.

The quantity of disinfectant she dumped into a bucket equaled the scalding water that followed. "First we scrub, then we spray." Fury mounted as she remembered Jewel and the flawless running of Charles's house in Wichita Falls. Regular pest control had been automatic there, as it should be in a place like Phoenix. Jewel would have a fit if she saw this mess. "Penny-pinching skinflint." Leah dropped to her knees, ignored the hot liquid in the bucket and scrubbed with both hands. "Probably thinks he's saving something for God by not paying to keep this joint up. Must be the only house in town where the bugs aren't professionally killed. Figures, though. Empty swimming pool in heat like this. Should have guessed when I saw that. Mean—"

The sound of a foot scuffing behind her stopped Leah in the middle of her tirade. She continued to scrub, her face down and rapidly reddening. If she'd had any sense, she'd have closed the door.

"Penny-pinching skinflint? Mean?" Guy questioned evenly.

Leah squeezed her eyelids together. All her careful plans to be calm and distant had gone for nothing. She must appear—and sound—about as businesslike as the cockroaches that provoked her outburst.

She pursed her lips and sat on her heels to wring out a cloth. "I shouldn't have said that." Oh, how she hated apologizing again. "But this kitchen is a disgrace. If someone inspected household kitchens the way they do restaurants, there wouldn't be enough demerits to check off on the evaluation."

"My," he said with mock surprise, "aren't we testy this morning? Didn't you sleep well?"

That does it. She struggled to stand, arms akimbo, while she glared at him. "I slept very well, thank you." She opened her mouth to ask him the same question and stopped.

His hair, neatly combed and curling forward beneath his ears, was still wet from the shower. He wore the clerical black she'd assumed he reserved for Sundays. Leah hadn't seen him in the garb since she first arrived in Phoenix. She passed the back of one hand over her eyes, closing out the appealing picture he made—green eyes glinting, his lean features deeply tanned against the stiff white collar.

"Cleaning kitchens isn't your job," he spat out suddenly.

Leah's heart flipped over. She'd never heard him speak so sharply. "I—" Her pulse thudded. "The job needs to be done, and I *am* supposed to be the housekeeper around here."

"If you can tidy up a bit here and there, terrific," Guy said far more softly. "But you're invaluable to me in the office. I don't ever want to see you on the floor like that again. Look at your hands." He clasped her wrists and held raw knuckles high enough for her to look at them. "You didn't even put on rubber gloves, Leah."

"I didn't think," she mumbled.

His jaw tightened, and he flattened his lips. Still holding her hands, he stepped back and took her in from head to toe. "What are you wearing?" he asked, amazement tinging his words. "The forecast is for one hundred and sixteen, and you're dressed up like an Eskimo preparing for a blizzard."

She lifted her head defiantly. "You exaggerate. This is a perfectly acceptable outfit for my type of work. Why are you wearing that?" She nodded at his severe shirt.

"We have a wedding today. Young Ben Perez and Sophia Yale are getting married. And what you have on isn't acceptable. It wouldn't be in the office, let alone on the kitchen floor—with that ridiculous apron over the whole thing..." The rest of the sentence trailed away.

"Finished?" Leah pulled away and poked at the bucket with one toe. "Whether you like it or not, I can't leave this mess the way it is."

"You can and you will." Guy rotated his shoulders, exhaling a long breath. "I apologize if I sound ungrateful. I'm not. But this isn't what I had in mind when I asked you to work for me. Call Wally and find out who needs a job for a few hours. That's how I've always gotten by with the cleaning—by calling someone in when I couldn't cope on my own.

"I'm sorry about the bugs. We do have them sprayed. The guy didn't show last month, and I forgot to do anything about it. That's why I need you—to help me keep on track. Call him, too, if you don't mind. The number's written down somewhere. But before you do anything, right now, in fact, please take off that—that *thing* and your jacket. All we need is a case of heat prostration.

"Incidentally, the pool will be filled. I'd forgotten that, too. Feel free to swim whenever you like."

"That's nice of you." She breathed deeply. How easily he turned the tables to make her feel small. "But there's no need to do anything special on my account."

"I want to," he said, then hesitated before adding, "You really shouldn't be bundled up in heat like this."

He remained in the doorway, clearly waiting for her
to do as he asked. Leah took off the apron and draped
it on top of the pots and pans. She made no attempt to
remove her jacket. And she wouldn't until Guy had left
and she was good and ready.

"There," she said. "Now may I get on with some
work? I will make the calls and get some help after I
straighten up what I've started."

He raised both hands in a gesture of exasperated de-
feat and turned to leave.

"By the way," Leah called to his back, "do you really
think brown boat shoes and no socks are appropriate
for the occasion?"

Guy swung around and looked down at the same
time. "Oh, no," he said. "Thanks—I might have forgotten. It wouldn't be the first time." His attention
lifted to her face, and his amused expression faded. "I
wish you wouldn't wear your hair up again. It's too
lovely to hide."

He disappeared rapidly into the hall, and Leah felt all
life go out of the room with him. She touched her chignon thoughtfully before making sure the pins were still
secure.

By early afternoon, Elsie Culver, a garrulous but
efficient woman Wally Timmons recommended, had
brought the kitchen to shiny perfection. Elsie also
cleaned the counseling office and both guest bedrooms
before she left, beaming at Leah's praise and delighted
with the suggestion of a weekly arrangement.

Guy had been gone all day. He kept his own ap-
pointment book, but the arrival of cars and the sound
of laughing voices had let her know the wedding took
place at eleven. Some time afterward, she'd watched

from the window while the bride and groom, followed by their guests, trailed to a reception in the small, separate hall beside the church. She'd smiled at the young couple's glowing faces and laughed when a minute flower girl, concentrating too hard on her dignified walk, landed on her bottom. Guy's appearance, just in time to scoop up the child and bounce her frown into giggles, brought a film of tears to Leah's eyes.

That had been an hour ago, and now she could hear distant strains of guitar music. What would it be like to dance with Guy at their wedding? Her crazy imagination was treacherous.

She pushed aside several letters from members of the congregation. They were mostly suggestions or thank-you notes to Guy and could wait. Physical activity was what she needed, something to obliterate the little flashes that constantly plagued her—the way Guy's smile narrowed his eyes, his strong hands forcefully wielding a shovel, gently patting a child's head. This was all so hopeless.

Restless pacing in front of her desk didn't help. He'd said he didn't mind her tidying up. Mrs. Culver hadn't touched his own disorganized study or his bedroom. Why not make some attempt to straighten them? At least the study.

Entering the room again took resolution. She let her eyes travel slowly over his papers, the brandy glass, still among them, and on to the chairs where they'd sat facing each other. She would not feel embarrassed again. Instead, she swept up the glass and headed through his bedroom to wash it out in the bathroom.

This is a mistake, Leah. The shower tile had dried, but his towel was still damp and twisted on a bar beside the sink. His clean scent hung in the air. Tentatively, she picked up a comb from the shelf and closed her hand around it while she looked at masculine trappings. A half-used bottle of after-shave, his razor. He seemed to surround her, awaken every half-forgotten instinct yet again without even being in the same room. She thought of being here with him, of sharing his shower, watching him shave, leaning against his naked back to fold him in her arms. The next sensation to assail her came close to panic, and she pivoted sharply away.

On the way back to the study, she averted her eyes from his unmade bed and tried not to look at the cut-offs and shirt he'd tossed aside the night before. He probably slept nude. She almost ran through the door, closing it firmly behind her.

Papers on the desk quickly assumed precise positions, shuffled and neatly stacked according to size. Folders, she filed alphabetically in a battered filing cabinet.

The jacket had remained firmly in place all day, but as Leah became more involved in her project, she shed the garment and tossed it on a stool.

By four she was ecstatic. The desk was solid oak, and with a coat of lemon wax, glowed warmly. So did the chairs and an old but venerable-looking credenza. The latter had also been buried with debris that Leah had straightened and placed behind sliding doors below. She'd brought off a transformation, and she could hardly wait for Guy's reaction.

She was admiring her masterpiece when she heard his footsteps in the hall. Her breathing almost stopped as she watched the door handle turn before he entered the room. He seemed not to notice her at first. One hand repeatedly finger combed his hair. His head was slightly lowered, and for the first time she noticed dark streaks beneath his eyes. The man was exhausted. Maybe he hadn't slept so well last night, either.

"Guy," she said softly, "are you okay?"

He started violently and stared at her. "Where were you?" he said sharply. "You weren't in your office, and I thought—" He closed his mouth and rubbed both hands over his face.

He'd been afraid she'd left, Leah thought, not quelling a surge of joy. Her car was on the other side of the church rather than in front of the house, and he'd jumped to the wrong conclusion. "I decided I needed a change of pace," she consoled. "And I remembered you didn't mind if I tidied up a little, so I came back here. What do you think?"

Guy took in the room very slowly. He walked to the desk, then the credenza, running his fingers over each surface. Then he touched the filing cabinet with a look Leah recognized as wonder. She'd really surprised him, she thought happily.

"Good Lord." He turned on her. "What have you done in here? Where are my—my—things? My notes and reference folders? What—" He riffled through a sheaf of paper on the desk. "These aren't in the order I left them. Nothing is. How could you do this to me?"

For several seconds Leah stood mute, goose bumps racing over her skin, her throat tightly closed. Then deep, engulfing heat started somewhere inside and flared to the surface. "You ingrate. There wasn't any order before I started making some. Your things are tidy and easy for you to use. Your reference folders are filed where they belong—in the cabinet. I spent three hours in here, sweating over what must be several years' accumulation of crud, and all I get from you is a bawling out."

"Hardly a bawling out. You surprised me." A white line formed around Guy's compressed lips. He strode to the filing cabinet and wrenched open the top drawer, almost overbalancing the whole unit. "You filed the folders where? Using what system?"

"Alphabetical, of course," she shot back.

"Alphabetical?" Guy's tone was bewildered. He raised a hand, palm up, then dropped it heavily to his side. "Alphabetical? Oh, no. That's the end, then. I'll never find them again. They're filed—when I decide they should be—according to subject. I suppose it never struck you to check how I did it before you started your Suzy Homemaker stunt. When are you going to understand that I don't want you to clean up after me?"

Leah's hurt welled up in her until she could hardly keep from crying. Papers and dull books were all he cared about. The hard work she'd put in to please him meant nothing. She opened and closed her mouth several times like a beached fish, searching unsuccessfully for something scathing to say before racing from the room and back to her office. *Callous, thoughtless ingrate.* She slammed the door and leaned against it for an instant before grabbing the nearest chair and dragging it to the bookshelf closest to the window. *Okay, okay,* she repeated in her head. *Calm down and get on with it. You promised you'd stick this out until someone else could be found for the job, and you're going to make it.*

Not bothering to take off her shoes, she climbed on the seat of the chair. Maybe she should have asked him before tampering with his personal stuff. But the gesture was well-intentioned, and he had to know that. He could simply have thanked her and covered up his feelings. He'd looked desperate. That made twice today he'd disapproved of her efforts. And she was turning into a snapping shrew. Why had she exploded at him that way? She blushed at the memory of her harsh words. There was too much tension between them; altogether too much.

No good putting off the top shelves any longer. She began to pull out pamphlets that had been stuffed between books. Whoever had been here before her must have been a slob. The pile of discards that she dropped on the floor grew rapidly.

"Biles," she read on the spine of one volume, "*Methods of Prayer*." She could rearrange it under B, or perhaps M for method, or would his lordship consider P for prayer a better classification. A footfall sounded outside her door at the same time as Leah balanced precariously on the back of the chair to reach something orange. Her fingers closed on the sheet, and she started to fall.

The room seemed to swing wildly as the bottoms of both slippery shoes slid on the narrow rim of wood. She heard her own scream, then saw Guy running, arms outstretched. His face was a blur.

"Leah!" His yell came a second before the windowsill cracked into her spine and she smacked into an ungainly heap between chair and wall. Several books rained on her hands and forearms as she shielded her head.

She heard the chair scrape aside and instantly felt Guy's arms surround her, his fingers smoothing her loosened hair away from her face. "Are you all right? Leah, say something. Your ankles—" He lowered her carefully to the floor and slid off her shoes, then gently probed each shin and ankle. "No one takes a fall like

that and comes out without a broken bone. Speak to
me, will you?'' he pleaded.

Leah's heart still hadn't returned to its normal place
in her body, but her senses were enough intact to revel
in his anxious face and the tender stroking of her limbs.
''I'm all in one piece, I think. Just shaken up.''

''Does your head hurt?'' He peered closely into her
eyes. ''Do you hurt anywhere at all?''

''N-no. I don't think so. Except for my back where it
hit the windowsill,'' she said, sighing.

Guy must have mistaken the sigh for a moan. ''You
do hurt. Far more than you're saying. I'm taking you
to the emergency room. We'll get some X rays.''

''No! No.'' She had taken a pretty good knock, but
being with him, seeing his concern, would soon ease any
pain. ''If I stay still for a few minutes, I'll be fine.''

''I don't think so, Leah. I'll feel better if someone
checks you over.''

''Guy,'' she said persuasively, ''please believe me. It's
not necessary. You just go back to whatever you were
doing. I'll rest here quietly for a while.''

He stroked two fingers along her cheek. ''Have I told
you how stubborn you are?'' His eyes were close, fath-
omless.

''Mmm,'' she whispered, turning her face until her
lips brushed his palm. ''But not quite so bluntly.''

''What are we going to do about us, Leah?'' It was a
rhetorical question, his own thought spoken almost
unconsciously. He followed the question by outlining
her bottom lip with a thumb. ''Going away wouldn't
solve anything. You see that now, don't you?''

She nodded, silently waiting.

When the kiss came, it was infinitely tender, sweetly
restrained torture that speared desire into her belly.

Afraid to break the moment, she held still, her head cradled in one of his large hands. Tingling sensations flitted along every nerve as he urgently, repeatedly, pressed his lips to her face and neck. He lifted his head, searching her eyes, and she saw again the agony, the inward battle he was waging.

"Leah, Leah," he groaned, and nuzzled into the hollow of her throat.

He seemed to rest there endlessly, his breath warming her skin. Finally, he stood and took her hands, pulling her up slowly.

Without shoes, Leah felt small. The top of her head was level with Guy's chin. She took a step closer until she could kiss the tanned vee where he'd discarded his collar and opened the neck of his shirt. His arms tightened convulsively around her, and she looked up to find his face tipped back, his eyes squeezed shut.

Leah wanted to smooth away the frown and kiss his mouth into a smile. And she wanted to ask him why he had to suffer, to make them both suffer, when loving and needing couldn't be wrong. Loving. She did love Guy Hamilton and always would. "Guy," she whispered, and waited until their eyes met. She couldn't bring herself to question his motives for disregarding the arousal she felt in his body or the passion she saw in his eyes.

A shuddering sigh rippled through him, and he kissed her again, first deeply, reaching, moving her head from side to side, then softly, his tongue flitting along the membrane inside her lips. His breathing was shallow, and she felt the rapid beat of his heart against her breast. Her own heart leaped erratically.

Leah reached up to touch tiny lines at the corners of his eyes, ran a fingertip along the groove beside his mouth and touched her lips to the dimple that formed there. What would he say if she told him she loved him? She shook her head, clutching him close instead. "It'll be all right," she said without conviction. "I don't know how yet, but we'll find a way in time." She must believe in what she said and make him believe it, too.

"I hope to God you're right." Guy held her to him. The fingers of his right hand splayed wide over her cheek, then tangled in her hair, and he bent to breathe softly against her ear. "Be patient with me, Leah."

Tears prickled behind her eyelids before a shuffling sound made her crane to see around his shoulder. Everything in her body froze. Elsie Culver stood in the doorway.

Chapter Six

Leah dug her fingers into Guy's side. "Elsie," she squeaked. "What a surprise." She bit her lip. What a dumb thing to say.

Guy straightened and turned to face the woman. Leah could see his breathing hadn't returned to normal, but he managed a smile. "Hi, Elsie. What can I do for you?"

"Mrs. Cornish said for me to come back later." Dark eyes moved quickly over Leah, taking in her stockinged feet before settling sharply on Guy's face. Leah didn't fail to notice the use of her married name when the woman had been eager for informality between them earlier.

Guy's arm, lightly circling her shoulders, shocked Leah. She tried not to stiffen. How could he be so nonchalant? "Mrs. Culver's right." The quaver in her voice horrified her. This episode could undermine Guy's position with his congregation. "I've asked her to come in once a week. But I didn't know your policy on payment, so I thought I'd better wait until I could talk to you."

"Ah." He nodded, still smiling at his curious parishioner. "I'm sure you know the going rates, Elsie.

Whatever's fair. You two can work it out together, and I'll sign the check. I'm glad you're helping out. I don't want Leah to overdo."

"I see," Elsie Culver said with an emphasis that suggested she saw far more than Guy's words might convey. She spread her feet in their sensible white lace-up shoes and poked at gray sausage-shaped curls. Every second felt interminable to Leah.

Guy cleared his throat and rubbed her shoulder. "Leah's been attempting to pull off the impossible and sort out this place single-handed. Just before you came in, I picked her off the floor. She was trying to do something about these crazy bookshelves—using the back of that chair for a ladder. Perhaps you can help me protect her from herself."

Neat, Leah thought. But not neat enough. Elsie's expression was knowing before she nodded. "I'll be glad to, Guy. Maybe I should wait until tomorrow to get the money and my schedule sorted out. Her being shaken up now."

"Good idea, Elsie." Guy's tone was sober. "She took a hard knock. I tried to persuade her to go the emergency room, but she won't listen."

Elsie was backing away. "Oh," she said, "I'm sure most of us know what's best for us, don't we, Leah? She'll be right as rain before you know it."

Striped polyester swished as Mrs. Culver left.

"Guy," Leah breathed, turning to him. "That was awful. Terrible. I've never felt so embarrassed or vulnerable."

"My congregation trusts me," he said, a distant look in his eyes. "They're good people—the very best. They aren't gossips, and Elsie won't question my explanation of what she saw."

"You mean you expect her to buy that story of my falling?"

Guy absentmindedly rubbed her back. "It wasn't a story. You did fall. How's the bump?"

"I'm probably going to be a bit stiff." Leah slumped into the chair, exasperated. "It'll pass. Right now I have more important things on my mind. You can't brush off what just happened. It could affect your career if a rumor starts."

"It could, but it won't." The windowpane rattled suddenly, and he went to peer outside. "What Elsie saw was hardly a breach of moral ethics. I was holding you. I'd like to hold you again now. If I could figure out a way, I'd hold you all the time."

"I . . ." Leah swallowed hard and resisted the temptation to go to him, wrap her arms around his tall, lean body and rest her cheek on his shoulder. "Guy, listen to me carefully."

"Weather's changing." The inflection in his voice didn't alter. He crossed his arms on the windowsill. "The wind's picking up."

Avoidance tactics wouldn't help either of them. "Okay, stand there and pretend we haven't said any of the things we've said to each other—or touched each other. Make jokes out of everything. But please be sure you hear every word I say."

His shoulders hunched slightly.

"Guy, do the members of your congregation know you're married?"

"Yes, of course."

Leah winced. He seemed determined to treat possible disaster lightly. "You told them?"

"Of course. When I took this job, I expected Susan to come with me. They thought they were getting a couple." He turned and leaned against the wall, tilting back his head. "I guess we all got a shock."

"All?" Leah's palms were sweating.

"My little flock and me." His toneless voice wrenched her heart. Whether he still loved his wife or not, the thought of his failed marriage continued to hurt him.

She must concentrate. "How did they take it when Susan didn't join you? What did you tell them?" She wanted him to say that he'd explained the complete circumstances of his separation.

He rolled his face toward her, and she saw his gaze center on her lips. His own mouth had set grimly. Guy wasn't as unconcerned as he'd like her to believe. "What was I supposed to say?" he asked tiredly. "That my wife decided going to school was more important than being with me? Or maybe that I'd been a lousy, preoccupied husband and bored her into not giving a damn about me anymore?"

"What did you say, then?"

He sighed and closed his eyes. "You have a way of making me feel so guilty."

"For God's sake, be straight about this, will you?" Leah immediately wished she'd phrased the question differently and had sounded less agitated. "Guy, I'm sorry if—"

"You have nothing to be sorry about, not with me, ever." He began to pace back and forth behind the desk. "I didn't explain. I should have, but I didn't. After I arrived here alone, there were questions about Susan, and I just fielded them. First, what I said was..."

"What?" Leah prompted quietly when he didn't go on.

Guy stared at her. "I said she had to finish up school. Another of my half-truths. Like the one I told Elsie Culver just now. Some example to my people, right?"

"Don't!" Leah went to stand in front of him and grasped his upper arms. "Why do you think you have to be perfect? You're just a man, Guy. Is that so terrible? Or could it actually make it easier for you to relate to other men's problems, do you think?"

His smile was lopsided as he watched her face. "So serious, and so wise. Sure, I'm only a man. Boy, don't I know I'm only a man." He laughed abruptly, showing beautiful teeth, narrowing his limpid eyes. "But madam, it's a fact that honesty pays in the end. Everyone here knows my marriage is over, although I've never told them. They would probably have liked to help me through the hard times openly, the way I help them through theirs. But I was too proud to admit I was as human and capable of being insured as they are. Also, our Mrs. Culver would have less to report if my permanent separation wasn't a taboo subject."

The sudden slam of the window made Leah jump. "Keep meaning to have Wally fix that," she muttered. "You are worried about gossip, aren't you?"

"Not really." His biceps flexed beneath her fingers, and he rested his hands lightly at her waist. "Please try believing people mean well. And remember, you can't make much out of a man picking a lady in distress off the floor, particularly when she's narrowly missed killing herself."

Leah slowly shook her head. "I'd better arrive on crutches tomorrow, you naive, trusting man. I know how good all these people are; they've certainly been good to me. But I also know that by the time Elsie Culver's story's been translated a few times, we'll have been making love on the kitchen table." She blushed furiously and tried to twist away.

Guy held her fast and stroked her burning cheek. "Everything's going to be okay, I tell you. You're reading too much into a very minor incident."

"I don't think so. I—"

"Well, I do. And I know these—"

Two of Leah's fingers, firmly placed on his lips, stopped his interruption. "Shh, Guy. Please, don't tell me again how well you know your people. I might scream. You love your work; I know you do. I may not have figured out much about what you do or completely understand everything expected of you, but I do know that a minister, particularly one in a close-knit community, can easily become the focus of speculation.

"If you do stir up controversy and somebody decides to make an issue out of your private life, you could find it hard, maybe impossible, to carry on here. I'm not about to be responsible for upsetting your career. I think we'd better arrange the employment ad we talked about last night."

"How about a drink?" Guy said as if she hadn't spoken. "You've had a busy day."

"Guy—"

"I could certainly use something." His eyes met hers briefly, flickered and moved away, but not before she read quiet desperation there. The man was trying to stay inside his own emotional comfort zone.

Someone had to keep a clear head here. "Thanks, but no. I've still got grocery shopping to do before I go home. And I am a bit sore."

Immediately, Leah regretted the reference to her fall. "You're sore." Guy took her hand. "I knew it. You should be lying down. I don't know what I'm thinking about. Come on. You can rest in one of the guest rooms, and I'll get you a cold drink." He started for the door. "And aspirin—you should have aspirin for the inflammation and the pain."

"Stop." Leah stood her ground. "I'm going home. The sooner someone sees me walk out of here, the better."

"I think—" Guy began, then pressed his lips together and sighed. "I think you're probably right. But Leah, if we can avoid a repeat of today—at least for as long as it's necessary—will you stop talking about leaving?"

"As long as necessary?" How was she supposed to interpret that comment? "You mean will I stay on and never interfere with your study again?" she quipped halfheartedly.

"You know what I mean." He dropped her hand and fingered his hair. "But I'm sorry if I seemed uptight with you about the study. I guess I've been on my own too long. I'm too set in my ways."

"I'll second that notion," Leah retorted heartily enough to make them both laugh.

"Beauty and tact—I'm certainly blessed in my... I'm lucky to have you, Leah. Remember what you said just before Elsie Culver barged in?"

She remembered every detail of the past hour in living color. "Why don't you tell me?"

"You said we'd work things out somehow." He came closer until she had to arch her neck to watch his face. "I admit today makes that seem like a difficult project."

"And you asked me to be patient, Guy. But you didn't explain what you meant by that." Leah stopped short of mentioning their earlier talk of openness. He was choosing not to risk telling her everything that was on his mind.

For an instant, Guy hesitated, and Leah held her breath, feeling him struggle with his own feelings. He inhaled slowly. "I meant what I said; that's all. Be patient; give us time to be sure what we want and what we should do about it."

She concentrated hard on slipping her shoes back on, keeping her head down. "And while we do that, neither of us will be tempted to push the relationship farther? I hope you're right. Or we may both suffer. I don't want the loss of your job on my conscience." She met his eyes steadily. "Okay, I'll stick around. I like it here. For the first time in my life I'm beginning to feel like a truly useful human being. But I won't live on pins and needles waiting for one of us to take a wrong step. And for the record, I'm not so available you can decide what my future's going to be—even on the short term. I'll make my own decisions about what's good for me." She paused for breath, waiting for his reaction.

The satisfied smile on Guy's wide mouth curled her toes. "I wouldn't have it any other way," he said, and picked up her purse and jacket from the desk. "You're absolutely right. It's best you have an early night. In ten days I'm due to leave for a retreat in Tucson. I'll be away from Monday to Friday, and I'm counting on you to run things around here.

"Tomorrow I thought I'd talk to you about setting up my appointments while I'm gone. If you do it, I'm likely to keep things straight, which I don't always manage by myself. In fact, I think it might be a good idea for you to take over that job permanently. I'll also have to arrange for you to be able to sign checks."

He guided her to the front door and opened it for her. "I'd like to make an early start in the morning, if that's all right with you."

Leah had mumbled an assent and set out for the other side of the church and her car before her mind clicked into full gear. A fiercely hot wind whipped her skirt around her knees, and she walked faster, willing herself not to look back, knowing he stood in the doorway, watching.

Again, she'd been outmaneuvered. All her brave announcements didn't mean a thing. He was steadily making her more deeply entrenched in her job and with him. There was no way she and Guy Hamilton would keep their distance from each other for more than a few days—or hours.

The Volkswagen's door handle burned her fingers. "Damn," she hissed, blowing on her hand. If she didn't watch out, she'd end up with more than burned fingers.

EACH DAY SEEMED WARMER than the one before. It had been a week since Leah and Guy had agreed upon what she knew was a tenuous truce. A hundred times, while poring over papers together, while he gave her instructions or asked his schedule for the day, their eyes met, and in the still seconds that followed, naked desire sprang between them. The prospect of his trip to Tucson next week filled Leah with a mixture of emptiness and relief. At least she'd be able to relax and think her position through for a while.

Today Guy was making sick calls and wouldn't be back before midmorning. Leah rested her chin on one fist. What did he do on sick calls? Speak of faith and God, she supposed. They really had so little in common—almost nothing. She cast about for a shared interest and was about to give up when she remembered his puttering in the garden. They both enjoyed the earth and growing things, although Guy didn't know she loved it, too.

The cranky doorbell reverberated through the house. Only strangers rang the bell. Leah stood and smoothed her cotton shirt and pants before opening the door.

Wally Timmons stood in the shadow of the overhanging roof, hat in one hand, an orchid plant in the other. He opened his mouth several times but seemed to keep changing his mind about what he wanted to say.

Leah took a bony elbow and urged him inside. "Wally, get in out of the heat. You don't have to ring the bell. No one else does. Come on in. I'll find you some iced tea."

He grunted and allowed her to steer him into the big kitchen, immaculate from Elsie's regular ministrations.

"Sit down," Leah insisted. "Set your things on the table and relax. You look beat."

"I'm not staying, Leah. Just came by to ask you a favor. Then I'll be going." His faded check shirt, freshly washed and ironed as always, sported a black string tie with a turquoise clip. Wally wore a string tie no matter what he was doing and was most usually seen with a straw cowboy hat tilted rakishly forward over crew-cut, iron-gray hair. Leah worried that he didn't eat properly, because he was cadaverously thin.

"You'll have some iced tea and some of this meat pie Elsie Culver made or I'll lock the door with you inside," she admonished. "First you eat; then you can ask me your favor."

He flushed, deepening the color in his bronzed and lined cheeks. His pale blue eyes crinkled at the corners. "If you say so, miss. You're a feisty one, like my Joan."

Tears sprang to Leah's eyes, and she busied herself with the pie. Likening her to his dead wife was the greatest compliment he was ever likely to pay. He'd talked about Joan once when Leah persuaded him to come and eat dinner in her apartment. She'd also learned the couple had lost a daughter when she was nine. The girl had died of complications following a tonsillectomy and would have been about Leah's age if she'd lived. Leah knew that Wally was unconsciously turning her into the daughter he no longer had.

"There." She put a large slice of pie flanked by a peach and some melon balls in front of Wally. "I'll join you in the iced tea. It's a scorcher today, and this house is never cool. Guy keeps hinting about new air conditioning, but he doesn't seem to get beyond hints. Think we'll get thunder again? We could sure use more rain."

"Could be. Leah, I was going to talk—" Wally stopped and fidgeted with his glass back and forth.

She finished a long swallow of her own drink and studied him curiously. Something was bothering Wally. "You were going to talk," she prodded.

He shook his head and speared a large mouthful of pie.

Leah waited, suddenly apprehensive. Could there be something wrong with Wally and he didn't know how to tell her? She drummed her fingers on the table.

He downed half his tea and straightened in his chair. "Would you see what you can do with this?" His voice was tight and crackly as he pushed the plant toward her. "I know you've got a way with the things. All those plants in your apartment grow apace, and you told me you used to raise orchids.''

Relief, then sweet sadness flooded Leah. She was relieved he hadn't said he was ill and touched that he'd brought the plant. "How nice of you, Wally. I haven't had one in ages.''

"It's nothing,'' he replied hastily. "Had it around for months and the durn thing won't do anything for me. Thought you might know what it needed.''

She stared directly at him until he lowered his face to the plate again and made much of scraping crumbs into a tidy pile. "I'll do my best, Wally,'' she said at last. The pot still had a bright, new price tag on its side, and she'd lay a bet the cash-register receipt was in Wally's pocket.

"You should have a bit of garden to mess with,'' he mumbled gruffly. "It isn't healthy for you to work in that stuffy office all the time. Wish there was more ground around my place.''

The door on the refrigerator didn't latch easily and began to swing open. Leah got up to close it. "I don't spend all my time in the office.'' Wally's suggestion surprised her, but he could be right. "Maybe I should ask Guy if I can help him around the grounds.''

She heard Wally clear his throat and turned to look at him. "You okay, Wally? You don't have a cold or something?''

"Nope. Never better. Just been a bit worried about you lately.''

His comment puzzled Leah. "Why? Because of my back? It's much better.'' She'd told Wally about her fall, and he'd immediately produced a bottle of lotion that smelled like horse liniment.

He made as if to stand, but Leah urged him back into the chair. "Is there something on your mind you're not telling me, Wally?"

"No." He spoke too loudly. "I reckon I was fussing about nothing. But you don't have any folks to keep an eye on you, so..."

"So you thought you would. Thanks, Wally. And I appreciate it. Everyone needs someone to keep an eye on them. I will do something about getting outside more. I'm sure Guy would let me help in the garden if I asked him."

He shifted and reached for his hat. "That's kind of what I wanted to talk to you about. You and—"

"Wally Timmons, you old goat. What brings you here?" Guy breezed into the kitchen. "Can't remember the last time I managed to get you over the doorstep. Of course—" he winked at Leah "—there didn't used to be a lovely lady to serve you iced tea, and what's that you ate—pie? Good to see you, anyway." He flopped into a chair, slid down and stretched out his long legs.

Leah wondered fleetingly how many ministers did their job in soft cotton shirts and faded jeans that hugged every fascinating male inch. "Tea, Guy?" she asked with an asperity that annoyed her. Around Guy her reactions seemed to take on their own life.

"Thanks." His expression was nonplussed. "You okay, Leah?"

"Yes, I'm okay. I'm terrific. Why is everyone so concerned about my health?" She plopped a glass in front of Guy before remembering Wally was watching. "Will you have some more of this, Wally?" she added more evenly.

"Not for me. I'd better be going."

He felt the tension in the room—who wouldn't? She and Guy created a charged current the instant they were within yards of each other.

"Who else is concerned about your health, as you put it?" Guy had sat bolt upright and stared intently at Leah.

"She's talking about me," Wally interjected. "I was just saying it isn't healthy for a pretty young woman to be shut away in an office all hours of the day—and night."

Silence hung heavy in the air for seconds while Guy and Leah caught each other's eyes. Was Wally making a point, or was she overreacting out of her insecurity?

Guy recovered quickly, settling back into a more comfortable position. "You think I work my staff too hard, huh? Maybe you're right. But this one's an eager beaver. What do you suggest I do?"

Wally stood and rammed on his hat. "What the heck," he grumbled to no one in particular.

"Wally—" Guy laughed "—I'm asking for suggestions."

Leah watched the old man turn his answer over in his mind before replying. She had the feeling he hadn't managed to tell her exactly what he'd come to say.

"What the heck," Wally repeated, and Leah smothered a laugh. Whatever was troubling him might take time to dig out.

Wally drew himself up to his full, spindly height. "Leah likes to garden. She used to do a lot of it where she came from, and she's got that little apartment of hers full of plants. There's greenery hanging and standing all over the place. But plants aren't the same as digging in the dirt, if that's what you like. You know that, and I know that."

Leah stared, fascinated. Wally's speech was the longest she'd ever heard him make, and Guy's absorbed attention suggested he was as taken aback as she.

"I didn't know Leah was interested in gardening, Wally. She never told me." Guy glanced at her quickly, then back to Wally. "Is there something I should do about it?"

Wally hooked his thumbs in his belt and slouched. "This wasn't what I came to—" He rubbed agitatedly at the back of his neck. "Oh, what the heck. She wants a piece of garden. Give her one and give her some company while she's working there, too. She's special, this one, unusual. And while you're at it, invite her out. Have her dress up and take her dancing. Young stud like you letting the grass grow under his feet— What's the matter with you? Aw, hell!"

Leah had turned on the faucet before Wally started speaking. Water splashed steadily into the sink as she watched him stalk into the hall. He shut the front door with enough force to make the walls shudder.

Guy remained in his chair, staring at Leah until the sound of running water caught her attention and she turned back to the sink.

She felt Guy come behind her. "That old guy really cares about you," he said.

"I'd never have expected him to explode like that. Or to suggest you should take me out or—" Embarrassment made her stop.

A strong hand gripped her elbow, and Guy turned her to face him. "Beginning to believe not everyone around here is a malicious gossip who doesn't want to see us together?"

"I don't know what I believe anymore." Leah shut her eyes.

He smoothed back her hair. "But you aren't ready to fly away and leave me?"

"I'm not ready to go anywhere, Guy." She met his gaze steadily. "I'm not secure where I am, either."

"I know that, Leah. But I keep telling myself you will be in time, that we both will be."

"Wait and see, right?" She wasn't convinced, but there seemed to be no alternative solution to what they'd started.

"That's it, I guess." Guy rubbed both hands over his face, then looked at her again. "You should have told me you like to garden. Have as much ground as you like. I'll be glad to work with you. It's good to have company out there." He gave a wry grin. "But I think dancing is a little more closeness than either of us should try to handle right now."

After he'd left, Leah picked up the orchid plant Wally had brought and took it to her office. She could still see Guy's face in her mind and feel his presence.

"Wait and see..."

If that was the answer, the way to find herself with him permanently, it would have to do. Life without him would be worthless.

Chapter Seven

Heat scintillated over the highway ahead of the jeep. Guy squinted and arched his neck. Sweat coursed between his shoulder blades. The two-hour drive from Tucson back to Phoenix had felt like two days. He was sticky all over, and a pain niggled at both temples.

When he turned off the Maricopa Freeway at Seventh Street and headed north into the city, a squeezing in his gut joined the headache. Every yard that raced beneath his wheels took him closer to the mushrooming dilemma he must face. The retreat had been different from any other he had experienced. Rather than the healing peace he'd anticipated, the three days he'd managed to stay away had been filled with a series of soul-wrenching revelations. Leah would wonder why he'd decided to return early. One minute he thought he knew exactly why; the next his brain became a confused jumble.

Time to think had been a blessing and a curse. Some of the hurt and frustration he'd never allowed himself to face after the breakup of his marriage had surfaced. There had been moments of panic when he'd deliberately remembered Susan, saw her gray eyes and white-blond hair, imagined her loose-limbed walk and the way she'd had of smiling up at him. They had loved with the abandon of the very young, never considering their happiness wasn't invincible. The vivid return of poignant old feelings had shocked and frightened him. He couldn't go through all that again with another woman.

At the intersection with Van Buren Street, Guy stopped for a light. He'd been unable to feel any rancor toward Susan even when they had parted. She'd been as sad as he, but for different reasons. For her, their love had died, and its passing had left her with an unhappy void. She'd openly explained her reasons for wanting to part, and he'd cried for her loss and for his and for his part in their failed relationship. He didn't know exactly how long he'd continued to love her, certainly for several years. She'd called him once; several times he'd called her. "I'll always care about you, Guy," she'd told him. "I'll always wish the best for you." But she'd stopped loving him, and in time he'd been able to relegate her to the past. In the last three days, he'd finally found a comfortable slot for her. A special but temporary gift, she was a real friend who had come into his life at the wrong time.

A blaring horn startled him into noticing that the light had turned green, and he jerked the vehicle forward. He was tired, and he wanted to see Leah. He checked his watch. Four o'clock. She should still be at the house.

The other clear discovery that had come to him during his quiet hours in Tucson had been the true depth of his growing feelings for Leah Cornish. His admission had brought flashes of intense joy. Until they had met, he'd been convinced he could never love or consider marriage again.

He visualized the official letter he'd received from Susan's lawyer in California a few weeks ago, stating that Susan Hamilton was filing for dissolution of her marriage. Mrs. Hamilton would prefer an uncomplicated proceeding, but if necessary, incompatibility could easily be proved. Cold, legal jargon. Simply, it came down to a bill of divorcement, and that sounded so much sadder to his mind. For Susan to decide on legal action after so long must mean she'd found someone else. Guy smiled faintly and rubbed sweat from the corners of his eyes. He was glad. She deserved to be happy. And when the divorce became final, he could seriously think of doing something about his own future. This time—if there was to be another time to give completely of himself—he had to be sure everything was right.

At McDowell Road, he took a left. Almost home. There were so many gray areas in his understanding of Leah. Two had glared at him persistently and would only become increasingly important if they decided to marry. First, she would be faced with the role of minister's wife, and for them to make a successful team, she'd have to be able to assume her part. Yet he didn't have any idea what she believed or even if she believed in anything at all. He'd waited for her to show some interest in the church, to attend a service, maybe. She had never mentioned faith or even entered the building.

Dust billowed when he turned the wheel at the corner of Fan Lane. The other concern was as big, if not bigger. She must become a complete person, capable of standing alone. Every day she took another step in that direction, but she still had a long way to go. She'd left one insular world for another. As far as he knew, she worked and went home—nothing more. Again, she'd

found a safe, enclosed haven and was steadily settling
into a pattern. If they married now, he believed their
future together would be happy. He also believed Leah
would draw back to resume her place in the shadow of
a husband, and he wouldn't allow that to happen. She
was too bright, too talented, not to be a person in her
own right.

Leah's yellow Volkswagen was parked in the shade of
the oleander hedge. Guy sighed with relief and pulled
in beside it. There was time to build a foundation for
their future. Marriage, or even a consummated relationship, wasn't an issue yet and couldn't be until he was
free. In the meantime, he had an idea how to broaden
Leah's world. He hoped desperately she'd agree to his
suggestion.

She wasn't in her office. The little room still smelled
of fresh paint. Her choice of stark white had surprised
him, but it opened up the small space. So did matching
vertical, slatted shades. The order she'd achieved made
him smile appreciatively before he recalled his own reaction to her efforts in his study. Well, she'd spoken of
wanting to "organize something," and he'd invited her
to try her talents on him. He winced. She'd looked so
hurt and puzzled when he hadn't been enthusiastic.

Her perfume lingered in the air. Guy breathed deeply,
and the muscles in his thighs contracted. He slung his
grip over his shoulder and headed for the other side of
the house, glancing into each room he passed. She could
be working somewhere outside, he guessed. There
hadn't been an opportunity before he left to discuss the
piece of ground she wanted; however, he had told her
to use as much as she liked.

He'd dropped the bag and stretched out on his bed
before he heard the splash of water in the pool. The

drape over the sliding-glass door was open. Lying on his side, propping his head, Guy could see sunlight bouncing in silver chips over the blue water and shimmering on the tanned shoulders of the woman who swam there.

Unconsciously, he pulled himself to the edge of the bed. She cut the surface smoothly in easy freestyle strokes. With each angling of an elbow, he saw a flash of her white suit.

At the far end of the pool, she pulled herself up to stand on the edge. Guy also stood and moved closer to the window. He knew she'd been swimming each afternoon since the pool had been filled, and he'd deliberately stayed out of the way until he was certain he wouldn't see her. He should have remembered today and kept his distance. This was what he'd been secretly afraid of, of seeing her, watching her and wanting her until he ached with the wanting.

She flicked water from her face and slicked the long, dark hair close to her head. Smooth limbs gleamed. Against the afternoon's cerulean sky, her slender body stood out in sharp relief. Guy traced each gentle curve and swell beneath the simple one-piece suit. He chewed his bottom lip. Joining her in the water on a blistering day would be perfectly natural, something no one could question—could they? The answer was obvious. Whether or not someone else questioned his motive was irrelevant. He'd know what drove him to her.

Leah made a clean dive, knifing into the water to head back in his direction. She moved with the economy of a practiced swimmer, and Guy closed his eyes. How often had Charles Cornish watched her in the secluded pool he'd probably had built for her alone? Guy detested the idea of the other man being with her and immediately detested himself for envying a man dead.

When Cornish married her, she'd been little more than a child, a beautiful, innocent girl. She'd somehow managed to retain the essence of that innocence and was undoubtedly far more beautiful now. Yet it was the very sense that she was naive and ingenuous that troubled him.

If she were more secure, better equipped to care of herself, would she need him? Would she still choose to be with him if she was exposed to other masculine company? Or had he become a convenient substitute for Charles Cornish, a man who, without her husband's wealth, still represented stability and protection? And was it possible, eventually, that she'd come to long for the luxuries she'd once enjoyed, then resent Guy for not being able to provide them? Thanks to his parents' legacy, he had a comfortable income to supplement his salary, but it didn't allow for many wild excesses.

Guy yanked the drapes closed. The uncertainties were multiplying, and he only hoped they'd both have the strength to face and work them through.

Leah saw Guy a second before he closed his bedroom drapes. She paused, her breath suddenly labored, her heart thundering. He wasn't due back until the day after tomorrow.

She glided to the wall of the pool. His shadow, dark through pale fabric, stayed unmoving until he raised a hand and appeared to rake fingers through his hair. He'd been watching her, and now he was shutting her out. Damn it all.

Leah pulled herself from the water. Was she such a threat to his pure soul? She frowned. Was she unworthy of the good minister, someone who might tempt, then sully him?

A desire to cry passed rapidly and was replaced by simmering fury. If he wanted her, as he repeatedly suggested he did, and he no longer cared for his wife, why didn't he get a divorce? He'd said his reasons for remaining married were complicated, but he didn't say why. Could he be clinging to his defunct marriage because it kept him safe from another permanent commitment?

The questions were endless, and Leah wasn't getting any answers. The only way she'd ever have a chance to understand this man, to get close enough to him to win his trust, was to confront him—as often as it took to get at the truth.

She sucked in a long breath through her mouth and marched to his door. The shadow had moved away, but she was certain Guy hadn't left his rooms. Her hard rap on the glass stung her knuckles. She blew on them, shook the hand, then stood with feet firmly planted and elbows akimbo.

Seconds unreeled. Leah could almost hear each one slip by. Her hand was raised to knock again when Guy pulled the curtain back a few inches, then opened the door. He didn't smile, and she saw his throat jerk as he swallowed.

"Hi," she said brightly. "Thought you weren't coming back from your retreat until Friday."

He rested a forearm on the jamb and pressed his brow against his fist. "Got all retreated out, I guess." His eyes held hers for an instant, then lowered to her mouth and down, slowly, hungrily, taking in her body. With his visual touch, her skin heated.

"How was it?" Leah managed.

Guy's eyes flicked back to hers. "What?"

"The retreat," she repeated. "How was the retreat?"

"I hated it," he responded flatly.

"Oh." Leah tried to read his closed expression. "Why did you hate it?"

"I think you can work out the answer to that one."

She crossed her arms tightly, willing her heart to slow down. "I think I'd like to hear you tell me."

He lightly traced her bottom lip with his thumb. "Mmm. Three days away from you was too long."

So why don't you find a way for us to be together all the time? "I'm glad."

"Are you?"

"What kind of a question is that?" she asked softly.

"A rhetorical one." Guy's voice was equally gentle. "I hoped you might say you'd missed me, too."

He was rapidly driving her mad. And words weren't going to be enough. She needed tangible proof of his feelings, a sign she could hold on to. "Guy," she said, pushing back wet strands of hair, "it's hot. You must be boiling after that drive. Come and swim with me."

The fist supporting his forehead clenched. A battery of expressions crossed his features before he slowly shook his head. "Thanks, but I don't think so. There must be a stack of work waiting for me, and I might as well get started."

"If you'd stayed in Tucson as long as you planned, you wouldn't be catching up with your work." She felt him drawing back, insulating himself from her.

"That was probably one of the things that made me so edgy while I was away. I knew how far behind I was getting. See you in the morning." He moved to slide the door shut, but Leah grasped the metal rim. "I really would like to get a few things done."

"What you mean is..." Her voice sounded strangled, and she lifted her chin. "What you mean is that you want to do things to keep yourself away from me. You're afraid to relax with me, to be close to me. Say it, Guy. Admit it."

His smile was weary. "I probably won't get to my sermon before Friday. Would you mind typing it on Saturday? I'd pay you overtime, of course."

Dull rage expanded in Leah. He refused to meet any issue head-on, and he had the gall to talk about overtime pay as if she were no more to him than casual help. And only a few minutes before he'd admitted to missing her too much to finish his retreat. He confused her, tied her up in knots.

"That'll be fine, Guy," she said, feeling muscles in her jaw tremble. "As long as you pay me, of course." She half turned away, then changed her mind and faced him squarely. "What kind of a God requires a man to prove his belief by living on a mental island?"

Guy said nothing but took a step backward, his complexion paling beneath its deep tan.

Tears stung her eyes once more. "You need someone, Guy. So do I. Doesn't it say somewhere in that famous book of yours that it isn't good for man to live alone?" Her throat burned. He must hear the crying in her voice. "That means you and me, friend."

Several running strides took her back to the pool. A blind forward lunge of her body sent her deep into the water, which surrounded her in its cool, echoing blanket. She swam hard, concentrated on her breathing, the blood pumping through her veins, her limbs pushing against the resistance. She mustn't think. His God. She'd thrown at him the one element that must mean most in his life. If she wanted to kill any chance they had of grabbing a little happiness together, she'd cho-sen the perfect weapon.

She'd lost count of her laps when she caught sight of long fingers and strongly muscled arms that matched her strokes entering the water. Guy swam beside her, his broad shoulders dappled with drops of liquid sun-shine. She hesitated, trod water an instant, then struck out again. They didn't speak, only kept pace with each other one length after another.

Finally winded, Leah slowed to a lazy sidestroke and watched him. The swimsuit he wore was a brief black slash around his taut body. He passed her again, and powerful legs sent a back-rushing current at her. Mus-cle and sinew, perfectly toned, stretched and con-tracted. A thrill of desire flew up her spine.

At the far end, he stopped with both arms spread along the wall while he waited for her. Blond chest hair, turned darker by the water, made a tantalizing pattern. The distance between them narrowed until she could have reached out to touch him. Leah held position, paddling, her eyes questioning his. Guy didn't smile. "Leah," he said, and offered her his left hand.

She felt a beat miss somewhere in some unplayed tune, a step falter in the dance, before she placed her fingers in his and let him pull her near. They swayed, gently bobbed, and he took her other hand. Slowly, they rotated, keeping the distance of their bent arms be-tween them. Leah gazed at long spiky lashes, into his clear eyes, and saw her own longing reflected there.

"It does say man shouldn't be alone," he whispered at last. "Do you read..." The question trailed off, and he pressed his lips together. "I don't want to be alone anymore. But we have a long way to go before we can do anything about it. You see that, don't you, Leah?"

She nodded assent as her brain screamed that she didn't understand anything but her need, their need and the way she felt with him.

Guy steadied her, then pulled himself up on the edge of the pool before hauling her up beside him. They sat, inches separating their legs, and swung their feet in unison. Leah could feel the warmth of his skin radiating into her flesh. Why did her throat have to hurt too much for her to speak? She ought to say something important.

"Neither of us can afford another mistake." Guy spoke low, as if more to himself than her.

"No." Leah glanced up at his clear profile. She wanted to tell him their being together couldn't be a mistake and to make him believe she was right.

He looked at her. "Let's not push this too hard." His hand hovered an inch above hers, then covered and held it on top of his tensed thigh. "Let's not go too far too fast and end up not even being friends."

Leah's heart swooped. His words made her hollow, a shell around the empty space she knew she'd become without him. "I never want us not to be able to see each other. I just... I guess I don't understand you. You won't let me."

His grip tightened. "I want us to understand each other. That's what this is all about. We don't understand each other yet. But we will, Leah, we will."

A stillness closed in around them—silence and warmth and the twin racing of their unspoken thoughts.

Leah turned her palm and lifted his fingers to her lips. She closed her eyes and felt him lean against her, guiding her head into the hollow of his shoulder.

His breathing moved the muscle beneath her cheek. "I feel so peaceful with you like this," he told her.

She wished they could stay as they were forever. "So do I. Guy, I'm sorry I said those things to you about—about—"

"God?" he interjected. "Not so hard to say. And I understand. Forget it. Just let me know if you ever want to talk more on the subject."

Leah didn't know what to say next. She coughed and looked at the sky. How did you admit to a minister, the man you'd fallen in love with, that your religious knowledge was limited to a few semiremembered Bible passages read as a child?

She straightened, suddenly tired. Being here with Guy was precious but tormenting. "It must be getting late. I could go over your appointments with you before I leave if you like." He would know she was running away from a further confrontation, but she needed time alone to think.

"The appointments can wait. I want to talk to you about an idea I had in Tucson." In a purposeful motion, he swiveled to sit cross-legged, facing her. "Have you ever thought about going back to school?"

Leah stared at him blankly.

"I mean to finish your high school requirements. How far from completion were you when you dropped out?"

She wound hair nervously behind one ear. More emotional battering. Now he was dragging up another part of her past she tried never to think about. "Less than a quarter," she mumbled.

"You're kidding," he said, laughing. "Why on earth couldn't you have stuck it out a couple of months longer?"

His incredulous amusement wounded her. He had no idea what her life had been like. "That wasn't a choice

I was allowed to make. We needed money immediately, not in a couple of months. There are times, Guy, when eating takes precedence over everything else.'' A small internal voice added, *And your mother's drinking habits and her need for cheap, flashy clothes to flaunt in front of her men*. But she kept the thought to herself.

Guy ran a knuckle along her jaw and clasped her shoulder, shaking her gently. ''My turn to be sorry. You'd think in my line of work I'd know better than to make sweeping judgments. But how about it?''

''What?'' Leah said.

''Going back to school. There are a couple of private colleges right in Phoenix where we could arrange for you to be enrolled for September to polish up and get your diploma. Then you could decide if you want to go farther.''

She shook her head. He was going too fast. ''You want me to go to school next month? That's only a couple of weeks away—less than that.'' Why? She'd been inept when she started working for him, but she thought he'd been pleased with her progress.

Guy tilted his head. ''Don't you like the idea? There's plenty of time to get you registered as long as you make up your mind quickly.''

''I suppose so,'' Leah said slowly. Another idea was dawning. This could be the next step in some plan to make sure she could make it alone if she had to leave. And she might have to leave eventually if they remained in Guy's self-imposed, don't-touch holding pattern.

''You don't sound very enthusiastic. Frightened?''

''No!'' she shot back with a vehemence that jolted her. ''No, I'm not afraid. Why should I be? But I'd like to know exactly why you're so keen on the idea." She raised her chin.

He looked puzzled; then his expression cleared. "Do you think I'm dissatisfied with your work or something?" When she didn't answer, he added, "That's exactly the problem, isn't it. Well, you're wrong. I've never had anyone as efficient as you working for me. You're terrific, a miracle. I can't believe what you've accomplished in a few weeks. And neither can I believe the way you taught yourself to type. I know you don't need more training to do what you do for me. But I want to feel you could make it anywhere, and for that you need to finish high school requirements and, possibly, think about something beyond that." He paused, watching for her reaction. "Hey, if you had less than a quarter to go, you must have been a grade ahead."

"Two," she said, and immediately blushed. "Didn't mean anything, really."

Guy cupped the side of her face. "It means, my humble little friend, that you are very bright. But we both know that, don't we?"

She ignored the question. "I wouldn't mind going back to school, I suppose," Leah said, sighing. Silently, she weighed her true feelings on the subject. Whatever happened with Guy, she did need to be able to care for herself. And to survive in a competitive world, she needed training and qualifications. "I'll do it," she announced in a voice that sounded authoritative and foreign to her.

"Great," Guy cried, grinning broadly. "Just great. Come on; this calls for a toast. Let's get some iced tea."

He dragged Leah to her feet and strode ahead toward the house. She trailed behind, studying his broad back and narrow hips, the long, strong legs. Guy Hamilton was steadily becoming the center of her existence. But his exuberance at her positive response to more schooling provoked a sickening constriction in her stomach.

At the door, his smile brilliant, Guy waited for her to catch up. Leah turned up the corners of her own mouth valiantly. His happiness was out of proportion, born of some much deeper meaning than the obvious one he'd offered. Leah thought she knew the true reason. She was one of his good works. Even though she couldn't deny the conviction that he desired her physically and cared for her in some special way, his consuming mission was to make her whole.

As they parted to change, Leah's nausea became a pain. He intended to patch her and mend her so that, if necessary, he could feel good about setting her free, like a bird after he'd mended its wing.

ON SATURDAY MORNING, Leah got up early. She dressed in lightweight jeans and knotted the tails of a pink checked shirt to leave an inch of midriff bare. Yesterday had been stiflingly muggy, an ominous stillness eventually giving way to lightning that tore the sullen sky into jagged swatches. For an hour Arizona's monsoon warning crackled, and distant thunder rolled before the downpour started. Then hours of sheeting rain in hundred-degree heat left the earth steaming and popping. Although the sun was shining now, today promised more of the same weather.

While she made coffee, she hummed. She wasn't going to spend the day alone, as she had every weekend since she'd arrived in Phoenix. Typing Guy's sermon might not be what most women would look forward to as a treat, but Leah did. She enjoyed working, and she would be near him—unless he had other plans for the day.

Her stomach dipped, and she pushed the thought away. He was bound to be around at least when she arrived.

Since she'd been alone, she'd slipped into the habit of skipping breakfast. The kind of thing people living alone did, she acknowledged, and rummaged in the refrigerator for a container of yogurt. The waistband of her jeans was loose. Time to start eating properly; she was already thin enough.

She glanced around her tiny apartment and smiled. It was the first place she'd ever had that was truly her own. With Wally's permission and aid, hooks had been fastened to the beam at the ceiling apex, and lush hanging ferns tangled their tender shoots with trailing philodendrons. A hoya's shiny leaves snaked jealously down to guard an inverted umbrella of fragrant pink blossoms.

Leah took her coffee and yogurt to a glass-topped bamboo table by the window and settled to watch birds flit noisily about their early-morning business in the ancient sycamore tree outside.

She realized she was still smiling, and a tranquil happiness stole over her. Yesterday, Guy had driven her through the rainstorm to an adult learning center in Scottsdale. The city suburb was a half-hour ride from St. Mark's. Guy had encouraged her to enroll in a private facility nearby and offered to help with the tuition. Leah had been adamant. The Scottsdale program was free, and she didn't want help. She certainly didn't mind traveling the extra distance.

Now that the step had been taken, she felt strangely excited. School had been an exhilarating challenge to her. Having to leave before graduation was a disappointment she'd never forgotten, and now she would have another chance. She shouldn't have needed someone else to suggest she go back. Too many years of not thinking for herself had left their mark.

A tentative tap, followed by Wally's distinctive "Haloo," broke her reverie, and she jumped up to let him in.

"Morning, Wally." She waved him inside. "Coffee's hot."

He gave her his nervous smile, driving the familiar deep wrinkles across his thin cheeks. "I had my coffee, thanks, Leah. Gotta get on the road." He held out a key, and she took it. "I'm going to be in Mesa for a week or so. Joan's sister and her family live there."

"I'm glad." Leah patted his arm. "It'll do you good to have a break. Don't worry about things here. I'll keep an eye on the place. Was there anything you particularly wanted me to do while you're gone?"

Wally rolled the brim of his straw hat in both hands. "I guess . . ." He crossed the room to examine the hoya blossom. "Darn, but you've got a way with growing things. I don't think I ever saw one of these bloom outside a greenhouse before."

Leah watched him, apprehensive without knowing why. "I don't have too many talents, Wally. I guess God decided I should have at least one. Was there anything you wanted me to do? You started to say something."

He swung around, a frown puckering his brow. "This isn't easy, Leah. I've been trying to tell you for days." The bony brown fingers had unconsciously worked a piece of straw loose in the hat brim, and now he studied it closely.

She waited, cold slicking over her skin. The day Wally
visited the rectory, she'd known he wanted to shed a
burden. Guy's arrival had stopped him; then she'd assumed Wally's outburst about her needing recreation
was the original purpose for his visit.

"I did get a patch of garden, Wally. I'm still learning how to cultivate the soil here—it's very different
from what I'm used to. Thought I might try vegeta-
bles, though.. You always get more than you can use
yourself, and there's certainly plenty of folks to share
them with."

He pressed his mouth into a straight line. The length
of straw had completely unraveled. "You're one in a
million, my girl. Someone who cares. It isn't fair."

Every word he spoke was becoming part of an incomplete puzzle. At last, Leah took a sinewy forearm
and led Wally to the chair opposite hers by the window. "Sit. And stop hedging. Say what you came to
say."

The thump with which he hit the chair seat spelled
reluctance. "You believe in God?" he blurted abruptly,
and immediately ran a hand over his reddened face.

"I—yes." Leah frowned. "Never had much time to
think about it, but I suppose I do in my own way."

Wally relaxed visibly. "Well, that's that one, then. I
told them you did."

"Them?" Leah asked. "Who wanted to know?"

The jerky pulling at his hat brim resumed. She had to
resist the temptation to take it from him before he de-
stroyed it completely.

"Wally? Who?"

He rocked his head slowly from side to side. "Just
some of the women. And Elsie Culver's husband,

George. He's not such a bad stick. Never works, though.''

Leah wasn't interested in George Culver's employment record. The cold on her skin had wormed into her belly. "That's all they said? Did I believe in God?''

Wally was on his feet, his features set in an angry mask. "Busybodies, the lot of them. The minister deserves to be happy, and I can't think of anyone I'd rather see him happy with than you.''

He stared at her fiercely, but Leah didn't offer any comment. Her heart pounded in her ears.

"They're just jealous. Every one of those women is half in love with the man themselves. But you've got to do something or he's going to get hurt.''

She found her voice. "Will you tell me exactly what they're saying and what I ought to do? Please, Wally.''

The hat was now a mangled mess. He met her eyes with anguished difficulty. "Guy's still a married man. He should have done something about that a long time ago, but it wasn't my place to talk to him about it. He's always been a private one about his own business. Never talked to a soul about why his wife never came—just stayed to himself. Not healthy for a young man.

"They're saying you two met somewhere else and started— They say you planned to get together even before you were widowed and the job at Guy's house is a cover for—'' Wally picked up her coffee cup and took a swallow, apparently without realizing what he'd done. The color in his cheeks had darkened. "What the heck.'' He backed toward the door. "You and Guy mean a lot to me. There isn't any sin in the pair of you—just a normal need between two young folks. But these biddies can rack it up. Guy could lose his job here if you don't straighten things out.''

Leah poked her hair with shaking fingers. "We haven't done anything wrong," she breathed.

"Whatever you do, it won't be wrong." Wally's scratchy voice hardened. "And it's only your business, anyway. But I've got to make sure you know what you're up against. They say the two of you are living in sin. That the married man who's supposed to be their spiritual leader is openly committing adultery."

Chapter Eight

"Guy!" Leah called. "Guy, where are you?" Her voice bounced, unanswered, through the house. The panic that had started while Wally made his pained announcements swelled to close her throat in a rigid vise.

She reached Guy's empty study and approached his bedroom. "Guy?" she asked tentatively. When he didn't reply, she knocked at the door, and it swung wide beneath her hand. She saw his unmade bed and the covers twisted on the floor; a glimpse beyond revealed a discarded towel and steamy air redolent of his clean, sense-twisting smell. But no Guy. He had showered and left the house.

The bubble in her throat broke into a hiccuping sob. "Where are you, damn it?" The jeep was still parked outside. He couldn't have gone far.

Tears sprang to her eyes, making blurry shapes out of the furniture as she stumbled into the hall and back to her office. She sniffed and dug in her purse for a tissue. He'd asked her to come. If nothing else, he should be here to tell her what he wanted done. And she needed him now. "I need you," she murmured aloud. "I *need* you."

The time... In her anxiety to talk to Guy, she'd left her apartment immediately after Wally. Now the clock on her office wall showed only eight-thirty. She'd agreed to start at ten. Guy wouldn't expect her to be so early.

A loud snap pulled her attention to the window. She saw through the blinds to an ashen sky streaked by a single golden shard of lightning. Thunder roiled, building to a muffled explosion before another crackling glow speared earthward. The rain might not take so long to come today, and Leah was glad. The still pressure in the air around her echoed the mounting tension in her head, and a wild storm would be a relief.

He could be outside working. The lightning was dangerous—he shouldn't be in the open. Leah ran through the front door and around the side of the house. The garden, the grounds, the pool—everywhere she searched was deserted. Her heart jammed against her lungs, and she rushed on, repeating her circuit until she stood, breathless, beside his jeep and her own Volkswagen.

The church... As soon as she thought of it, she noticed that the white building's door stood open. He often went there in the morning—maybe every morning, for all she knew. Several times she'd met him as she arrived for work when he was returning from the church.

Scattered drops of warm rain hit the path. Leah started to walk, watching wet splotches slam pale concrete and spread, faster and faster, until their outlines merged. The top of her hair and her face were damp by the time she inched cautiously through the entrance of the low stucco structure.

Guitar music, played with strong intensity, surprised her. The building was cool and dimly lit. Leah tiptoed

es adjusted
n pews be-
flickered in
liantly em-
ltar. Apart
d on it and
ah noticed
an who sat

cradle the

ipping the
From here
hed down,
and. Guy
used, jaw
g his eyes
lly, before
oined the
Each un-
bbed her
desperate
n, but she
gers, but
d.
Here Leah
immersed
pt as part
touching,
he hadn't
any other
could she
d, untal-
eting pe-

riod when he neede

but physical attracti

A final, haunting

guitar between his

though she couldn'

warmed her face. Le

slip back to the hou

her tennis shoe on

fore Guy's head wh

"Hello?" He sear

"Leah! Hi. I didn't

He held out a ha

room for her. Leah

approached. She le

of his and sank dow

smile and glowing

tween their two live

if she stood outsid

never able to enter?

Leah studied the

didn't know you pl

ful. Your voice is b

"Shucks, thank

laxed and glad she

tioned her religiou

seeing her in the ch

shared his beliefs.

Leah hated destr

lot we don't know

He made little ci

so much, I think

gether and know le

She had to chan

reason for being he

to talk to you. Wally came to see me this morning. He—
he—'' The rest of the sentence wouldn't come.

"What's wrong?" Guy sat straighter. "Look at me."

"Oh, Guy." Slowly, she brought her eyes to his. "I
should never have come to Phoenix. You were kind
enough to be interested in me and write to me after
Charles died. That should have been enough. Why did
I try to cling to you? Why did I have to charge in here
and mess up your life?"

He frowned. "You've been crying. Sweetheart, please
tell me what's happened." Strong but gentle arms
wrapped her tightly against him.

"The worst, Guy. That's what's happened." She
whispered weakly against his throat. "I've gotten you
into deep trouble, just as I knew I would."

He tilted her chin up. "You aren't making a whole lot
of sense. How could you cause me any trouble?"

"By giving in to my own selfishness." Leah pushed
roughly away, turning her head to avoid the startled
look in Guy's eyes. "We can't go on with this," she
said. Another tear trickled down her cheek, and she
covered her mouth with a shaky hand. "I'm a danger
to you, and I won't hurt someone I—I care about."

Guy put an arm around her tense shoulders. "Okay.
You've got my undivided attention. And I want to know
why you're crying. I can't stand to see you like this."

"The whole parish is buzzing with rumors about us."
The air seemed too thin. Leah clenched her teeth to stop
them from chattering. "Wally's worried sick you'll lose
your job. And so am I."

His sigh made Leah stare at his lifted profile. "You
fuss too much, my friend," he told her. "So does good
old Wally."

"No, Guy, no. You aren't a fool or naive; you can't be. Only an innocent would believe this situation isn't as volatile as dry tinder." She spread her fingers over his cheek and pulled his face around. "Elsie Culver wasn't fooled when she found us together in my office. Poor Wally almost choked trying to get out what's being said."

Guy entwined the fingers of one hand with hers and shook his head. "I've heard the same things Wally's heard, and I'm not worried, little one. Not *too* worried. Please, don't let this upset you. These are good people. They're human, that's all. It'll all blow over."

"Damn it." Leah balled both fists against his chest. "Sometimes I wonder if you and I live in the same world." She pounded him once, twice, but gently, helplessly. "Don't tell me again how good the malicious gossip mongers in this parish are. I know they are, somewhere underneath. But I also know they're capable of doing you harm by taking away what matters most to you—your work. Your whole world could come crashing down around your ears if whoever runs this joint fires you."

"Whoever runs this joint?" Guy's laugh was almost drowned out by an endless bass thunder roll. He bracketed her face in his hands. "You're marvelous. Sounds like the world's coming down around us, anyway. Your hair's wet, my gloomy prophet. Must be raining already. As soon as it passes over, we'd better get to the house so you can dry out."

"Don't you care?" Frustration threatened to suffocate Leah. "Or are you so blind you don't really see what's going on here? For goodness' sake, if Wally heard—good old faithful Wally, who doesn't have time for chitchat—the story must just about have traversed the state by now." She rallied her courage before adding, "They think we're having an affair."

Guy held her shoulders lightly, searching her features, his eyes sparking with some emotion she couldn't read. "Do you know who really runs this *joint*, as you put it?" He lowered his lids a fraction before going on. "God does. And he's not about to allow us to be punished for nothing."

Leah stiffened. She couldn't get into a theological discussion with him; she didn't want to. She pressed her lips into a firm line.

When Guy looked at her again, she recognized the light in his eyes—fervor and a deep desire for understanding she couldn't give him. "We aren't having an affair," he said. "As long as we know that's true, there's nothing to fear—from anyone. Trust, Leah. That's all I ask. We don't have to go over why I believe what I believe or whether you agree. Maybe one day, but not now. For now I'm asking you to put the burden on me, because I can handle it, and *I'm* not concerned."

"But Guy—"

He cut her off. "No. No buts. I love this congregation, and they love me. We'll work it out. Shall we see how hard it's raining."

There was no arguing with him. He *was* oblivious of the real world. Leah waited while he stowed the guitar in a cupboard and let him lead her by the hand to the door. She'd intended to insist she get out of his life and out of Phoenix. He made it impossible to push her conviction of impending disaster. If she suggested going, he'd only remind her she'd promised not to and make her feel like a suspicious heel.

"Its not too bad out there." Guy smiled back at her in the entrance. "Let's make a run for it."

TWO HOURS PASSED before Leah finally sat at her typewriter with Guy's sermon. While she'd been in the church, rain had beaten down two hydrangea bushes she'd planted in a corner bed by the pool. Staking and tying hadn't taken long, particularly with Guy's help, but then they'd decided to shore up a row of seedling orange trees as a precautionary measure.

Working beside him, Leah had felt an overwhelmingly poignant closeness. Together they'd scooped at wet mud, their hands touching often, their eyes constantly seeking each other's, their laughter joining while tension steadily ebbed. Afterward they had washed up in the kitchen sink and laughed again at their dirt-streaked faces. Special times—little capsules of happiness she must treasure and guard as memories for the uncertain future, when they might be parted forever.

"Any questions?" Guy loped in and came to stand behind her. "I'm going over to the Krauses'."

Leah glanced quizzically up at him.

"Mrs. Krause is the woman who had a hysterectomy," Guy reminded her. "She's been home a while and insists she's coping, but I doubt it. Her husband may even have taken off—he disappears from time to time. One of these days he'll forget to come back altogether, and that mightn't be such a bad idea. At least she'd have one less mouth to feed and know where she stands.

"Anyway, I'm going to take her kids to the zoo at Papago Park. The rain's stopped, so we should be okay."

"Yes," Leah replied, disappointed he wouldn't be around as she'd hoped, then guilt-ridden at her own selfish reaction. "If I have any problems with the sermon we can go over them later."

He touched her shoulder fleetingly. "Thank you, Leah. We're beginning to make quite a team, aren't we?"

"I guess." Leah rolled paper into the typewriter.

"Nothing else we need to discuss now?"

She bent her head. "No, you'd better get going."

"Yes. Leah—" His words trailed off as her face came up. "See you later, then."

Leah felt a nerve in her cheeks twitch. "Goodbye," she said hastily. "Give those little Krauses a good time. They probably don't get too many."

He hovered at her elbow. "Right. I guess I'll go, then."

"Mmm." She nodded, starting to type, her head down again.

"See you later?" He backed away.

"Later." Leah managed not to look up until she heard the front door close. She released a long breath when the jeep's engine turned over and rumbled steadily away.

She slumped in her chair and drove both hands into her windswept hair. Emotional tension scrambled her thoughts and filled her with sweet tumult that threatened to suffocate her. He'd been no more anxious to leave than she was to see him go.

"Trust," he'd said. Believe everything would be all right. Leah wanted to believe she and Guy were meant to be together despite each roadblock thrown in their way.

The typing went slowly. Guy's handwriting deterio-
rated as he became immersed in his topic, and Leah
stopped frequently to pore over a sentence.

"Believe." Leah banged out the word and paused.
She'd already discovered that reading too closely while
she worked slowed down the process. But now she
pushed back her chair slowly and reached for the next
page of the homily.

"We don't hurt those we love," Guy had written.
"We don't see evil in those we love." She slid farther
down in her seat and crossed her feet on the desk.

"Love and trust. That's what it's all about—the
whole ball of wax." Her eyes skimmed words more and
more rapidly. When she reached the bottom, she
dropped the sheet to her lap and reached for the next,
and the next, until the final page lay crumpled beneath
her clenched fingers.

"Believe. Believe in each other's basic goodness.
Without charity there's no hope. If we look for crud,
expect distrust, we'll find and deserve them. The pure
heart trusts, and evil cannot thrive there."

He'd written his message more to her than to his
congregation. The conviction grew within Leah and
swelled until her pulse pounded the truth in her ears.
Guy might not even have realized what he was doing,
but he'd said the same words to her earlier, begged her
to trust, tried over and over again to assure her his people were good. But he knew she didn't trust, didn't believe, and had left her alone here with his plea for her to
change.

She'd never be able to live up to his standards.

Chapter Nine

Leah's dashboard clock read two minutes to midnight. She'd driven for hours, walked for hours and driven again. Her course had been aimless while she struggled with decisions she could no longer evade. She was exhausted and had no idea exactly how long ago she had left Guy's house and his untyped sermon, trying to run from what she must do now.

She turned into Wally's driveway, and her heart jammed in her throat. Guy's jeep was parked in front of the porch, and she could see his tall, shadowy form leaning on the hood. Too late to keep on going; he'd already seen her.

Before she had time to stop the car completely, Guy pushed upright and strode toward her. The headlights picked up the planes and angles of his strained features and his tousled hair. As she applied the hand brake, he wrenched open the Volkswagen's door and all but hauled her out bodily.

"Leah." He swung her in front of him, and his grip on her arms hurt. "For God's sake, Leah. Where have you been? I've been looking for you for hours."

She had begun to shake, and her jaw ached with the effort to control its quivering. She would not look at him.

"When I got back from the Krauses', I found my sermon on the floor and no sign of you. Nothing. No message. No you." His voice broke. "You're shivering. What's happened?"

"Nothing," she whispered, trying to pull free.

Guy shook her and brought his face close. "Tell me what's happened. You look awful."

"Thanks."

"Oh, hell. I'm too beaten for this. At least you could have left a note. I've died over and over in these past hours. You might have been in a hospital—but I checked every one in town, so I knew you weren't. Then I was terrified I'd find you in some ditch—injured or...or dead." Clearly exhausted, he dropped his hands to his sides. "Come on." He recouped visibly and reached for her elbow. "Let's go inside where we can talk. If I don't get coffee, I'm going to keel over, and you've got to need something—sleep above all else, I should think."

She ought to tell him, here and now, that her first instinct of the day had been the right one, that she intended to follow it, to get out of his life immediately. But the lead that seemed to have replaced blood in her veins dragged her down and weakened her resolve. Mutely, she walked with him up the steps to her apartment and let him take her key.

He flipped on the switch to the tiny entryway light and instantly slid a hand beneath her hair to clasp her neck. His piercing appraisal of her made Leah want to hide. She had to be a total wreck. Every pore in her skin felt clogged with grit, and mud from earlier in the day had dried on her tennis shoes and ankles. Her hair, long since dried but unbrushed, was a tangled mass.

"Sit down," he ordered shortly. "Before you fall down. I'll put on a kettle or something." He hadn't been back to her apartment since the day he'd helped her move in but seemed oblivious of his surroundings. "Then we'll talk."

"Guy," she began, not moving. "You're the one who looks as if he needs sleep." Stress had pinched his face and made it appear sharp. White lines ran from each flaring nostril to the corners of his compressed mouth. Guilt at causing him to suffer twisted her insides, but she closed it out and made herself go on. "I'm fine. Please go home and forget about me. It'll be best for both of us, honestly."

His laugh was hollow. "Forget about you? You really don't know a whole lot about me, do you? I'm never going to forget about you. What's the saying...? 'When the going gets tough, the tough get going.' Well, lady, you're looking at a tough man, an obstinate man. You may flag along the way, but be prepared to be picked up and dragged on by me for as long as it takes."

Leah shrugged despondently. She was too tired to argue. Her suitcases and the boxes she'd used to transport her few household necessities from Texas were stored in the coat cupboard. While Guy hovered, she dragged them out and opened the first case on top of the sofa bed.

"What are you doing?"

Leah ignored him and went to the closet. She grabbed an armload of clothes without bothering to remove their hangers.

When she turned toward the couch, Guy blocked her path. "You're going to answer me. What do you think you're doing?"

"If you can't work it out, there's no point in my trying to explain."

"Oh, I can work it out, all right. Only it's not going to happen. You think I'm going to allow you to run away without even giving us a chance to discuss the sudden change in you since I left this morning. No dice." He lifted the clothing from her arms and dumped it over a chair back. "Why did you stop in the middle of typing my sermon?"

"I *can't* talk about it, Guy. Don't you understand I've had enough of this emotional wringer I've been put through for weeks. Look—" She met his eyes, then glanced at his mouth and swallowed hard. "I can't be what you need. When I found you this morning, I intended to tell you I was leaving Phoenix. I should have gone weeks ago, the minute I realized the position you'd be in as long as I stayed. But now I am going, and nothing you can say will change my mind." She'd picked up a dress and started stuffing it into the case when he placed a hand very gently over hers.

"How about if I say I think I love you?"

Leah stood quite still. Nothing moved, not Guy, not a muscle in her own body, not a waft of air. Time hung, suspended, before she crumpled, cross-legged onto the floor.

"It isn't fair," she mumbled, hunching over.

Guy sank to his knees beside her and stroked her bent head. "Why, sweet—why isn't it fair? Because I said I thought I loved you?"

"Because every time I try to clear up this chaos and make a fresh start for both of us, you do or say something that muddles me up again." She looked at him squarely. "I can't pretend anymore. I can't be your sexy saint, or whatever you want me to be. Held but never completely possessed. Waiting without knowing what I'm waiting for. Do you have any idea why I couldn't go on with your sermon?"

"No. I asked, but you wouldn't tell me." He swiveled to sit on the rug and lean back against the couch where he could observe her.

"Every word you wrote was aimed at me, wasn't it?" She raised her face. "All the stuff about trust and believing and not hurting people we love— You weren't talking to your congregation but to me."

The green eyes stared back fixedly. "Wrong," he said at last, flatly. "If you had really thought through what I wrote, you'd know exactly what I meant. Aren't you the one who kept telling me my people were gossips— some of them, anyway—'malicious gossip mongers' was the phrase you used yourself only this morning."

Leah rubbed her face hard. "And you told *me* they were good. You've kept telling me they were good. So what was I supposed to think you meant? Who was I supposed to assume you were writing to?"

"My fault again," Guy said bitterly. "Where did you go?"

She buried her eyes on folded arms atop her knees. "I drove around," she said indistinctly. "And walked. I don't know where I went."

Her wrists were gently clasped. He ran his hands up her arms until he could pull her gently onto his lap. Cradled, folded against his faded blue shirt, Leah allowed her tense body to relax slightly. She smelled him, heard his heart, steady beneath her ear, and felt his warmth permeate her flesh.

"I was writing to my parishioners, Leah. The Elsie Culvers who stare up at me every Sunday."

The absentminded grazing of his rough chin across her brow soothed her. "But you said you weren't worried about what anyone else said." She snuggled closer, raising a hand to trace the stubble of his beard from sideburn to neck. "You said you weren't concerned."

He sighed, then tightened his arms around her. "Sometimes I talk a good story. I am worried, and I am concerned. And knowing they'd do this to me hurts like hell."

Leah shifted and slipped from his arms to sit facing him. "You weren't straight with me." She gripped his shoulders. "You pretended. I can't figure out what you want from me, Guy. It's obvious I'm a problem here. I'm willing to go, but you say you want me to stay. *I* want to stay. You say you *think* you love me." After a moment's hesitation, she rested two fingertips on his mouth. "What does it all mean? What do you want me to do?"

Guy kissed her palm, then flattened it against his chest. "Wait for a while. I can't give you some deep, well-thought-out meaning for the way things have happened between us. We met by chance, more by chance than most people do. I was drawn to you then, but you were out of my reach. When you were free, some thread of what we both felt that first night brought you to me. Maybe our paths have been steadily converging all our lives, or maybe we're just two people reaching for each other out of loneliness." He crossed his arms around her back and spoke beside her ear. "It takes time to be sure. And I guess what I'm asking is for you to give us that time and to be willing to wait until I'm free to consider a complete relationship."

"You don't have to be free in the legal sense before I can know if what I feel for you is real. You've been alone for six years. How can it be wrong for us to be together?" She was pleading, but she didn't care.

"It's wrong for me." The timbre of his voice, dipping lower, chilled her. "And it could turn out to be a mistake for you if you discover I was only a convenient man to turn to. There are other men in the world. You need to be sure it's me you want. I need to be sure."

The moment buzzed with the complete absorption that enclosed them. Leah couldn't bring herself to even discuss the possibility of caring for another man.

She straightened until she could see Guy's face. "You're talking as if we were discussing the rest of our lives."

"Aren't we?"

Leah's stomach made a slow roll, and a lump formed in her throat. "Yes." She searched for a way to say everything in her heart but couldn't find the right words. All he had to do was reach out his arms, to take her—as far and as fast as he wanted. Although she'd never be more ready for Guy, she knew they would wait until he was as sure as she.

His face, resting sideways on his knee, was inches from hers. When he spoke, warm breath fanned her cheek. "You start school next week. A whole new world is going to open up for you."

"If I stay." She couldn't look away.

"It's time to face some hard facts, Leah. You should be able to go it on your own. Finishing school will make that easier. Don't run off and start looking for another safe place to hide. You've got too much on the ball to waste yourself."

She moved to grip her shins. "I know I need to be self-sufficient." Defiance rippled through her. "I'm not searching for someone to look after me, if that's what you're afraid of."

His eyes measured her for some time before he replied. "No, I don't really believe you are. But if it's right for us now, it'll be right in a few weeks or months or however long it takes. Let's take our time and be very sure."

Leah let out an uneven breath. "You said you thought you loved me. Didn't that mean anything?"

"You know it does." He smiled and pushed strands of hair behind her ear. "I'm just pointing out that we have to explore all the angles and keep them straight."

"Then..." She pressed finger and thumb into the corners of her eyes. "Then, while we're being logical and analytical, we'd better remember that I'm pretty certain I love you."

"I hope you find out you do," Guy replied softly and without hesitation. "Are you as drained as I am? I could sleep sitting up right now."

Leah nodded. If she wanted him, and she did, there was no choice but to do things his way.

"Do you suppose we could haul out this bed of yours and just lie together?" he asked. "I don't know if I can drive for a while."

She opened her eyes and blinked at him. "I guess we could do that. Sure you're not afraid I'll ravage you?" Her owlish grin brought Guy's answering chuckle as he pulled her to her feet.

"Funny lady. You terrify me. Stand back while I fix this thing."

When they lay side by side on top of the covers, Guy tentatively threaded an arm behind Leah's neck and pulled her head onto his shoulder. She felt so good, so soft. Weary as he was, a flicker of arousal seared him. He closed his eyes and stroked her hair, trying to unwind.

"Guy." Her voice was muffled against his shirt.

"Mmm." One of her jean-clad knees had automatically hooked over his thighs. This might be more than even iron-willed Hamilton could handle. He held very still. "What were you going to say?" he prompted. She'd fallen silent while she fiddled with one of his shirt buttons.

"Can't remember exactly." Her hand went to rest at his throat. "But it was probably something about not wanting anyone else but you."

She sounded fuzzy, thank God. With any luck, she'd fall asleep, and then he'd better get out of here. Tiredness was probably the only thing saving them right now. In the morning, when they were both wide awake, the story was likely to be different.

"Will you promise me something?" Guy whispered into her hair. "The next time you're upset about something, would you please tell me before you decide to drive all over the state? I don't think my blood pressure could take another strain like today."

Regular breathing was Leah's only reply. Her body had gone limp. Her hand slid gradually from his chest, and she half turned onto her back.

The room was dim, lit only by the meager globe in the entryway. Guy waited several minutes before carefully disentangling himself until he could sit on the edge of the bed.

He slid his shoes back on, keeping vigil over Leah's supine form. Heavy lashes flickered, and he held his breath, but she didn't wake.

Her lips parted, and he felt his own do the same and imagined his mouth pressed to hers, to every part of her. Unable not to, he watched the gentle rise and fall of her breasts. The fire in his groin was instant. He wanted to be inside her, surrounded by her.

The air, when he left the apartment, was too warm to cool his heated skin. At the bottom of the steps, he paused to look at a black sky that seemed pinned in place by glittering star tacks.

He gritted his teeth. His damned principles were tearing him, and her, apart. As soon as the divorce was final and he could be certain Leah wanted him for himself, there'd be no more holding back.

FIVE DAYS LATER, on her first night in school, Leah sat doodling in the margin of a notebook sheet. It was five days since she and Guy had lain together and she'd awakened alone, disappointed to find him gone. She smiled to herself. Although nothing direct was mentioned, they were more at ease with each other, and she'd begun to dream of the future—with Guy.

The bell for break rang. Leah filed out of the classroom and followed other students to a commons area. So far, her first night at school had been a snap.

She'd found a math evaluation simple. The ease with which she remembered her facts had both surprised and pleased her. Next would come English, and again she didn't anticipate difficulty.

Along with a teenaged boy, she was one of the youngest class members. Leah scanned the couches and chairs in the room until she located the boy, then grimaced. She hadn't been mistaken when she'd thought he was having difficulty staying awake at his desk. Now he was scrunched down in the corner of an orange plastic couch, his eyes closed.

Leah strolled to sit at the other end of the same couch and poured iced coffee from the thermos she'd brought. Over the rim of the cup, she studied Dan Ingalls. She knew his name from the roll call. He was dozing lightly, his thin wrists and hands twitching occasionally.

Everything about the boy was thin, too thin. Thick, straight black hair fell forward over a broad forehead; his brows were as dark as his hair and finely arched. A handsome kid. She'd noticed the brilliance of his blue eyes when he arrived ten minutes late for class. She'd also noticed the tight line of his wide mouth, the too-old, too-troubled set of his features. Now relaxed, he looked very young and vulnerable.

Leah's attention wandered to shoulder bones, prominently obvious through a clean but threadbare shirt. His knees poked at the worn fabric of corduroy jeans. She drank more coffee and frowned. Something intangible drew her to this boy. Her heart contracted. The something was a sensation that she had something in common with him. At his age, he should be in a regular high school, not trying desperately to keep his eyes open in a roomful of extension students.

She shifted her purse and pile of books to the floor and cleared her throat. The boy started violently, his eyes instantly wide and staring.

"Sorry." Leah smiled. "Did I wake you up?"

His elbows locked, both hands braced on the seat. "No. Just resting my eyes," he lied, and a trace of pink spread over his pallid cheeks.

"That's all right, then," she said matter-of-factly. "Would you like some of my coffee?" It might keep him awake even if it didn't put meat on his bones.

"I . . ." He slackened his arms. "It's okay, thanks."

"Please," she insisted. "There's an extra cup, and I made too much as usual. I'll only have to throw it away." She poured, then handed him the other cup before he could refuse.

"Thank you." One hand gripped the other biceps tightly while he drank. He showed no sign of speaking again.

"How old are you?" As soon as the words were out, Leah clamped her teeth together, expecting him to withdraw completely.

"Eighteen," he replied flatly, and took another sip of coffee. "You?"

Leah laughed. "I deserved that for prying. It's just that you're obviously so much younger than the rest of us old fogies. But fair play. I'm thirty, soon to be thirty-one."

A suggestion of a smile turned up his mouth. "That's pretty old okay. Next you'll want to know why I don't go to school in the daytime, right?"

She felt her own cheeks redden. "I really wasn't being nosy. I quit high school at seventeen, and tonight I've finally taken the first step toward finishing. Guess I looked at you and saw a bit of myself. Only—" Why would she spill all this to a stranger who couldn't possibly be interested?

"Only?" he repeated, finishing his drink.

Leah refilled the cup and fished some coins from her purse. "Only something tells me you've got more guts than I had." She pushed to her feet, feeling his eyes follow when she crossed to a vending machine.

Deliberately, she made sure he couldn't see her insert her money and receive a granola bar. She moaned and thumped a chrome panel while she surreptitiously dropped in another coin before scooping out the second bar.

Grinning and shaking her head, she returned to her seat. "Here." She tossed one of her purchases to her companion. "My fist must be pretty potent. First I didn't get anything, then I got two."

He glanced sharply from his hand to Leah's eyes. She smiled benignly, guessing she hadn't fooled him. After a moment's hesitation, he tore off the wrapper and demolished its contents in two bites. Again, her hunch had been right. He was hungry.

"So why don't you go to school during the day, Dan?" she ventured when he finished eating.

His blue eyes took on a wary, hooded appearance. She was going too fast, and his life was none of her business, anyway.

He sniffed. "I'm Dan, and you're Leah something or other. You got the name from the roll. I wondered how you knew for a minute."

"Leah Cornish." Her muscles untensed slightly.

"Maybe I like to sleep late and goof off all day—fishing, playing golf, who knows?" The ceiling, with its square white tiles, held his attention.

Leah moved her books fractionally with one foot. "Sure, that's where you get that fantastic tan. I had to go to work, that's why I dropped out of school. There was just my mom and me, and we needed the money. I never thought of carrying on at night and probably couldn't have made it if I did."

"I may not be able to." His eyes shot to her face, and he blushed violently. One slender finger rubbed at the space between his brows. "Fell into that one, didn't I. I guess you and I do have something in common. You can find me at the Serve U Right grocery store, over on

Central, any morning between seven and nine. I stock the produce. Then, in case you're into hotels, I park cars at the Benton Plaza until five. Cowboy hat, slick Western gear and all—you wouldn't know me in that uniform. I don't know me in it.''

A pang of sad helplessness began its steady procession to Leah's heart. Helplessness and an intense yearning to help Dan. Memories of her own non-existent childhood flooded in, the years when she'd shone as a student despite total lack of support from a family. Then the sadness at having to walk away a few months before she would have received her diploma.

"Did you do this last year, too?" Her voice sounded tight.

Dan shifted restlessly, and Leah sensed she was getting too close to the walled-off section of his life. She remembered so well her own anger at the world and her unwillingness to accept any kind of interest or understanding from the strangers who were all she had, apart from her mother.

His shoulders hunched, and he seemed to make a decision. "I worked nights last quarter. That didn't cut it for the money we need. I'm with my mom, too—but I've got a brother and two sisters. The girls are pre-school age, so by the time Mom paid for baby-sitting, she wouldn't make anything if she went to work. There, Leah, now you've got the whole scoop on me. Not so interesting, huh?" he finished with a defiant jut of his chin, and picked up his books. "Must be about time to get back in there."

She reached to grip his arm. "You're going to make it, Dan. Let me know if there's anything I can do to help."

"Oh, I'm going to make it, all right." An expressionless mask slid over his face. "I'll end up as chairman of the board somewhere. Thanks for listening. Guess I was a bit weak tonight. I don't usually spout off my life history."

Back in the classroom, Leah noticed Dan had moved to a seat closer to the door. By the time she'd gathered her possessions at the end of the session, he'd disappeared, but she couldn't get him out of her mind.

Her heels clipped across the asphalt parking lot on the way to her car. She kept her head down, half immersed in what she'd learned and the prospect of a heavy schedule in the weeks to come and half preoccupied with Dan Ingalls's problems. Intuition told her she was probably the one person he'd ever confided his whole situation to, and then only in a moment of weakness, when she'd caught him off guard.

"Well, how'd it go?"

At the sound of Guy's voice, her face snapped up. He was standing beside her car, both hands sunk deep in his jeans pockets.

"What...oh, very well, thanks. What are you doing here? Where's the jeep?"

Close enough now to see him clearly beneath a lamp standard, his sheepish expression amused her.

"I caught a bus over." He rolled onto his heels. "Thought maybe you'd give me a lift home."

Leah struggled to keep a straight face while sweet warmth suffused her insides. He'd wanted to be here when she got out on her first night. She could hug him. "I'll think about it," she said laughing. "But let's get this clear. You decided, spur of the moment, to take a bus ride that just happened to end up here?"

"Well—"

"Then," she interrupted. "Then, when you were about to catch the bus back again, you remembered I was taking classes here tonight and thought it would be nicer to ride home in my sumptuous Bug than a stinky old bus. Have I got it right?"

He exhaled audibly. "So I'm behaving like the mother of a kindergartner on the first day of school. So I deliberately came to meet you because I wanted to make sure you were okay." His right toe scuffed loose gravel. "And I also wanted to drive you home, because I don't like you wandering around in the dark alone," he finished in a rush.

Several passing students were turning curious faces toward them. Leah hurriedly opened the passenger door and motioned Guy inside. "We're attracting a crowd. Get in. I'll drop you off on my way home."

"I can go all the way with you, then walk back." Guy protested. "It's only a couple of miles."

"Get in," Leah retorted, and walked around to the driver's side. Once settled, she switched on the ignition and studied his face in the glow from the dashboard. "Everything went beautifully tonight, Guy. You don't have to worry about me, because I'm going to love going to school again."

Being cared for with a depth Guy couldn't disguise filled her with deep joy. But tonight she'd acknowledged something else. She wanted to stand on her own feet. If and when she and Guy decided to make a joint life, she would not come to him as little more than a childish dependent.

He grunted as they headed west. "If you hit a rough spot with your studies, will you let me help?"

"Of course. I'm counting on it."

At the church, she drove him all the way to the rectory and waited for him to get out. When he didn't move, she reached across the console and kissed his cheek. "Thanks for caring about me." She gripped the steering wheel. "Night, Guy. See you in the morning."

He opened the door, then turned back and pulled her roughly into his arms. "You're something. Do you know that? And I think I'm crazy about you."

Leah's attempted laugh didn't quite come off. "You think a lot of things, sir. Maybe you should try making up your mind about a few of them."

His mouth came down on hers in a fierce kiss, his tongue reaching far into her mouth. When he drew back to look at her, Leah's heart was a drumroll. She pushed her fingers into his hair. Guy rained a hundred tiny, brushing kisses over her face and neck, ending with another sound possession of her lips before he swung from the car and strode into the house without looking back.

After several seconds, Leah's heart slowed to a normal rhythm, and she drove slowly home. Guy's attempt to excuse his concern had been transparent. He had a protective urge toward her that wouldn't quit, and she loved it.

Chapter Ten

The next ten days sped by. Leah went to school four nights a week and began to find herself wilting earlier in the afternoon as attacking her homework before work in the morning became a routine. But with each class her self-confidence grew, and she looked forward eagerly to every new challenge—and to the shy friendship she was building with Dan Ingalls.

He had gotten into the habit of sitting with her during recesses. Sometimes they hardly talked at all. But occasionally he revealed a little more about his family, and she grew less reserved over her own early life.

Leah was convinced Dan didn't get enough food for his gangly eighteen-year-old frame but knew the granola-bar ruse wouldn't work twice. He'd agreed to share a sandwich she brought one night, then turned up the next time with two overripe peaches Leah knew must have been castoffs from the grocery store. She'd eaten the fruit, fighting back tears as she did so. How did you help a desperate boy without wounding his pride?

Tonight was Friday, and she had a plan. Despite her persistent pleas for him not to, Guy continued to show up after every class session and drive with her as far as the rectory. He had a natural flair for plugging in to other people's problems and for gaining their trust. If she could persuade Dan to go out with them for a hamburger, she might begin solving two obstacles to her peace of mind: Dan's need for more food and the discovery of a solution to his money worries. She hadn't felt right discussing the boy's concerns behind his back, but if she could get Dan to talk himself, Guy was likely to cast around for a solution.

The final bell sounded, and Leah grabbed the bag she'd bought for her books. She scurried up the aisle, searching anxiously for Dan, who had done his usual disappearing trick. Why hadn't she invited him out during recess?

In the hall, she broke into a run, turning the corner in time to see Dan's tall, angular back at the top of the building's front steps. Her shout came as a breathless croak, and by the time she burst into the fresh air, he was gone.

From her vantage point, Leah scoured the lot, watching each moving figure. Then she saw him and froze. *Good Lord.* She knew he lived miles away, at the far end of Indian School Road, but he was pedaling through the side gate on an ancient bicycle.

Now she really would cry if she didn't get a hold on herself. She hid her eyes with one hand and bit into a quivery lower lip. His father had been dead a year. Apart from his mother, he was the only one old enough to be of any real help to his family. He was struggling to work at two jobs, finish school and sandwich homework in between. And to top it off, he must be riding the old bicycle miles and miles every day to save bus fare. There'd been no one to help her out of the pit when she was a struggling teenager—until Charles had come along. Dan's plight was twice as desperate as hers had been. Surely she could find a way out for him.

"Hey, Leah."

At the familiar sound of Guy's voice, Leah uncovered her eyes and watched him jog in her direction. Slowly, she joined him, and as he draped his arm around her shoulders, she knew what she had to do.

"Carry your books?" Guy laughed, reaching for her bag. His smile dissolved as he looked down into her face. "Why so sad? Something go wrong?"

"Nothing's wrong—with me. Can I stand you a hamburger?"

He jolted to a stop. "A hamburger? Didn't you get dinner? You've got to eat—"

"I just want an excuse to go somewhere and talk," she interrupted brusquely. "Not your place, not mine. A bar, anywhere. I need your help—and your full attention."

Guy frowned but didn't ask any more questions while they walked to her car.

THE FOLLOWING AFTERNOON, Guy helped Leah into the jeep and set out to find the Ingallses' house on the far side of town.

"I've watched Dan get more and more exhausted," Leah said when they made the turn to head north on Seventh Street. "And he's irritable. He snapped at the English teacher last night, and I'm starting to worry they'll kick him out."

Guy glanced sideways at her. Wind blew through the open sides of the jeep, whipping her hair into a dark cloud around her face. Her deep blue eyes were shadowed with worry. "You're sure he'll be at work when we get to their place?" he asked, returning his attention to the road. Every time he looked at Leah, he had to quell an urge to touch her, and his condition was getting worse.

"He doesn't get off from the hotel till five. I thought I told you that." Her voice came to him in snatches. So did wafts of her perfume.

The night before, at Oscar Taylor, a trendy bar and grill in the plush Biltmore Fashion Center, she'd poured out Dan's story. Again and again, while wooden fans whirred overhead and her fingers made tight little patterns on a marble-topped table, Leah had gone over points that clearly opened wounds in her own memory. It hadn't taken any time for Guy to recognize that Leah's bond with this boy came from the experiences of her own young life.

Phoenix was having one of the hottest Septembers on record. The thunderstorm season had slowed, but the intense heat continued. Today Guy wondered if he shouldn't consider getting rid of the jeep for an air-conditioned vehicle. He twisted his head toward Leah again and found she'd rested her head back and closed her eyes. Her skirt slid above her knees, revealing long, smooth legs.

He gripped the wheel a little tighter.

"We should be able to talk to Dan's mother before he gets back," Leah said. "I want you to meet him, too, but I think we'll get farther without him at first. From what he's told me she's a very reasonable woman. He told me how she worries about his schooling. Sometimes I think he'd give it up now if it wasn't for her."

The sun blazed white, almost bouncing over the surface of broad Indian School Road, with its low-lying buildings and singed shrubs. Leah had found Dan's address in the telephone book, a tiny house on a small street angling off behind a row of stores.

"Looks like the place." Guy parked at the curb behind a weeping willow, its graceful boughs unmoving over an arid expanse of sand and scrub grass that made up the front yard. "I suppose this isn't what you want to hear, but I'm nervous."

Leah squeezed his hand. "Why shouldn't you be? At least we know we're on the same wave length. But the worst that can happen is that she tells us to get lost."

Guy stared at her for a moment before climbing out. She didn't expect him to be a superman, only himself.

Side by side they walked up the path. Leah rang the bell as Guy righted a toppled red tricycle.

The door opened several inches. "Yes."

Both lowered their eyes to a small face that appeared at handle level in the narrow crack. Guy managed to smile warmly. "We wanted to see your mommie. Is she in?"

A knee wriggled back and forth beneath pink shorts as the little girl considered what to say next. A shock of black curls cascaded to her shoulders and bobbed with the movement of her body. She appeared to be about four. "I've got to ask what you want," she said guilelessly, her blue eyes wide.

Sympathy stabbed at Guy. The mother was probably afraid of debt collectors, or just plain afraid—of everything. He hunkered down to the child's level. "Would you tell your mommie we're friends of Dan and we'd like to talk to her about him?"

Immediately, the door swung wide, and they were confronted by a petite woman with the same shock of black curly hair as the child. On one hip, she carried another little girl, who couldn't have been more than

two. Guy's heart twisted. So much unhappiness. So
many lonely people no one could reach.

"Dan?" the woman said sharply. "What about Dan?
Did something happen to him?" Her face had paled,
and her hand rubbed unconsciously, rhythmically, at
the baby's leg.

"No, Mrs. Ingalls," Leah reassured quickly. "This
is nothing like that. I'm in the same class as Dan over
in Scottsdale, and we've gotten to know each other.
This—" she hooked an arm through Guy's "—is my
friend, Guy Hamilton. I also work for him. Could you
spare a few minutes, do you think?"

The woman shifted the child to her other hip and
nodded agreement. They followed her into a shabby but
clean living room where she sat in an unraveling cane
rocker and waited until Guy and Leah perched on mis-
matched straight-backed chairs.

"What did you say your name was?" Mrs. Ingalls
addressed Leah.

"Leah Cornish. Dan's a wonderful boy, Mrs. Ingalls."

"My name's Connie." She smoothed the skirt of a
yellow checkered housedress. "What's all this about
Dan?"

Guy had deliberately kept quiet while Connie Ingalls
gained some ease with Leah. Now he bent forward to
rest his elbows on his knees. "This is almost more about
you than Dan." He smiled down at the smallest child,
who had crawled from her mother's arms and stood
staring up into his face. He held out his hands, and she
clambered onto his lap.

"That's Mary," Connie said. "She doesn't usually
take to strangers."

"Guy has a way with children." A blush flashed up Leah's neck when Guy caught her eye. So, he thought with satisfaction, she watched him when he didn't know it. "But it's children we came to see you about really, isn't it, Guy?" she ended lamely.

While Guy outlined the plan he'd come up with since last night, the other child, Anna, coaxed Leah to a shoe box in the corner and proudly displayed a doll made of a white athletic sock. He kept one eye on Leah's easy manner, the way she sat on the floor to interact with the girl, and quickly explained his own plight at the church nursery.

After Connie absorbed the fact that he was a minister, he told her about his ongoing difficulty in finding and keeping permanent staff and how he needed someone to oversee and manage the facility.

Connie looked blank. "What does this have to do with Dan or me?"

"Well." He coughed. Leah was now tucking a handkerchief blanket around the sock doll as Anna leaned contentedly against her, one thumb in her mouth. "Well, Connie, Leah was telling me how Dan works at two jobs and has a hard time of it getting through his homework. She also explained the obvious; it would cost you more in day care for your children than you could earn most places. So I wondered if you would do us all a favor by running my church nursery."

Worn hands wound and unwound in Connie's lap. "I don't know what to say."

"Say you'll do it," Guy pressed. "You'd bring the girls with you, of course. The pay's not terrific, but you'd all get your food there, and Dan could drop one of his jobs so he'd have a better chance at his schooling. You have another boy—how old is he?"

"Bob's twelve." She leaned forward, hope beginning to dawn in her eyes. "He comes home from school and takes straight off to do his paper route, anyway. He'd be all right till I got home."

Leah stood up suddenly, holding Anna's hand. "What about transportation? Do you have a car? I could come and get you in the morning, then bring you back."

Connie shook her head. "You've done enough. We like the bus, don't we, girls? Don't you worry about that." She frowned. "Did you already talk to Dan about this?"

Guy and Leah fell silent and looked at each other. Anna wrapped an arm around Leah's leg, and she absently ruffled the girl's shiny curls. *She's got a way with children, too,* Guy thought. *Maybe we'll have—* Not now; it wasn't the time to think about himself.

"Dan doesn't know, does he?" Connie's delicate brows drew together. "He'll think it's some sort of charity and get mad. He's like his dad..." The words trailed off.

The child on his lap had knelt to watch Guy's face closely. He tried to look around her, then laughed when she firmly clamped a small hand on each side of his jaw. "Well," he started, and Mary touched his moving lips. He kissed the end of her nose and caught her to his chest, where she snuggled happily.

A sniff snapped his attention back to Connie, who swiped impatiently at the corner of one eye. "Stupid," she said harshly. "Don't have much time to think about it. But Ed—that's my husband—never had much time to hold Mary before—before he died. I expect Dan told you he had lung cancer. They say children come into the world with needs built in and one of them's love—from more than one parent who's always too uptight to give them enough. Seeing Mary like that—" she nodded at Guy "—with you, makes me wish I could give them more, get them around more people."

"Oh, Connie, don't." Leah crossed to the older woman and sat on the floor beside the rocker. "Listen. This job will be just what you need. It'll get you out of the house. The girls will have other children their own age to play with. And you'll all be around a lot of good people." Her voice wavered, and she immediately glanced at Guy, smiling self-consciously through tears that welled in her eyes.

He smiled back knowing she'd unconsciously called his parishioners good but that she meant what she said.

"But Dan..." Connie began.

Anna had gone to rest against Leah's back and wrap her arms around her neck. Leah clasped the little hands beneath her own chin. "Dan will come around," she said firmly. "He's proud, but he loves you all too much not to see that this is a perfect situation. Leave it to Guy; he's great with young people. He'll explain everything to him, and Dan will be glad; wait and see."

Guy has a way with children.... He's great with young people. He sat back, still hugging Mary. Leah was excellent with children, and she was the one who had wheedled her way into Dan's confidence, something he'd probably have found more difficult himself. This woman had strengths she refused to recognize, an almost soul-wrenching specialness, yet she was still willing to slip into the background behind a man she cared for.

"Mom! I'm home. Where are you?"

The sound of a door slamming and Dan's voice turned the living room scene into a motionless tableau.

Connie fixed a smile on her face, but her hands held the chair arms in a death grip.

"Wait till you see what they were throwing out." Dan strode into the room, head down in a grocery sack. "This bread's still fresh and—" He glanced up, his eyes fastening on Leah. "What are you doing here?" Dull, angry red suffused his face and neck.

"Hi." Leah kept a tight hold on Anna's hands. "I brought a friend of mine over to meet you. Remember I told you about Guy Hamilton, the man I work for?"

The boy's hostile blue stare shifted to Guy's face, then flicked away. "Sure." He was prickly, surly. "How'd you find us?"

"Dan, they..." Connie began.

Dan shook his head sharply, cutting her off. "Let them tell me, please, Mom."

"Telephone book, silly," Leah retorted with artificial lightness. "We decided to go for a drive and ended up coming here."

Guy looked at the ceiling. She was a lousy liar—D-minus variety.

Dan shoved the brown sack on a Formica-topped table and stood stiffly behind his mother. "And I'm Little Bo Peep. I never asked you to come snooping around after me. What is he?" He indicated Guy. "Some sort of do-good social worker?"

Guy flinched. This was going to be tougher than he'd thought. He opened his mouth, but Leah's next move took center stage.

She swung Anna into her arms and stood, feet planted firmly apart. "You listen to me, Dan Ingalls. Pride's one thing. Being a damned fool and making other people suffer because of it is another. I was where you are today once. I found a way out—marriage. It

probably wasn't the best escape route, but it was the
only one that came along. I've told you all about me,
and I know a fair amount about you. I want to help you
like someone helped me. Can't you stop being so pig-
headed and accept that for what it's worth? Guy's no
do-gooder, and neither am I..." She coughed and
covered her face with her spare hand.

Guy got up quickly and set Mary down. He went to
put an arm around Leah, who turned her face against
his shoulder.

"Okay," Guy said quietly. "We're letting this get out
of hand. There's nothing going on here that we can't all
walk away from, so what do you have to lose by listening?" He hated sounding harsh, but the right effect was
produced. Dan visibly subsided. "Let's all sit down and
talk," Guy added.

An hour later, mentally whipped, Leah followed Guy
from the little house. Mary and Anna had been soundly
kissed and hugged by both of them, and Connie stood,
glowing, in the doorway. Dan, deflated but smiling,
waved from the shadows behind his mother's shoulder.

"Long route home?" Guy asked when they waited at
the intersection with Indian School Road. Late-
afternoon sun rays turned mica sidewalks to sheets of
glitter. "I think maybe we need to unwind."

"Whew," Leah responded, locking her hands behind her head. "Long way home sounds good to me.
That was something. When you told him you were a
minister, I thought he'd pop a blood vessel."

"Poor kid," Guy snorted. "He's got a lot to work
through. Including the fact that despite his father's
strong religious beliefs, he died and left his family
alone. That didn't help him warm up to me."

"You were magnificent with him." Leah put a hand on his thigh and felt the muscle move as he changed gears and the answering shudder deep inside her own body. She began to withdraw her hand, but Guy held it there, and they drove in silence for several minutes.

"Will it be all right, Guy?"

He looked questioningly at her; then his expression cleared when he must have realized she was talking about the Ingallses rather than their own situation. "*Everything* will be all right." His grin was wry as he applied both hands to the wheel and drove beside the pink mountains that edged Phoenix's Valley of the Sun.

"Connie's going to settle in just fine," Leah continued, trying to sound convinced. "But I can see trouble with Dan if he thinks anyone's doing him a favor or he's not paying back every little kindness we try to show them."

Guy sighed. "You ought to know what I'm going to say next, little one."

She did, at once, but studied the landscape instead of answering him.

"Trust."

She smiled despite herself and punched his shoulder playfully. "I'll try." And she would, but not without constant wariness.

At St. Mark's, Leah declined Guy's invitation to come in for a while. She wanted to get ahead with some of her schoolwork.

He slammed the door of the Volkswagen behind her and crossed his arms on the window rim. "Ma'am," he said solemnly.

Leah met his clear green eyes and felt herself begin to sink. "Yes, sir?"

"Would you do me the honor of accompanying me to dinner one week from tonight. That'll be a Saturday, and I thought we could take a run up to an intimate little place I know on Squaw Peak. Of course, if you're busy, I'll understand."

His tone was light and bantering, but Leah saw the way his fingers curled tightly into his palms. Her own mouth felt like a dust bowl. "And how do you know about intimate little restaurants," she quipped with a coolness she didn't feel.

Guy wrinkled his nose. "When Wally got back yesterday, I asked him to suggest someplace."

"Our guardian matchmaker?" Leah said. "Wally has to be the world's most unlikely fairy godmother." They both laughed until tears ran down her cheeks and Guy rested his forehead on his arms.

Leah turned on her engine. "Thank you," she managed. "I'd be delighted to have dinner with you. It's time we both broadened our horizons."

She drove away without looking back. Guy had asked her out for dinner. A real date. He was taking the first tentative steps toward a courtship.

Chapter Eleven

"Meet me on the patio." Leah scanned Guy's note quickly. What now? She'd just got back from running errands, and all she wanted was the impossible—a long, cold drink and some sleep. Her schedule was beginning to wear her down.

She slid a box of office supplies on top of the cupboard behind her desk and headed for the back of the house via a sliding-glass door off one of the guest bedrooms. This was the room where she changed when she went swimming, and it had begun to feel almost like her own.

Guy's back was to her, his fair head bent forward over a book. Leah pursed her lips. Guy was always reading something. She wished she had half his brains. Maybe then the new concepts that seemed to come at her faster with every hour in school wouldn't take so long to master.

She allowed herself a selfish moment to feast on his broad shoulders and the way his hair curled at the top of his collar. Then she walked beside him, "You wanted to see me, Guy?"

He started. The book must be engrossing, although it looked vast and dusty to Leah. "Yup. Sit down and have some tea. Made it myself, so it's bound to be fantastic." He'd opened his shirt almost to the waist, and sunlight bronzed the hair on his chest.

Leah deliberately studied the dancing blue water in the pool as she plopped into a chair and accepted a sweating glass. "I can't stay long. I just got back and my in basket looks like I died a month ago."

Guy laughed. "You're too industrious. You've been looking tired. I want to talk about that and find out how you think things are going around here."

More and more, he included her in discussions about parish affairs. She could feel him consciously relegating responsibility to her, allowing her to share in decisions. And he never missed an opportunity to offer help with her studies. They'd started working together regularly in the garden, and Guy always found a way to turn their conversation into a question-and-answer session.

"No comment?" he asked. "Are things that bad?"

She realized her silence had lasted too long. "Sorry. I was thinking. Of course things aren't bad. They're great. Connie Ingalls is as happy as a clam, and I've never seen the kids so well organized and content. Wally told me the parishioners are delighted with the change."

Guy turned his face up to the sun and closed his eyes. "*Goes to show.* Whatever you give, you get back a hundredfold."

His philosophy again, his faith. Leah inwardly drew back, closed out the worried little voice of doubt and searched his face instead. Vulnerable in relaxation, he looked younger. His beautiful mouth, slightly parted showed a glimpse of white teeth and his silver-tipped lashes cast fanlike shadows on his cheekbones.

"Any problems you think we should be addressing?" He opened one eye to squint at her.

Leah thought a moment before shaking her head. "None I can think of, except—" She pressed her lips together.

"Except?" Guy sat up and turned his full attention on her. "Except what?"

It was now or never. Might as well get it over with. "My schooling is interfering with my doing the job properly. I'm beginning to think it was a mistake to go back." There, she'd said it.

He snapped the book shut and slid it onto the table. "I was half expecting you to say something like that. I've felt it coming, but I don't understand why, and—" His hand closed around her forearm. "There's nothing wrong with your work. You just said yourself how smoothly everything's running around here."

She ran her tongue over the roof of her mouth, gathering every scrap of courage she possessed. "It's getting tougher and tougher to juggle everything, Guy. I might have to quit the extension program. I need to give my full attention to my responsibilities here." Her heart started to thud hard. Surely he would understand she didn't want to give up, that it was a case of being sensible.

Guy stood and rammed his hands into his pockets. He stared at the sky until Leah thought her head would pop with the waiting. "No," he announced at last. "I know I don't have any right to tell you what to do, but I'll do my damnedest to stop you from quitting. What's the real problem? What aren't you telling me?"

Leah felt like an errant kid called on the headmaster's carpet. "Geometry," she said, and immediately curled up inside. *Dumb excuse; why not be honest?*

His stare bored through her. "Sure, Leah—you're going to give up school because you don't like geometry? Come on."

"Okay." She squeezed her eyes shut. "Okay, you want a blow-by-blow misery list, I'll give it to you. It isn't just geometry or English or any individual subject. I am struggling in some areas, but the main thing is I can't handle my schedule. I get up when it's still dark and work for three hours before I come here. You'll agree I don't have the luxury of deciding whether or not to earn a living. And don't think I regret that—I love it here. But by the middle of the afternoon I'm half asleep, and on four days a week I have to gather up enough energy to go to school *after* I finish work. The nights when I don't go to school I try to catch up with things around the apartment and do *more* homework. I'm whacked, Guy, and I'm not making it."

Guy began to pace, furious concentration furrowing his brow. "I'm sorry." He stopped abruptly in front of her. "I don't know what I've been thinking about. Of course it's too much. I get so involved in other people's problems I forget the one who—" His throat moved convulsively, and a horrified awareness darkened his eyes.

"Don't," Leah cried, knowing he was remembering his neglect of his wife. "This isn't your problem, or your fault; it's mine."

"No, no." The metal chair creaked beneath his weight as he sat and buried his face in his hands. "Please, let me work this through." He lifted his eyes to hers. "You'll be finished with the learning center in a few weeks. For the rest of that time, I want you to pack in the parish business at noon and spend the afternoon doing homework. I'll be around to deal with any problems that come up and to help you.''

Leah opened her mouth to protest, but Guy reached to silence her with a quick kiss. "You're more important to me than anything or anyone else. I'm so proud of everything you've accomplished."

Trembling weightlessness invaded her legs. "You've already done too much for me. I can't take any more from you."

His fist came down on the armrest. "You can, and you will. Think. How would it look to Dan Ingalls if his idol quit? Could you blame the kid if he did the same? He's down to one job, but he does still have to manage that and be the man around the house for Connie and the little kids."

She covered her eyes. "If you wanted to make me feel like a creep, that was the way to do it. Why am I so weak?"

Fabric swished, and he was beside her, holding her tightly. "You aren't weak, my love. Just a perfectionist who's gone on overload. And I *have* been blind in some ways, although I was concerned that you seemed tired. Just say you'll do this my way from here on, please. It'll all work out for the best, believe me."

Leah wrapped her arms around his shoulders and rested a cheek against his neck. Peace stole over her. She would do anything for this man.

"Is the answer yes?" he asked against her ear. The wide circles he made over her back began to awaken responses she mustn't allow.

"Yes." She pulled away, averting her face. "But just for once I wish it was me doing something for you instead of the other way around." Emotion clogged her throat. "I've always known the world was made up of givers and takers, and Guy—'' She willed herself to look at him, biting back shame at her own spinelessness. ''I thought one day I'd manage to change sides. But I'm still a taker, aren't I? I'm sorry, but I am working at it.''

Guy felt blood drain from his veins. If he didn't get out of here now and think, he'd say all the things he was determined not to say—yet. He traced the bridge of her nose with a knuckle and gave her a determinedly cheerful grin. She didn't have to know he was dying inside. ''I can tell you how much you give until I'm blue in the face, lady, and you won't believe me. But I'll say it, anyway. You *give* all the time. If you stop to think, you'll know I'm right.''

Her blue eyes were clear mirrors heavily shadowed by her dark lashes. She held trembling lips tightly closed.

Oh, God. ''Leah,. I have to attend to a couple of things. Why don't you swim, or rest? Or start on some schoolwork, if it makes you feel good?'' He bounced to his feet, backing away at the same time. ''We'll touch bases later, all right? Will you do that?''

Her whispered ''Yes'' reached him a second before he reentered the house.

So who did *he* get to talk to? Who did any ''pillar of strength'' talk to when he himself was confused and hurting? Guy paused beside the desk in his study, braced his weight on outstretched hands and hung his head. So far he'd managed to find enough guts to invite Leah out to dinner on Saturday night. Big deal. They were together most of every day, and he hadn't been able to open up and tell her where he stood, his hopes and dreams for them or his hang-ups.

Damn. While he'd been so tied up with his own world, he hadn't even noticed how strung out she was becoming. What did he have to offer a woman on a full-time basis? He'd already blown one marriage; would he do the same if he got another chance?

The room seemed to shut him in, the walls steadily pressing closer. Guy headed for the front door. He'd climbed into the jeep when he noticed Wally raking a fresh load of pea gravel beside the social hall.

The old man saw life clearly and knew where he'd been and where he was headed. When his wife died, he'd come to Guy and stumblingly asked for an ear to listen to his bewilderment. Wally had known, with that wisdom of the honest, that his pain and emptiness must be faced and shared or it would suffocate him.

Guy's walk from the jeep to the social hall seemed one of the longest he'd ever taken. Wally didn't hear him coming and continued to rake, sweat gleaming on the back of his thin, wrinkle-crazed neck.

"Wally—" Guy's voice sounded loud in his own ears. "Got a few minutes?"

The rake stilled instantly, and Wally swung around, shading his eyes. "Hello there, Guy. Didn't hear you. What's up?"

Resolve fled. "Oh, nothing really, ah . . . Good load of gravel?"

Wally looked puzzled. "Gravel's gravel."

"Well, then—that's good." He scuffed at a clod of dirt. "Hot again today."

"Hot most days," Wally said.

Guy felt sick. "Monsoon season's about over, I guess."

"I guess."

"Wally . . . how's Joan's sister?"

Wally slowly rested the rake against the wall and hooked his thumbs into his belt. "Same as when you asked me the other day, after I got back from Mesa. She's fine.''

Guy smiled. He was making a fool of himself. ''There was something I was going to ask you about.''

''I figured there was.'' The straw hat was shifted to the back of Wally's head. ''So why don't you stop horsing around and spit it out.''

''Because.'' He shouted the word, and heat flooded his face. ''Because I don't know how, damn it. I need some advice, and I don't know how to ask for it. Go on, have a good laugh about that one. I won't blame you. I might even join in.''

Wally indicated a nearby bench, and they walked to sit in silence.

After several minutes, Wally stuck a sharp elbow in Guy's ribs. ''How about starting at the beginning. Seems like that might be best.''

''I think you already know the beginning.'' Sweat drizzled down the side of Guy's face. ''For six years I've only been a husband on paper. You've got to know my marriage ended in the physical sense even before I came here. My fault. I never learned how to give a woman the attention she needs.''

A grumping noise came from Wally as he shifted his weight. Guy sighed; he was probably embarrassing the man.

''An old codger like me doesn't know much about this stuff,'' Wally began gruffly. ''But I'm not blind. I can see when two young folks are all tied up with each other. You're scared; that's your trouble. And all the talk around the parish has got you going in circles. Leah says you reckon it doesn't, but I know better.''

Guy draped his elbows over the back of the bench and stared at the toes of his shoes. No point in arguing against the truth.

"You don't know what to do next, do you?" Wally added.

"I sure don't," Guy muttered, flicking stray pebbles from the seat. "We need some sort of life away from this place, but I've never been good at—at courting a woman, I guess you call it. How do I know when something's right? I can't go through what I went through before. And I can't put Leah through it. Oh, hell." He leaped up and shied a rock against the closest palm trunk. "The best thing I can do is back off and let her find someone else."

Wally's laugh was a bark. "Oh, sure. You'll back off. In the pig's eye you'll back off. You're in too deep, but too thickheaded to admit it. I tried to tell you what to do weeks ago, then figured it was none of my business. Now you've asked me. You just came from her, right?"

"Right." Guy sank back onto the bench, his hands hanging between his knees.

"And you're both miserable?"

"You've got it."

"Then go back in there and do something about it. Take her somewhere and forget all this." He spread his arms wide. "I got a hunch the jawing around here's about died out, so you can forget that."

Guy chewed his lip. "I hope you're right. I am taking Leah to dinner on Saturday night."

"Great," Wally said, and slapped Guy on the back. "Good idea. But take her somewhere *now*. You're both walking around like love-struck kids, and until you sort things out between you, you won't be any good to the rest of us."

"Wally—" Guy sighed. "She was going to quit school because she was so tired. I didn't even notice she was burning out."

"Disgusting," Wally replied solemnly. "A man shouldn't make human mistakes—not you, particularly."

"This is serious."

"Sure it is. So *do* something about it. Take her out of herself. Give her all your attention for a while and you'll see her come alive again."

Guy crossed his arms. Here he was, asking a man more than twice his age how to go about letting a woman know he cared about her. "Shoot," he growled. "I don't know how to do it. I've spent too much of my life tied up with my work."

Wally's characteristic "What the heck" split the air with as much force as any curse. "Think about what she likes," he exploded. "Think, man."

"I am thinking. Nothing's coming, or I wouldn't be here making a fool of myself."

"You don't make a fool of yourself when you show a friend you need help. That takes guts."

Guy shrank inwardly in the face of this man's hard-learned wisdom. "Do you have any idea, anything at all, what I could do?" he asked humbly.

Wally grabbed his elbow and propelled them both to their feet. "She likes plants. The weirder, the better. She's crazy about orchids, and they don't grow well in normal conditions around here. Take her to that desert garden place—over in Papago."

"What if she says no? She's tired."

"Don't take no for an answer. Drag her into that jeep of yours and sweep her away. No woman can resist a little force now and again. Tell her how good she looks.

Listen to what she says. And don't talk about church goings-on or school or anything but the two of you." Wally clamped his mouth shut abruptly and tilted his hat back over his eyes. "I gotta get on with spreading that gravel. I've already said too much."

"I BET YOU NEVER SAW a saguaro as big as that?" Guy said, whisking Leah along a path past a jungle of giant cacti. "What's that called—the spiky thing? I see them all over, but I've never known the name."

Leah adjusted her sunglasses and tried not to look aghast. "It's just a yucca." She panted, running to keep up. "Arizona's state plant, remember?"

"Ah, yes," he replied, and paused to stare intently at the speckled, swordlike leaves. "Beautiful."

She quelled the impulse to say she didn't find yucca beautiful; interesting, maybe, but not beautiful. Ever since Guy had rushed back into her office and insisted they were going to the Papago Desert Garden, he'd kept up a steady stream of conversation and constant motion. Tired before they began, she was now drained, mentally and physically. She'd give anything to find out what was in his mind. And it wasn't cacti or yucca.

"The orchids are in those greenhouses." Guy pointed to two identical buildings near the entrance. "Like to see them?"

He was already steering her rapidly to the right. "I'd love to," Leah managed, and immediately felt an infuriating bubble of laughter well in her throat. Hysterical. She must be losing her mind. Or Guy was—or maybe both of them.

Inside the first glassed-in building, the familiar humid air made her stop and breathe deeply. Everywhere she looked, lush foliage had been used to form a natural backdrop for dozens of orchids.

"Like it?" Guy watched her closely. "Are they like the ones you used to raise?"

Leah smiled. "My little greenhouse wasn't quite up to this, but I did have some of these varieties, yes. And I love it in here. Feel that air—and look, birds. They've got tropical birds in here."

Guy followed her glance to where a brilliantly plumed parrot perched on a giant philodendron creeper. "Did you have birds?"

"No!" She threaded an arm beneath his to soften her amused reaction. "No, Guy. This is big-time. Once, Charles took me on a trip to Canada, to British Columbia. We went to a conservatory in a place called Queen Elizabeth Park. There was this huge dome full of tropical shrubs and flowers, and the birds were everywhere. I can still close my eyes and remember the scents. Gorgeous."

Guy became still. "Can you close your eyes and remember Charles?"

She couldn't believe he'd said it. He sounded jealous. Leah pulled her arm away and frowned up at Guy. "Yes," she said slowly. "I still remember Charles, with or without my eyes closed. He was a kind man, the best, and I was married to him for eleven years. Can you still remember Susan?"

Pain washed over his features, and she had to hold back an impulse to comfort him. "That's different," he said.

"Why?" she asked very softly, her stomach plummeting. "Because she was your wife and therefore more important than my husband? You're not making any sense."

"Forget it." He walked on, and Leah had to hurry to catch up.

"I'm not going to forget it, Guy." She dodged in front of him on the narrow pathway. "Don't turn away. Why did you want me to come here with you today?"

His laugh was derisive. "Because I wanted to give us a chance to get closer."

She swallowed and laid a hand on his chest. "Thank you. I want that, too. So what's wrong?"

"Nothing." His eyes were riveted on her. "Except the faraway expression on your face when you spoke about good old Charles just now. You'd think the man had been a saint rather than—"

"Don't," she cut him off. Her breath came in painful jerks. "Please, don't. You didn't know him the way he was when we met. I don't think anyone ever knew him the way I did. And even if he'd been a monster, which he wasn't, he was my husband, and I won't let anyone drag down his memory. He loved me, Guy. He had a lot of faults, but who doesn't? You? Me? I don't think so." She crumpled abruptly onto a huge stone frog. "Forgive me, please. I sound like a righteous boor."

Firm hands grasped her shoulders, and she was pulled against Guy's solid body. "You're the one who needs to forgive me, as usual. I just can't stand the thought of anyone else mattering that much to you."

Leah gritted her teeth. *But you aren't willing to commit yourself to me. You're still too afraid.* "I think we're both pretty worn out. Let's call it a day."

She let him hold her hand, although every inch of her cried out for solitude.

"The place we're going to on Saturday is called Beside the Point." Guy's attempt at nonchalance didn't quite make it. "Should be nice."

They reached the exit turnstile. Leah clicked her jaw nervously. Hot as it was, her skin was clammy. "That's something I was going to talk to you about, Guy. I can't make it Saturday."

He halted, trapping her between the metal railings. "Can't go? Of course you can go. You said you would."

His expression was a mixture of male ego incredulous at rebuff and disappointed small boy. Leah panicked. "I don't have anything to wear, and anyway, it's my birthday." Her mouth remained opened. Of all the excuses she could have come up with, that had to be the most ridiculous.

Slowly, Guy pulled her close until she stood toe to toe with him. "Saturday is your birthday, huh? Great. All the more reason to celebrate." His grin was suddenly wicked. "In fact, instead of just dinner, which would certainly not be enough for the occasion, I suggest we drive up into the mountains for the day. Have you been to Sedona?"

"N-no. I mean—"

"You haven't? Perfect! I'll take you. And you've given me the perfect idea for a birthday present. Come on. The Biltmore Fashion Center will still be open. I'll buy you a new outfit for the occasion." His hand at her waist propelled her forcefully across the parking lot.

"I can't let you do that." Her voice jarred as he bundled unceremoniously into the jeep.

All the way back to town, he brushed aside her arguments, finishing by telling her how unhappy she'd make him if she wouldn't allow him the small pleasure of buying her something. By the time she followed him through the plate-glass doors of Saks, self-consciously trying to order her windswept hair, she was limp and beyond further debate.

She stood awkwardly by while he considered the store directory. "One floor up," he announced, and grabbed Leah's hand as he resumed his meteoric pace up the left side of the escalator. He took the steps two at a time past mildly surprised patrons.

"Guy," Leah hissed at the top. "Where are we going? Everyone's staring at us."

"You, you mean. Don't blame 'em. You're gorgeous."

She shook her head helplessly and followed him across bottomless carpet, feeling more like someone who'd come to clean the place than shop there.

"Designer!" Her heart sank. "Guy..." she started again, but he was already flipping through racks of wildly expensive creations. Why hadn't she kept her big mouth shut? She'd shopped in plenty of stores, and departments, like this. Times had been different then. No way would she let Guy buy her an outfit, and *she* certainly couldn't afford anything here. She wasn't sure she could afford to breathe the rarefied air.

"What do you think of this?" He held up a gauzy dress with a handkerchief hem and spaghetti straps. The colors resembled an evening rainbow.

Leah gave him a gentle smile. He was so special, so gracious and giving—and he had exceptional taste to boot. The dress was a knockout and would have a knockout price to match.

"Well?" He opened wide, questioning eyes.

She hooked an arm through his. "Listen," she whispered. "You have spectacular taste. That is absolutely the most scrumptious creation I've been within miles of for a long time, but—''

"But you don't like it." He cut her off with a frown and started rifling through the rack again. "Maybe this one's the wrong size."

"No, no." She laughed, holding his wrist. "I love it. And it happens to be the right size. But take a look at the price tag. Go on, look at it."

He did, and his frown deepened.

"See?" Leah tried to ease the garment from his grasp. "I don't need anything like that. Anyway, since we're going to Sedona by jeep on Saturday instead of out to some fancy restaurant, I won't need something special to wear."

Guy looked down into her face for a long moment, his dear, slow smile spreading to warm every feature.

He hung the dress back on the rack, and Leah let out a grateful sigh. When he turned back to her, he was still grinning.

Leah narrowed her eyes. "What's the joke?"

"No joke," he shrugged innocently. "I'm glad you can spend the day with me on Saturday, after all."

"I never said—"

Guy tapped her bottom lip. "Oh, but you did. You just said that since we we're going to Sedona, you wouldn't need a fancy new dress. Don't tell me you're the kind of woman who lets a man down twice in one afternoon?"

She tried to think of a snappy comeback, but nothing came. "Let's get out of here, you operator." Leah punched his hard stomach playfully and marched toward the down escalator.

Chapter Twelve

He took the box from behind his back and laid it quietly on her little table by the window. Arriving an hour early, even on the pretext of getting out of town before the weather heated up, wasn't done, he knew. But he'd hardly slept all night and hadn't been able to wait a minute longer to see Leah.

At least the surprise element of his appearance had distracted her and she hadn't noticed the oversized package, semihidden behind his back. When she'd opened the door, sleepiness still glazed her eyes as she stared at him, disoriented, and clutched a short cotton bathrobe together at her throat. She'd looked soft, so incredibly sexy. Not blurting out his news immediately had taken superhuman control.

She was clattering mugs in the tiny kitchen. "Got to have coffee while I dress, Guy. Can't make it without coffee." She sounded fuzzy, and he smiled affectionately. How would she react when he told her what he'd found among his unopened personal mail after she'd left yesterday afternoon? He was a free man. The official notice in his pocket informed him he no longer had a wife.

"How about you, Guy?" Leah called. "It won't take me long to get ready, but why don't you have a cup of Cornish morning mud while you wait."

"Boy," he said, laughing, "with an endorsement like that, how can I refuse?" The perfect moment to break his news would come when they were alone and separated from the mundane trappings of their everyday lives.

"Here you go."

Her voice, behind him, caused Guy to swing around abruptly. Barefoot, her white robe with its ruffled edges barely reaching mid-thigh, she was like some beautiful, exotic butterfly. The robe was all she wore. Its thin fabric clung to her body and molded full breasts, their tips clearly defined and erect.

Leah's eyes met his when they returned to her face, and a rosy glow touched her cheeks and lips. Total understanding of his thoughts passed between them, and she smiled gently when she offered him a mug. "I'll get dressed, and we can hit the road. I'm looking forward to seeing more of the scenery outside town."

Guy surrounded her wrist and set down his mug before taking hers away. "I've got something for you. For today." Just the contact of their two skins inflamed his desire. He consciously slowed his breathing. "The box." He indicated the pink-wrapped package. "Open it."

"You—Guy, I told you not to buy me anything. Thirty-one-year-old ladies don't need birthday presents." She went to run a finger over a length of lavender ribbon. "What is it?" She grinned, and the little-girl excitement popped to the surface.

Guy laughed. "You look more like eleven than thirty-one right now. Open the thing and see. No, wait—"

One large hand splayed on top of the box. "I can't resist giving a hint."

Leah tried unsuccessfully to pry his fingers loose. "Guy, don't tease."

He gave a theatrical sigh. "Okay, but the man said you can change them if you don't like them. I bought you a set without pruning shears, since we already have a couple of pairs. But if you want your own—"

"Guy Hamilton, you beast." Her fists, pressed against her hips, made the robe gape, and Guy felt lightheaded with the effort not to touch her.

"Open it." His voice caught, and he cupped her jaw, leaning to part her lips gently with a kiss that sent his heart into four-four time. She stood on tiptoe and wrapped her arms around his neck. Their bodies fit together perfectly. Guy squeezed his eyes shut. His response was about to become evident to them both. He set her carefully away from him. "That was instead of a birthday card."

Her mouth, thoroughly kissed now, was moist and dark. After a lingering look, she stroked his jaw; then bent to concentrate on unwrapping the package.

"Oh, Guy, you shouldn't have done this." Her breath escaped in a long sigh as she pulled the rainbow gauze dress from its tissue cocoon. "It's so beautiful. I loved it when you showed it to me the other day. But it cost a fortune, and you can't afford it." She immediately clamped a hand to her mouth, blushing furiously.

Guy choked on his laughter. "I should think you'd be embarrassed. How do you know what I can afford? Just because I don't drive a fancy car and bop around in trendy duds, you think I'm a pauper, is that it?"

She shook her head mutely and gave him a wry grin.

"Good," he retorted. "Because I'm not. Actually I'm an eccentric millionaire. Now, I want to see you in that cheap little number. The saleswoman assured me, it's perfectly casual enough for a day's driving in the mountains." He pinched his nose. "'Actually, sir, this was undoubtedly created with *ultimate* versatility in mind. The lady will feel *utterly* comfortable wherever she wears it.'"

Leah kissed the corner of his mouth quickly and hurried into the bathroom, smiling broadly and fondling her present. He'd pleased her, Guy thought with satisfaction. They were starting off the day on the right foot; he was thinking about her first instead of taking her presence for granted.

He sat down and mulled over the questions that had plagued him all night. One sip of coffee proved Leah hadn't been kidding when she called it mud, but he took several swallows before abandoning it. His tight muscles and nerves began to unwind. She'd always had that effect on him, and here, among her greenery and the evidence of her light and airy touch, he felt her presence even when she wasn't in the room.

His fingers curled around the folded envelope in his pocket. The news had come earlier than he expected—a blessing and a possible curse. It might have been better if he hadn't known until she finished school. He picked up discarded gift wrappings and crumpled them inside the dress box. Now he could do what he'd wanted for so long—ask her to marry him, become her lover. His gut flattened against his spine.

A piece of ribbon had fallen beneath the table. Guy picked it up and rolled and unrolled one end. Familiar slivers of uncertainty gnawed at the back of his brain. She was emerging whole, for the first time in her life; he felt it, and he couldn't let anything interfere with that, including his longing to be joined with her forever.

Leah had thanked him for helping her—more often than he cared to remember. If he asked her to marry him and she accepted, would it be out of gratitude? Guy discarded the idea. She was as in love with him as he was with her; that wasn't an issue. Her possible desire to give up school and any attempt at autonomy was. She'd already talked of dropping out. Their marriage might convince her she should give up on further education. He'd seen her in the role of subservient wife before; it was a natural position for her. He couldn't, wouldn't, watch her slip into his shadow and stagnate.

"What do you think?" Leah breezed into the room, still barefoot, and made a twirling circle for him to view the dress from all sides. Her hair flew. Her eyes picked up a violet hue from the vivid fabric. Some sort of glossy stuff on her lips made them shine, and her tanned skin glistened. As she moved, the exotic scent of autumn roses in sandalwood floated to him. Every sane thought fled.

"Well?" She stopped, breathless, arms outstretched. "Do I keep it or exchange it for a pair of pruning shears?"

"You, my comedienne, grab a pair of sandals and anything else you need, then get me out of here before I do something you could take me to court for."

"TLAQUE—WHAT?" Leah brushed hair from her eyes and peered at a blue-and-yellow-tile sign set into a white stone wall. Guy was edging the jeep into an impossibly small parking space crisscrossed with exposed tree roots.

He reached to take several papers from the glove compartment. "Tlaquepaque," he said, engrossed in reading. "You say it, T-lockey-pockey."

Leah glowered at his nonchalance. "How do you know? I suppose you speak fluent Spanish."

He grinned, his eyes invisible through dark sunglasses. "My talents are endless." One long forefinger stabbed at the paper he held. "Actually, this is a pamphlet about the area, and it tells you how to say it."

"Fraud." Leah laughed and hopped to the dusty red earth. "What is this place, anyway?"

"You'll see."

Guy led her beneath a carved archway into a cobbled courtyard ablaze with beds of flowers and centered by a bubbling fountain. Through inner archways she could see similar courtyards lined by two-story buildings, lush foliage cascading from their upper balconies. "Guy, this is lovely. All the little shops. Feels very Mexican and foreign. I expected Sedona to be a sleepy backroads place."

He pulled her to his side to allow a horse and buggy to pass. The driver wore a top hat, and his cargo consisted of two laughing young couples. "I understand Sedona used to be pretty sleepy," Guy explained. "Some man bought this piece of land on the edge of town and turned it into an arts-and-crafts village with a purely Mexican flavor—even trucked in authentic village bells, wrought-iron railings and so on all the way from Mexico. People come from all over to visit the place."

Leah instantly fell in love with the quaint atmosphere. Every tiny shop, with its treasure of unique paintings, pottery or jewelry, beckoned her. Handmade quilts, extravagant blown-glass creations, crystal

shapes faceted to catch ever-changing colors—the se-
lection was unending.

"Look at that." She grabbed Guy's arm and pointed
to a window at a beaten silver necklace of interlaced
hands, a continuous chain of touching. "What a beautiful idea."

"Let's get it" was his prompt reply, and Leah had to
stop him from marching inside the store.

"I've had one fantastic present today, thank you,"
she insisted firmly. "If you're going to try to buy me
everything I admire, I'd better keep my mouth shut.
How about lunch? It's almost one."

He glanced back at the necklace, then reluctantly
gave in. "I don't see why I can't give you some things
if I want to. But okay, have it your way. Lunch. How's
Mexican food sound, since that's the theme around
here?"

Forty minutes later, full and deliciously mellow, Leah
squinted at Guy over the salty rim of a margarita glass.
"Rincon del Tlaquepaque Restaurante Mexicano," she
announced with satisfaction, reading from the front of
the menu. "How's that?"

"Perfect." Guy covered her right hand on the red-
and-white checkered tablecloth. "Spoken like a na-
tive."

Leah chortled. "Practiced while you were in the
bathroom. I've never had a margarita like this before."

"Mmm." He eyed her critically. "They say they put
egg whites in them and that's why they're thick and
creamy. But from the sound of you, two had better be
your limit. Something tells me you aren't a drinking
woman."

She waggled the fingers of her left hand airily. "Need
a little practice, that's all." Their arms touched, and she

leaned close to smile into his incredible eyes. "Have I told you—" Another swallow of the smooth liquor slipped easily down her throat. "Have I told you you have the sexiest eyes I ever saw?"

"You're tipsy," Guy whispered, and pulled her against his shoulder. "You must have the lowest tolerance for alcohol on record. Let's walk."

He was misreading the cause of her happiness, but Leah followed him obediently from the open-air terrace, back into a cool courtyard. Giant sycamores towered above them, and cottonwood and cyprus cast shadows over the paving.

"Feel up to a little hike?" Guy asked. "There are some easy trails we should be able to stroll up and get a good view of the whole area."

Leah nodded cheerfully, resisting the urge to tell him she'd follow him anywhere.

"Hey, look at that." He stopped so abruptly that she bumped into his back. They'd reached the shop where she'd admired the silver necklace. "See?"

Without giving her a chance to locate the object of his interest, he pulled her through the door into a dim interior.

As Guy spoke quietly to the clerk, Leah frowned. If he thought she would let him buy the necklace, he was in for a disappointment. She hadn't completely forgotten the rules of propriety.

He stood by the window until the case was unlocked and something small given to him. The ring he held up was gold, made like the necklace of hands joined in an endless circlet.

Leahs awareness cleared. Her heart contracted sharply, and the air around her took on the crystalline quality of high country's winter snap. She couldn't meet Guy's eyes.

He took her right hand and slid the ring on her third finger; it fit snugly. "A bit tight," he said quietly. "But I like it. Will you let me give it to you?"

"Yes," Leah said, then added more loudly, "yes, thank you. It's lovely, the loveliest thing I've ever seen." The traitorous tears misted her eyes. In his own way, he was trying to tell her something, to give her a sign. And for now she needed no more.

Their walk back to the jeep was made in silence, as was the short drive to the outskirts of Sedona, where Guy parked again and came to help her down.

"Are you up to it?" He indicated a trail of switchbacks leading between jutting pink mesa scattered on their lower reaches with scrubby trees and tumbleweed.

Her answer was to set out, nimbly avoiding fallen rocks and larger boulders along the way. The ring on her right hand seemed a circle of cool fire. Every second she fought the impulse to stare at it. Her wedding band had been heavy platinum, studded with six diamonds and flanked by an engagement ring so massive it dwarfed her hand. Selling the set after Charles died had made her feel cynical, ungrateful, until she fully acknowledged her reduced circumstances and decided her late husband would have understood.

An unconscious gesture, left hand caressing right, savored smooth gold and found it more pleasing than any fabulous jewel. Goose bumps flashed across her skin. Was she disloyal to a kind man's good intentions? Guy caught up, towered over her, smiling down, and her doubt fled. There was a time to get on with life, and for her that time was now. He took the lead, and she followed in his footsteps.

They scrambled on; Leah's open sandals, although flat, were unsuitable for climbing, but she didn't complain. The rock face became shallow scarps, like terraced steps running in ridges around the closest mesa. "If we get to the other side of this," Guy shouted over his shoulder, "we should be able to see forever."

He was right. "Oh, Guy," she breathed, flattening herself against rust-colored stone. "The sky. It's so blue, it burns. And it's...infinite. This whole setting looks like something out of a Western movie."

"That's why they make so many movies here," he replied. "Can't you imagine wagon trains down in that gulch." Below, a sheer ravine plunged to a wide gap between mesa. "And men on horseback thundering past. Clouds of dust, sweat, leather chaps, lariats—"

"Yes," Leah interrupted, laughing, "and 'yahoos' all over the place. I've seen those shows, too. Right now I feel as if we're the only two people left alive in the world. It's so peaceful."

"Do you suffer from claustrophobia?"

Guy's left-field question startled Leah. "Why, no. What a weird thing to ask up here."

"There's a cave immediately above us." He was craning his neck, shading his eyes. "At least I think there is from the shadow. Stay here if you like. I want to take a look. Won't be a minute."

Being left alone in the middle of nowhere, even for a minute, didn't appeal to Leah. "Hang on," she gasped. "I'm coming. I love caves." *Liar.* She never even remembered being in a cave.

The shadow Guy had seen was cast by a jutting overhang above an aperture just high enough for him to enter upright. Inside was a smooth hollow, like a bowl lying on its side, the floor covered with a fine mixture of dusty silt and sand.

"This has to be the strangest cave I've ever seen," Guy marveled. He slowly paced the perimeter, running his hand over the walls. "Looks like some giant punched a hole when the rock was still soft, then rotated his fist back and forth. Hah! A prehistoric potter." He appeared enormously pleased with his analogy as he scanned every inch of his find.

Leah cleared her throat. "Your potter was kind enough to provide us with a seat—our own eagle's eye vantage point on the world." She sat on a slab in the cave entrance, swinging her feet and supporting her weight on her arms.

"In other words, cut the gibberish and come sit with me." Guy flopped down beside her and matched the rhythmic swinging of her legs.

"I wish we never had to go back." Leah tipped up her face and closed her eyes. "I like it here."

A sudden breeze whipped the light skirt from her knees, and Guy stilled her hand before she could pull it back in place. "That first night—in Texas," he said. "Did you know I'd been watching you for some time before you saw me?"

Her lips parted; then she swallowed. "No, Guy, I didn't know. I heard something and it frightened me. That's all."

He watched her mouth, then flicked his eyes to hers and covered her with a visual caress. "The lights in the water made your dress transparent around your legs. When the wind blew, I wished I was the wind and touching you."

Leah's chest felt compressed by some enormous weight. She breathed deeply, her bodice suddenly unbearably tight.

Guy turned sideways and stroked her bare thigh lightly, repeatedly, from knee to groin until she shuddered and arched her back. He kissed the hollow of her throat, and feathered tiny nips along her collarbone and up to her ear.

Leah bent her head, and he kissed the back of her neck. "You're driving me slowly—no, rapidly mad," he rasped. "I don't think I can take the waiting anymore."

Her heart made its own thunder. "You don't have to." He'd pushed her skirt high; his steady caress of her leg continued. His sleeve cuff was folded back. Vein and sinew, flexing beneath the tanned skin of his hand and forearm, the way his wide watchband rode low and caught the light—every minute detail about him fascinated her.

The message was clear. He wanted to make love to her, here, in this high place apart from the rest of the world. Leah reached for the buttons on his shirt and undid them steadily, feeling muscle jerk on contact.

"This isn't what I planned. I wanted to bring you somewhere marvelous for the first time we were together."

Leah laughed deep in her throat and pushed the shirt from his shoulders. "And this isn't marvelous?" She glanced at the breathtaking panorama.

Guy shifted and ran the tip of his tongue along the line of her parted lips. The heel of his hand made wide circles over her stomach and pressed downward, sending shards of primitive longing through her body.

Almost violently, Leah rained kisses over his torso, savoring the smooth, salty skin at his sides, and fingered his hair-roughened chest and the hard, contracted flesh of his belly above his jeans.

"My God," he groaned. "I'm scared."

Leah flinched as his fingers dug into her upper arms. "Why? This is right, Guy. I know it is."

He pulled his lips back from his teeth, squeezing his eyes tightly shut. "You don't understand, little one. You've talked to me a thousand times about remembering I'm only a man—and I am. Six years alone is a long time."

She covered his body with gentle, constantly moving hands. Could he think he'd be unable—? *Fool.* He was concerned about his ability to maintain control, nothing more.

"Don't worry," she whispered, kissing a flat nipple. "Everything doesn't have to be perfect at once. We'll make it right." He didn't know the narrowness of her experience or the length of her own abstinence.

"I don't deserve you." His kisses were instantly fierce, possessing her mouth, rocking her face with their intensity. Breathing heavily, he held her close in trembling arms, his lips tracing her brows, her closed eyes, her cheekbones and jaw.

The narrow straps on her dress fell easily from her shoulders, and Guy gave his attention to the hint of softly swelling flesh that rose and fell ever more rapidly above her neckline.

"Guy." She lifted his face. "I want to feel you against me. Undress me, please." A slight angling of her body gave him full access to the small buttons that closed the dress from neck to hem.

The sensation of the one finger he slid downward, between her breasts, brought her nipples to straining crests. He slipped each fastening open carefully, his restraint etched in the taut lines of his face.

Guy paused, nuzzling her ear. "Can I make love to you, Leah? Will you let me love you in all the ways I've dreamed of?"

She couldn't answer. Her voice seemed frozen in her throat. Leah took Guy's hands and tucked them inside her dress to surround her breasts. Guiding him, she lifted herself to him, making his taking her giving. He rubbed tongue and lips back and forth over thrusting fullness, then pulled back long enough to tug the dress down to her hips.

Warm air, and Guy, caressed her naked flesh. Pressed to his body, Leah slid beyond choice, beyond decision, to a fury of passion from which there was no turning back. The contrasts of their skin, their textures, urged her on and drove her to rotate her breasts with wanton deliberateness against the stimulating roughness of his chest.

Their exploration was frenzied, insatiable, until their bodies took on a mutual heat, a delicious feverishness. "Stop." Guy panted, holding her wrists. "Where? Not here."

He looked around, eyes glazed, before pulling her to her feet and farther into the cave. Their discarded clothes made a tumbled heap on the sandy floor, and Guy quickly shucked jeans and underwear in one sweeping motion, before kneeling in front of Leah. Still clad in skimpy bikini panties, she took in his form, the symmetry of him, his complete arousal. Blood pounded in her ears.

"Guy." She tried to sink down with him, but he clamped her hips and held her fast. "Guy, I want you, now."

His hands slipped upward, curving across her back, bending her over him until he could take the tip of first one, then the other breast into his mouth. His gentle teeth and firm tongue weakened her legs until he had to stop her from falling.

Guy recognized her fervor but wouldn't surrender to it. If he let go now, it would be all over before she could possibly be satisfied. She was so lovely—golden where the sun had touched her, ivory where a swimsuit had hidden her skin. Her breasts were full, with a tantalizingly translucent quality. Holding back was taking more of his will than she'd ever know.

He rubbed a cheek over her ribs and blew gently against her navel, then, with constraint that made his arousal a pain, slid down the skimpy white panties. He followed his spanned thumbs with his lips, down, down, to the center of her. And she cried out and drove her fingertips mindlessly into the rigid muscles of his shoulders.

"No." Her voice was small and distant. "What—? Guy, no." And when her perfect body convulsed, he eased her to the ground, smoothed her tangled hair from her face and kissed her lips.

"It's all right," he whispered. "With someone you love, anything that pleases you is all right."

Her eyes flicked open, wide and wondering, and her hands groped for him. She bent her knees and guided him between her thighs and inside her. "Don't wait any longer, Guy."

He'd allowed his own eyes to close. Now he stared down into her eyes and saw his own wanting, needing, mirrored in deep blue—a reflection of his own raw desire.

Their two bodies moved as one, the pace increasing until incoherent love utterings, dragged from their hearts, became a language as ancient and primitive as the dance of their joined flesh.

He lasted longer than he'd dared hope, and at their shared climax the outpouring of his continence purged him of tension and left him heavy, warm and infinitely calm.

"I love you," he heard Leah whisper very far away, and wrapped her close.

He muttered a reply but never knew what it had been. Their limbs remained entwined, and he rolled onto his back, pulling her on top of him. Leah's head fit perfectly into his shoulder. Her heart beat a rapid, answering tattoo to his own.

Languor threatened to take him into sleep. He forced his mind to hang on while he stroked her and kissed the top of her head. She needed to feel him still with her.

The sun had slid lower in the sky when Leah finally rolled away from him and dragged his shirt to the cave entrance, where she knelt, gazing out.

Guy turned on his side and propped up his head. She looked like a wood nymph, her hair a shimmering mass, her spine straight above a tiny waist and flaring hips.

"What do you see out there?" he asked, and smiled when she peeked over her shoulder at him. "Any giants making magic caves?"

"No," she replied, sighing. "There's only one magic cave, and we found it."

He laughed. "We made it magic, my love. Before us it was just a plain old hole in the wall."

Leah fell silent, and Guy reached for his jeans to re-
trieve his watch. Locating the wrong pocket, he found
the long, official envelope instead and drew it out.
Surely this was the perfect time he'd known would oc-
cur.

A rustle at the cave mouth made him glance up. Leah
had turned toward him, the sun's back light hiding her
face. There was a tenseness about her that suggested a
welling up of emotion. "What is it?" he asked, forming the envelope into a cylinder.

"You make me whole, Guy," she said. "All I want
is to be a part of you. Nothing else will ever matter
again. Tell me you don't regret what's happened."

"I don't regret it." The inside of his mouth became
as dry as the sand beneath his bare feet. "You make me
feel wonderful, too. But don't say nothing else matters
to you but me. That's a pretty big number for a man to
carry around."

She stirred, her posture unyielding. "You don't have
to carry anything. Just love me."

He did love her. God, he loved her—too much. He
shoved the envelope away and searched until he found
his watch. The right moment hadn't come.

"Guy?"

He had to answer her. "I do love you, Leah."
Checking the time gave him a chance to hide the tears
of frustration in his eyes. "Hell, look how late it got.
We'd better get out of here if we're going to be through
the mountains before dark."

Her awkward, hurried movements as she dressed
wrenched his heart. He'd confused her, left her not
knowing where she stood with him. But he must make
sure she completed school and saw herself as a separate
entity. If he told her now what he longed to share, she

might stop growing. He had to wait a little longer—at least to get her over the one hurdle she'd started to jump. Then he could reassess what to do next.

Holding her hand, he led the way back down the trail. Neither spoke aloud, but their thoughts seemed to scream. Was he wrong not to tell her he was free and wanted to marry her? Guy agonized over the question with every footstep. He couldn't be wrong. Waiting would be as hard on him as it was on Leah.

He stopped abruptly and brought her fingers to his lips. "I love you, my darling." At his words, her features relaxed. He kissed her brow and then her lips before setting off again at a faster pace.

Just a little while longer, he reasoned with himself, but every atom of his being warred against waiting one more second to claim Leah.

Chapter Thirteen

The only light Leah could see at Guy's house came from the meager bulb beside the porch.

Tonight had been the first time he hadn't come to meet her since she'd started school. Even in the days immediately following their trip to Sedona, when the atmosphere between them had been charged and volatile, he'd still been there, lounging against the Bug, at the appointed time. As if by unspoken agreement, they had never mentioned the few hours of joy they'd stolen in a place and time that gradually took on an unreality for Leah. Slowly, they'd slipped back into their old routine—except for the probing glances that passed between them when they weren't wary and the occasional desperate kiss that left her throbbing and shaky.

She climbed from her car and hesitantly approached the rectory door. Why hadn't he come, tonight of all nights? She'd made it. So had Dan. They would receive their high school diplomas by mail within ten days.

In the parking lot outside the learning center, Dan, more carefree than she'd ever seen him, had guided her around in a sedate waltzlike dance before breaking into a wild, whirling jig. Afterward, they leaned on each other, panting and laughing and, Leah knew from

Dan's searching eyes, both looking for and wondering about Guy.

She plucked an oleander blossom from the hedge, stalling, and stepped back to scan the windows once more. Then she rang the bell, afraid if she let herself in and he'd fallen asleep, he'd mistake her for an intruder. Seconds tripped by, then minutes.

Leah checked the hood of the jeep and found it cold. He had left the rectory in the middle of the afternoon without warning or explanation but evidently had returned a long time ago. She tried the bell once more, then knocked before using her key to enter. Unfounded apprehension chewed at the pit of her stomach. What did his change in routine mean?

The dark hallway and the stillness intimidated her. Yet she couldn't bring herself to violate the gloom with light. Guy must have wanted darkness. He'd come back tired from wherever he'd been and fallen asleep. That was the answer.

But Leah couldn't go home without making sure he was safe. Her tennis shoes made faint squishing sounds on the terrazzo floors. The guest-bedroom door was closed, but the counseling-office door was ajar. She turned sideways, staring in as she passed, then walked backward to the corner.

Jumpy idiot. The pounding of her heart filled her throat.

Guy's study door was open, as was that of his bedroom, and she edged slowly as far as his desk. "Guy," she whispered toward the bedroom. "It's me, Leah. You okay?"

A sudden blast of air and the sound of rattling drapery hooks shocked her. Every nerve in her body jangled, and she approached the bedroom, forcing herself nervously inside on legs that felt as if she were dragging them through deep water.

The draft came from the open sliding door to the patio and turned the single big curtain into an eerie, moonlight-filled balloon. Leah's attention flew to the bed, searching for Guy's shape, half convinced she would see him there, murdered by some mad stranger.

The bed was empty.

Relief was immediately snuffed out as she tried to decide what to do next. The patio. Guy wouldn't just open the door and leave it that way. He must be outside.

Walking on tiptoe now, she crossed flagstones to the edge of the pool and peered fearfully down into obsidianlike water. Good God, her imagination was on overload; she was a hair away from total panic.

"Anybody'd think you were in church."

At the sound of Guy's voice, Leah's body jolted with enough force to almost throw her into the pool. She spun around, her clasped fists knotted against her belly. Rapid swallowing was all that stopped her from throwing up.

He sat on a chaise longue, his legs outstretched. "You know how people always tiptoe and whisper in church?" he said hoarsely. "No, maybe you don't. Well, Leah, hi. Why are you creeping around in the dark?"

She couldn't believe what she'd heard or his behavior. And she was angry, suffocatingly so. "You scared me, Guy Hamilton, all you can do is make wisecracks. What are you doing out here in the dark?"

"I'm doing what I please. This is my house in case you forgot—or it is for the moment."

Leah neared him slowly, sniffing the air suspiciously but smelling no trace of alcohol. "I haven't forgotten whose house this is. But what do you mean, it's yours for the moment?''

''Nothing.''

The moon glimmered on his hair as he turned his face away. Her irritation fled. Something was very wrong. ''You weren't there to meet me tonight,'' she offered redundantly, and pulled a chair beside his. ''I missed you.''

''I forgot,'' he replied without inflection. ''But I seem to remember your telling me you didn't want me there, anyway.''

Irritation flickered again. ''Guy, that was a long time ago, after the very first class. You didn't let what I said then stop you once afterward. Why tonight—the last night? Even Dan hung around pretending to be checking over that wretched old bike of his when I knew he only wanted to see you.''

''The last night?'' A clicking sound came from Guy's throat.

''Yes.'' Every muscle ached. ''The last night, and we both found out we're getting our diplomas. Dan was talking about trade school or maybe even a community college. I was kind of wondering about college myself.'' Her throat closed, and she struggled for composure. ''None of it means a thing without you. Without you I'd never have started or finished even this much of my education. And it was you who made it possible for Dan to carry on.''

''I should have been there waiting,'' he muttered. ''We should have celebrated.''

A muffled sound snapped her upright on the edge of her chair. He couldn't be crying. ''What is it?'' She leaned over him, touched his cheek and found it wet. ''Oh, please, Guy. Don't shut me out.''

He covered his face with the splayed fingers of one hand. "I messed up, Leah. I didn't handle a single thing right. All these years I believed my own faith was strong enough to rub off on anyone I touched, carry them through—make them see each other the way I do. I accepted everyone else's weaknesses and failures, and I thought they'd do the same for each other and... and for me." The chair squeaked as he swung his feet to the floor and hunched over.

Instinctively, Leah reached for him, paused an instant, her hands hovering inches from his bent shoulders, then clasped him in a grip that made her arms ache. A sickening idea was forming in her brain. "Does this have something to do with us?"

He remained silent, his head heavy on her shoulder.

"It does," she said, sighing. "Someone's making trouble for you because of me. I knew this was going to happen."

"A petition," he muttered indistinctly. "They called me over to the McCleods' house and showed me this endless list of signatures they'd collected."

"Oh, Guy." Leah began to tremble convulsively. "I warned and warned you. You wouldn't listen to me. I knew there could be trouble. What did it say—this petition?"

"It doesn't matter. I should have been there to meet you and Dan tonight instead of sitting around her wallowing in self-pity. It's—"

"Guy, don't—" she broke in, but the glitter in his eyes stopped her momentarily. He was desperate. "It does matter. I care about what happens here, and so do you. I should have made you listen."

He held her hands. "This is your real beginning, Leah. You can go as far as you want to go now." His teeth glinted as he tipped his head up. "I dreamed of this for you, and I'm happy. Make the very best you can of yourself, my love.''

''My love.'' It was the first term of endearment he'd used in weeks, and Leah's thirsty soul drank it in. But he was skirting reality again. ''We have to talk about what happened to you today,'' she said softly. ''There's no way to avoid an issue forever. We talked about that once, Guy.''

His forefingers rubbed the insides of her wrists. ''Tomorrow I'll go to see Dan. Or maybe I'll call him and get him over here to talk. We've never discussed what he really wants. He's bright. He can do very well with the right chances, and I'd like to help him. I'd like to see him go to college.''

''Oh, Guy, Guy.'' Leah shook her head slowly. ''Helping every needing soul who passes your way won't shut out your own problems. Please—'' Her voice rose. ''Please tell me what happened today and what it means to you—to us.''

He stood and faced the pool, his hands deep in his pockets. ''I was informed that I'm a bad influence, a rotten example to my *good* people. More importantly, I don't give their children the right example.''

''All because Elsie Culver saw you hold me that day?'' Leah was outraged. ''After a few months' imaginative embellishment, one tiny incident has mushroomed into some grand, illicit passion?''

''They have more than that to go on,'' Guy said. ''Swimming together in this pool—''

''Once!'' Leah interrupted. ''And again, ages ago.''

''Listen. You asked what they have on me, so hear me out. We were seen together having drinks. At least a dozen instances of the two of us together in your car—at night—were documented, and—''

"You driving back from school with me," she exploded.

"Listen, will you?" he ground out. "And think. We were 'observed' shopping at the Biltmore Fashion Center, where we appeared 'unsuitably animated' and 'unconcerned about the impression we created.' This, of course, shows my 'completely inappropriate tendency toward extravagance and materialism,' in addition to my 'lack of the decorum expected of a church minister.' Someone I don't know must have helped with the wording of that lot.

"And we left early one Saturday morning a few weeks ago, and I didn't get back to the rectory until the middle of the night," he finished, the words snapping through clamped teeth.

"We got back at nine." This was crazy, all crazy.

Guy flopped into the chair again. "You got back at nine. *I* didn't feel like coming here and thinking all night long, so I went for a drive. How was I to know my big-hearted flock had set up a surveillance system to monitor my movements?"

"They did that?" Leah breathed. "They've been watching you. Watching both of us all this time. What do they want you to do?"

Guy's laugh was bitter. "Ideally, I think they'd like to see me stoned and run you out of town. Or maybe the reverse. Failing that, it's shape up or ship out, Hamilton. I do things their way—to the letter—or their damned petition goes to my superior and I'll be lucky if I'm allowed to preach in some mission in Outer Mongolia. And you've been so fantastic with all of them. I can't believe it. I had to leave the McCleods' house without saying anything. I was afraid I'd lose it all if I opened my mouth.

"Poor old Wally was here when I got back, worried to death because he knew where I'd been. He wanted to help me. He'd come to warn me earlier, but I'd already left. I took his head off, darn it. I'll have to go see him."

Goose bumps had sprung out on Leah's arms and legs. She shuddered violently. "Then that's it," she said flatly, getting up.

"What?" Guy stared up at her.

"I've got to get out of here, of course. The decision's been taken out of our hands. I've said this before; now I've got to follow through. I won't be responsible for ruining your career." As she spoke, she backed away. She would cry soon, and long, but it mustn't be in front of Guy.

"No!" he shouted. The next instant he towered over her, his strong fingers wound around her elbows. "If you go, they've won. We'll be admitting everything they think of us is true."

Leah bent her head and said, "It is true, Guy."

She heard him swallow. "It's not the way they've made it out. What we've had isn't something obscene and unnatural. We—we care about each other, and that's beautiful. It would be wrong for you to go."

"If you thought all this, why were you sunk in some kind of black pit when I found you out here? You just said you have to do things their way."

He was quiet for a moment before kissing her forehead quickly. "I hadn't had time to think everything through properly. That, or I couldn't without having you here with me to make me realize I won't let anyone do this to us."

She wanted to agree, to throw herself behind him and fight, but she didn't believe they could win. "It'll be easier on both of us if I leave."

"Stay, Leah. Please do it for me. I need you just to be yourself. Behave naturally and carry on. That way you'll be supporting me. If you go, I'm branded as some sort of monster, whatever I do. Surely you see that?" His breath escaped slowly. "I'm admitting to you that without you I'm not going to make it, anyway. Together we can weather whatever comes, and then I'll be able to get my own head together again and decide what to do next."

Leah carefully pulled free of his grip. "I'd better get home. Wally will be wondering where I am." They both knew she would stay in Phoenix as long as necessary. Why spell it out or dwell on the fact that they probably had no future together? "Guess I'll see you Monday. Have a good weekend."

"Thank you," Guy said quietly.

As soon as she was gone, he went inside and lay on his bed. He loved her so much. Every tiny detail of their lovemaking had flashed through his mind a thousand times since they'd been together. The weeks of not touching her or holding her had been hell, but the waiting should have been over tonight. Tonight he'd planned to ask her to marry him.

If his world hadn't suddenly been turned inside out, he would have met her and taken her somewhere quiet to toast the successful end of school and to offer her the sapphire engagement ring he'd bought. He reached up to lift the box from a bookshelf above his bed. Resting on one elbow, he popped open the lid. Ghostly light from the window bored laser shafts into the center of the three stones inside.

Her eyes were the color of these gems. Every day since he'd bought the ring, he had studied it covertly, visualizing it on her slender finger. She'd never taken off the little band he'd found in Sedona. It sent a spear of happiness and longing into his gut every time he looked at it or saw her smooth its surface. But he had wanted to give her this real sign of his love and the life he planned for them to share.

For a few insane seconds at the McCleods', he'd considered announcing he was a free man and that he and Leah were to be married. Then reason had blessedly taken over. If he'd followed his instinct, then told her, perhaps just now, she would think he was using her to climb out of his predicament. She probably did think as much regardless. A sudden offer of marriage when his professional neck was on the line would seal her opinion, and he wouldn't blame her.

He was crying again. Hot tears ran down his temples, and he turned on his stomach, clenching the ring box in his fist. "Messed up" had been an understatement. He'd done a bang-up job of ruining both their lives. Why hadn't he told her the minute he received notification of his divorce and taken a chance on what she might do? Why did he always feel he had a clearer view of how others would or wouldn't react than they did themselves?

Guy didn't know the answers to any of his questions. He knew only that he loved his work—and Leah. And becoming her husband now would take a miracle.

Deep inside, he was convinced he could beat the threat to his job. An open discussion with his superior, and time, was all that should take. But Leah? She was unlikely ever to trust him again—or to take that step he so longed to see her take toward even a tentative faith.

The salt taste of his tears was in his mouth, and he ground his back teeth together. He couldn't give up on making it through with Leah.

Chapter Fourteen

The phone rang as Leah walked through her office door on Monday morning. She dropped her purse on the desk and leaned to pick up the receiver. "Good morning. St. Mark's."

She heard the caller breathing for several seconds before Elsie Culver's familiar, high-pitched voice scattered down the line. "Will you still be at the rectory tomorrow morning, Mrs. Cornish?"

Leah massaged her right temple. Three sleepless nights and the miserably confused hours between had left her with a constant, dull headache. Elsie Culver was all she needed right now.

"Mrs. Cornish," Elsie prompted, "are you there?"

A long, slow sigh flowed from the bottom of Leah's lungs. "I'm here, Elsie. And I'll be here tomorrow. What can I do for you?"

A muffled voice in the background, then a scraping sound, let Leah know Elsie wasn't alone and had covered the mouthpiece to confer with a companion. Leah tapped a fingernail on hard plastic and quelled the urge to hang up.

"Tomorrow's my day for cleaning," the other woman finally announced. Then, with a smug note, she added, "But under the circumstances, I'll put it off until I hear from the minister. I suppose he's talked to you about our little discussion on Friday?''

Leah's temper threatened to snap. "He did mention something," she managed through gritted teeth. "Don't give tomorrow another thought. We'll manage."

As she dropped the receiver into its cradle, she sensed someone behind her and swung around to see Connie Ingalls hovering in the doorway. One look at the dark circles beneath Connie's blue eyes and the disheveled mass of her usually well-ordered black curls, shot fear into Leah. Mary and Anna stood each side of their mother, clinging to her hands. Their little faces were solemn.

Connie opened her mouth to speak but immediately choked on wrenching tears that shook her whole body.

"Connie!" Leah sped to grab the woman's shoulders. "What's happened? What's the matter?"

The ragged sobs only increased as Mary and Anna wrapped their spare arms around Leah's legs.

Helplessness overtook her. She needed Guy. "There's no room to sit down in here. Let's go to the counseling office; then I'll find Guy." A sliver of apprehension invaded her at the thought of facing him, but she shoved it aside.

Connie let herself and the girls be led down the hall and settled in a huddle on a couch. Her tears had abated to irregular hiccups. "I shouldn't have come here," she said. "But I can't work at the nursery until I find out what's happened to Dan. And I don't know what else to do."

Leah froze. "Something happened to Dan? Oh, Connie, why didn't you let us know? Where is he?"

"That's just it." Connie's sobbing began again, but more quietly. "I don't know where he is. He left yesterday afternoon, and he hasn't come back. The girls

and I looked everywhere we could, but they're too little to walk far, and I ran out of places to go on the bus.
Besides..." She trailed off, looking at her balled hands.

"Yes, yes, Connie. Besides?" Mary had toddled from
the couch, and Leah swept the child into her arms.

"I didn't have any more money," Connie whispered, and hid her face in both hands.

Leah blinked rapidly. "Stay here," she told Connie
gently. "Guy will know what to do."

She found him in the garden, attacking the soil with
a spade as if pounding dirt would satisfy some deep
anger. For a moment, she watched him, absorbing into
her own heart the disappointment and agony she was
sure drove him. Then the pressure of Mary's trusting
little fingers tugging at Leah's collar broke the moment.

"Is Uncle Guy mad?" Mary asked in a loud whisper. She jammed a thumb into her mouth, and her
smooth brow crinkled.

"No, just busy," Leah reassured, then shouted,
"Guy, can you spare a few minutes?"

His head shot up, and his instant, welcoming smile
made her swallow. He was relieved and incredibly
happy to see her. The past two days had been hell for
both of them.

"Coming," he called, sticking the spade upright in
the earth before brushing at old work pants as he
walked toward them. "Hi there, little Mary. How's my
girl?" He kissed a dewy cheek and, ruffled the girl's
hair, but all the time he kept his eyes on Leah's. "It's so
good to see you. If you hadn't shown, I'd have hunted
you down. I don't know how I managed not to come to
you over the weekend, but I figured I had to give you
breathing space."

She hugged Mary tightly. "Not now, Guy. We've got trouble, and this time it isn't because of anything we've done. Come on! Connie's inside, and she needs you."

Guy was strides ahead of Leah and Mary by the time they reached the counseling office, Leah having filled him in on what little she knew about Dan's disappearance.

Leah offered to take the two little girls away and leave Connie and Guy to talk alone. They both insisted she stay.

Guy made Connie repeat, word for word, what she'd already told Leah. She added that Dan had come home from the hotel job the previous afternoon, then left after an argument. Insistent prodding from Guy didn't produce more information except that Dan had walked out before, several times, but always returned after a few hours.

"Where would he go?" Guy repeated, talking to Connie but shooting a frustrated glance at Leah, who shrugged helplessly. "Please, Connie. If you won't give me anything else to go on, how can I help? I can go cruising around searching for him, I suppose. I will, anyway. But if I don't find him pretty quickly, we'll have to report him missing to the police."

"No!" Connie exploded. "No police. He's always been such a good boy—a man now. I won't have the police putting his name in their books."

"All right, all right," he calmed her. "But *help* me."

"He likes the mountains." Total exhaustion had turned Connie's face gray. "And he took his bike. He could have headed out into the hills. I went all over the town, so I don't think he's here."

"He likes mountains?" Guy lifted both palms. "Where would I start?"

Connie bit her lip. "We went to Squaw Peak for a picnic once—when his dad was still alive. We've often talked about what a happy time that was. Dan would never go back afterward, but maybe..."

Guy leaped up. "I'll try there first."

"They turned off all the lights."

Anna's words, clearly spoken, gained her the attention of every eye in the room.

"Shh," Connie muttered, hugging the child. "She's just tired and confused," she added to Guy and Leah.

Guy frowned and went to kneel in front of Anna. "What do you mean, sweetheart, 'They turned off all the lights'?"

Anna curled her knuckles against her mouth, her face turned up to her mother's. "Mommie said not to tell. But they turned off the lights, and—" She began to sniffle. "We—we couldn't cook or use the fan. And when Mommie tried to call about it, the phone wouldn't work, either." Her voice ended in a shrill wail.

"Okay, Anna," Guy soothed. His features were a set mask. "We'll make everything all right again. Connie, they cut everything off for nonpayment of bills, didn't they? Why didn't you tell me?"

Perspiration appeared above Connie's mouth; she looked sick. "Because you've done so much for us already. Things got better for a while, but then our rent went up, and I couldn't make it."

"You could have told me," Guy said. "We'd have figured something out. I suppose this is what sent Dan running like some mad thing. He's had all he can take, poor kid."

Leah was clasping and unclasping her fingers, and both little girls scrubbed their eyes miserably. Guy surveyed them all and shook his head. "This is as much my fault as anyone's. If I'd kept my feet on the ground and

my eyes open, I'd have realized you and Dan still might
not make enough to get by. But I wish you'd come to me
before things got so out of hand, Connie. Go home,
please, in case Dan shows. Leah will call and arrange to
pay your utility bills and get the power and phone re-
hooked. Later on, we can make some permanent decisions."

"I left the McCleods' eldest girl in the nursery,"
Connie muttered. "I didn't know what else to do, and
there wasn't anyone but you to turn to."

Guy helped her to her feet. "I'm glad you came to
me. Try not to worry. I'll get someone over to the nursery, then run you home and see if I can find Dan. Leah
will stand guard here."

He left, ushering the bedraggled little band ahead of
him. Leah caught his brief backward glance and smiled
encouragement. His job called for him to be all things—
minister, mentor, the final straw to clutch when all else
failed. A giant order for one man, too much for any
man without human, as well as spiritual, support.

She made the necessary calls to the utility companies
and wrote checks to cover Connie's outstanding bills.
Then she began her vigil and tried, unsuccessfully, to
work.

By midafternoon, the weather had taken on an un-
usually heavy atmosphere for the time of year. A pew-
ter-streaked sky beyond the window suggested a
rainstorm, rare for November.

Two calls from Guy, checking to see if she had any
news, only deepened her gnawing dread. The house
seemed to close in around her, and Leah wandered outside. An oppressive silence hung over the grounds and
the buildings, and the palms seemed hardly to sway.

Useless. She felt absolutely useless. All she could do
was hang around an empty house and wait. Dan's face,

laughing as it had been on Friday night, came clearly into her mind. His happiness hadn't been allowed to last long. She wanted to see him, to make sure he was all right.

Guy's flower beds were still a blaze of color. Chrysanthemums and clumps of ice plant crowded each other out. They needed thinning.

Leah forgot her tailored gray slacks and went to her knees on the concrete pathway. After a half hour she had arranged at intervals several small piles of plants. She sat on her heels and regarded the uprooted flowers. Too bad to throw them out. Maybe she should make them into bouquets and give them away.

She had severed the stalks and filled her arms with blooms before she acknowledged the obvious. She had no one who would want her gift except Wally, and even he might find her offering strange.

A car sped by on Fan Lane. Its engine noise startled Leah, then plunged her into depression. If only Guy would come back and say Dan was safe.

Churches always had flowers, she thought. During her childhood, peeking into a church at the end of her street had taught her that. She looked at her gay armload, then at the white structure across the way. Funny, now that she thought of it, she didn't remember seeing any flowers the one time she'd been in the building.

Hesitantly, she walked down the path and beneath the palms to the wooden door of St. Mark's. She maneuvered her bundle from arm to arm to turn the handle.

Once inside, Leah had to locate the power panel to the left of the door. First she flipped on every lever, flooding the empty building with glaring brilliance. She turned off all but a few lights near the altar.

Finding herself on tiptoe as she moved along the center aisle, Leah remembered Guy's comment about people's behavior in church. She immediately planted each foot with a smart click and dumped her burden beside the front pew. She grinned a little, and it felt good. Guy would smile, too, if he'd read her thoughts.

She hadn't been wrong; there weren't any floral arrangements. A cluster of green plants stood at each side of the altar, but there were no cut flowers in the church. Perhaps the parishioners wouldn't like it if she filled their place of worship with all this gaudy color. Guy might hate it, too. No, he wouldn't. Instinctively, she was sure Guy would love flowers in here, just as he loved them outside. She needed vases.

The first cupboard she checked yielded nothing but a stack of dusty old books and the guitar Guy had played. Leah ran a finger across the strings, winced at the discordant noise she produced and closed the door quickly. Three other cupboards failed to produce anything she could use. She was torn between abandoning her project and going back to the house for containers when she located a box of milk-glass vases and a metal jug in an alcove.

Further armed with a bucket of water from an outside faucet, Leah began to assemble cheerful, if not skillful, groupings.

While she worked, she thought of Guy and of Dan. If she were Guy, she'd be on her knees, praying for Dan's safety. Unconsciously, she threaded her fingers together. How did you pray? She glanced around the cool, pale interior. Peaceful. If she could pray anywhere, it should be here, but no one had taught her how. Maybe you didn't need to learn something like that.

"I just wish Dan would get back safely," she blurted out loudly. Then she added, "Please." It wasn't much, but it was the best she could do. This was a time when she couldn't afford to miss out on any possible help from anywhere.

Somewhere she'd heard the comment that God didn't make deals. But who knew what God did? If everything turned out all right for Dan—or even if it didn't—she might just start trying to be friends with Guy's boss.

She had just put two vases of flowers, one tall, one stubby, on the right side of the altar when the sound of the door opening was followed by squeaky steps on the linoleum floor. Leah was almost afraid to turn around. When she did, she hesitated long enough to take a deep breath and whoop before rushing headlong against Dan's tall, thin body.

"Where have you been, you little stinker?" She surrounded his ribs in a bear hug and felt his long arms awkwardly close across her back. Pounding him, keeping her head down on his chest, she started to cry. She'd cried more in the past few days than the rest of her life.

"Aw, hell, Leah," Dan pleaded. "Don't cry; please don't cry. I'm sorry I did this to all of you."

Leah released him and stood back to take in his length. "You look awful."

"Yeah." His wide mouth turned down. "That's what Mom said."

"You went home already? Good. Your mother was frantic. You should get back there to her, Dan—after you tell me where you've been." She pushed him into a pew and sat beside him. "Have you eaten?"

He smiled a little wanly. "I went to see my mother, remember. You think she didn't immediately start cramming food into me." The blue eyes, underscored with dark smudges, slid away. "Food Guy bought. We didn't have it yesterday."

The right words would never be more important with this boy than they were now. "It made Guy feel good to be able to help out. We both care about you all. You're very special to me, Dan. You know that, don't you?''

He shook his head and crossed his arms on the back of the next pew. "I don't know why. All you've done since you met me is put out. Now Guy's out there driving around for nothing. *I'm* nothing. I can't even try to let him know I'm okay."

Leah wiped slick palms on her pants. "Guy will be back soon, I'm sure. The last time he called, he said he'd give it another hour or so, then come home and decide what to do next."

"How long ago was that?"

"I don't know. An hour, maybe longer."

"Mom said he was looking in the mountains, Squaw Peak. But I'd never go there."

"No," Leah said. To deal with this situation, she needed wisdom, Guy's kind of wisdom.

"Leah—" Dan's throat moved, and he pressed his lips together. "Why do some people have nothing but rotten luck? My dad—my dad—" He covered his eyes.

She rubbed the sharp bones in his back. "Just say it all, Dan. Get it out. All the junk inside only grows until it chokes you."

He nodded, keeping his eyes closed. "My dad wasn't much older than me when he married my mom. They didn't have beans, but they were happy, and he was the kind of man who was always expecting good things to happen. When I remember him, I remember him laughing, not—not the way he was when he died."

He paused, and Leah saw him gathering together the little pieces of his past and the confusion of his present and trying to fit them together. She knew there was nothing she could do or say to help him.

A shallow breath shuddered noisily past his lips. "He and mom went to church when I was little. Bob went with us, too. We were always so poor, but Dad gave to the church, and he prayed, and nothing good ever happened to him. I hurt him when I wouldn't go anymore, but I don't understand any of this." He made a wide gesture. "I can't feel anyone here. At least not anyone who gives a damn about me. On Friday night I thought I could see something worth having in the future. For about twenty-four hours I was just like my old man. Dreaming. There's nothing for the don't-haves in this world; only it takes some of us longer than others to realize it. My dad *died* without realizing it."

"Dan..." *Oh, God. The right words, please.* "Dan, you're no more of a 'don't-have' than I was. I don't even have a memory, any kind of a memory of a father to hang on to. He was a drifter, and one day when I was still a baby, he drifted right out of my life. My mother was..." The damn tears welled again, and she could hardly breathe. "My mother was a whore who worked in a restaurant and brought home a succession of men after she finished work each night. I grew up listening to them through the walls of a two-room apartment. Then, when I was nineteen, I married the first man who asked me. I was lucky. I'll never stop being grateful to Charles. He loved me. He gave my mother enough money to make some sort of new life. And he *never* threw up at me how I'd come from the gutter.

"I got a chance, and I'm not ever going back to the gutter. Now I've started making something of myself. So have you. This thing that happened over money at home will pass; you'll see. You and I are going to be the best we can be, and we'll make our own good luck." She was weary, but she must press on. A flicker of light in Dan's lackluster eyes suggested she was making inroads. "I never went to church as a kid. Although I often wondered about it. Charles and I went a few times. I didn't know why he wanted to go or what he thought about when he was quiet there. I just used to stare and wonder if I looked okay, because that was important to him. But this is a peaceful place, Dan. I still don't know what I believe, but I *can* accept that Guy's found something special I'd like to have a part of. Maybe it wouldn't be so bad to come in here sometimes to think. I might just try it one day. In fact, I'm going to do it for sure. Why don't you, the next time you feel like running away?"

He spread his arms along the back of the bench. "I might. Know where I was?"

She raised her eyebrows.

His laugh was hollow. "At the airport. I rode all the way out there just to sit and watch planes take off and land all night and wish I was on one of them going somewhere. It didn't matter where. I even thought of going to some railroad siding and jumping a boxcar, like you read about. Didn't have the energy or the guts. I fell asleep, and some guy picking butts from the ashtrays woke me up at about eleven. It took me the rest of the time I was gone to find the courage to go home."

Leah laughed and blinked. "If I cry much more, I'm going to flood us out. I'm so glad to see you, Dan. From the day we met, you've been like the brother I never had. Relax, kid. With Guy's help, we'll work it all out. Time you started thinking about more schooling, not skipping town."

"Why don't you and Guy get married?"

Leah's insides dropped away. Her skin crawled. "That's a weird question," she managed around a pain in her throat.

"And none of my business, right?" Dan shrugged. "Only you two are obviously crazy about each other, and if you were married, we could all relax."

She tried to stand, but he held her wrist. "Mom and old Wally and me, and a lot of other people who think you're great, are getting pretty sick of worrying about the two of you. So why don't you just do it? That'd be the way to shut up all the rotten gossip."

She smiled tightly. How did you explain that you were willing but the other party wouldn't take the necessary steps to make it happen. "Don't worry about us. It's time you got back to your mother and the kids. But we'll talk tomorrow, okay?"

"Okay." His eyes were suddenly old, appearing to see deep inside her head. "Tomorrow."

"You bet it'll be tomorrow, kiddo." Guy had come beside them unnoticed and was gripping the end of the pew, glaring at Dan. "You've put your mother through hell, and Leah and me." He sat beside her and gathered her tightly against his side. He was filthy and wild looking, his pants spattered with mud.

Leah unthinkingly held his hand. "Go easy, Guy. Dan's had a rough time, and I understand. He's already talked to Connie, and he's going home again now. We all need to back off and get some perspective."

Guy watched her mouth as she spoke, then stared into her eyes. His fingers twined more tightly into hers. Leah wondered how long he'd been in the church, listening, before he approached them.

"Wise, as usual," he said. "When you start looking for someone to care about, Dan, one on one, try for a lady like this. Now get home. While I was running around like a dog after its tail, I came up with a doozy of a solution to your little financial foul-up. Working for me part-time. Wally should be doing less, and you can fill in. It'll work if it doesn't kill you in the process. Get some sleep and prepare for battle."

All three slid to stand in the aisle, and Guy wrapped an arm around Leah's shoulders as they watched Dan leave. The door closed with an echoing thud. Their twin breathing was the only sound in the silence that rushed in.

"I'm bushed," Guy groaned. "I went by Connie's on my way back and found out he'd shown. The electricity's back on, and they'll have the phone by morning. Sit with me a minute. My muscles are screaming for a hot shower, but all I want to do is be here with you for a while first."

She made no attempt to stop him when he pulled her onto his lap and lifted her face to his. "You're beautiful," he said. "Have I told you that lately?"

"Not lately," she replied breathlessly.

"Well, you are. And I've decided what you should study in college."

Leah leaned away. "Oh, thanks. And what's that?"

"Crisis counseling, of course. You're a natural. I know that boy might still be gone if he hadn't wanted to come back and talk to you."

"You give me too much credit, but thanks. He'd never have been able to walk away from his family." Guy's palm, massaging her shoulder, made thought almost impossible. "You should get that shower and some rest," she added.

"Mmm." He looked past her, a speculative expression narrowing his eyes. "Did you do that?"

"Do what?" She craned around and instantly guessed he was referring to the flowers. "The flowers? I hope it's all right. I had to do something, so I started thinning beds and couldn't bear to throw all of those gorgeous things away. Was it all right to put them here? I can easily take them—"

His hand, cupping her chin, immediately followed by a swift but intense kiss, cut her off. "They're lovely. Could be the loveliest thing I've seen in this building, next to you. I'll have to get you to do floral arrangements in here all the time."

He was avoiding the disaster steadily closing in around him. Leah followed Guy from the church, forming arguments, avenues to broach their dilemma, but discarding each one. She couldn't be the one to bring up the subject.

The rain she'd expected was falling steadily, and they ran to the house, arriving breathless and laughing, their shoulders damp.

Guy wiped moisture from Leah's face with his hand. "Don't go away," he pleaded. "I've hardly seen you today, and I can't stand to be alone again. If you leave, I'll only come and hammer on your door."

She flattened a palm on his chest. "I won't go yet. Shower; then maybe we'll talk for a bit."

"Why can't we talk *while* I shower." His eyes turned the color of green slate before he added, "Through the door, of course," and grinned.

Muscles in Leah's jaw trembled. "I guess we can." She was afraid, as much of herself as of him. They couldn't afford more mistakes, not now, not here.

He whistled as he led the way, then sang in an unusual grainy, intensely masculine voice that broke in a heart-twisting way. She closed her eyes fractionally and felt the magnetic force field between them. The heavy heat had started deep inside; the thrilling ache, in her thighs. She straightened and lengthened her steps. They were going to talk, nothing more.

"I'm going to strip off these disgusting rags," Guy announced, going into his rooms. "They may have to be burned later." His shirt hit the floor before he made it into the bedroom.

Leah automatically picked it up. "You are one of the most untidy people I've ever met," she remarked, thinking at the same time that it was totally true.

"I know," he replied complacently. "Guess I'm not completely perfect, after all."

She balled up the shirt and hiked it at his back, but he turned just in time to catch it. He'd tossed the crumpled checked cotton back before she had time to recognize the move as a diversion. Guy used the split-second advantage he'd gained to grab her waist and back her to the bed.

"Guy!" Her knees buckled, and she was flat beneath him, his face a few inches from hers. "We can't do this. I mean—you know what I mean."

"I know exactly what you mean." Firm lips covered and parted hers. His tongue found the farthest recesses of her mouth, teasing, until she began to relax and return his ardor. His naked chest and shoulders felt cool beneath her searching fingers, his muscles hard and his skin, when she lowered her face to kiss his neck, tasted deliciously salty.

His thigh pressed between her legs, and she turned her head sharply, the familiar wanting flaring out of control. She nipped his shoulders and arched her back when he stroked her breasts through her silk blouse and bra.

Abruptly, he seized her hands and captured them above her head. "Time out while we can still think. I'm going to shower. You can hide your face or watch, whichever appeals." He straight-armed over her, gazing down; then the bed rebounded with the loss of his weight.

"While we can still think." Leah lay very still, trying to form the simplest thought that didn't relate to the clamoring sensations in her body. Then she scrambled to sit cross-legged in the middle of the bed and propped her chin in the palm of one hand.

Guy aped a series of Adonis poses until she collapsed with laughter, which slowly subsided as he removed the rest of his clothes. He stood for an instant, his eyes silently telling her what he wanted, before going into the bathroom.

Leah was left with the mental vision of his straight back and wide shoulders, his tensile legs, like those of an athlete and sprinkled with blond hair.

The sound of dashing water, then the glass door bumping against rubber, was followed by Guy's voice, raised in song once more. By the time Leah reached the outside of the shower doors, she wore only her lace bra and panties.

His body was a tall outline, not moving, simply standing, head thrust back to allow water to jet against his face. She reached back to unhook the bra and dropped it on the counter beside the sink, intensely aware of the fullness and weight of her breasts. The panties followed, and she stepped into the enclosure behind Guy.

Chapter Fifteen

He hadn't heard her. When she laid her palms flat on his back, she felt muscle and sinew jolt. Guy stood very still, elbows uplifted, his hands locked behind his neck.

Leah smoothed his wet body. The steamy air filled her lungs and shortened her breaths. She reached up to trace his arms and shoulders. Lightly, she feathered her fingers down his spine and fanned outward over his ribs to the glistening skin at his sides.

"I love you," she whispered, and circled his narrow hips, pressing her breasts to his back, massaging the hard plane of his belly. There could be no more holding back. This might be their only time together. Although she cared with every tiny fragment of her being, whether or not he loved her in return, she still savored, reveled in, her own declaration.

Guy moved slowly and covered her hands, guiding them over his groin to unyielding thighs and back to his stomach. "I love you, too, Leah. So much it hurts. Hold me, sweetheart."

Spray beat from his shoulders onto her hair and face. He reached back, pressing her ever closer, and she touched him with a total intimacy that sent a shared tremor through their molded bodies. She touched him as a woman in love and as a lover intent on pleasing and being pleased. They loved each other, and the knowledge set her free. Once, he'd told her nothing could be wrong when given or taken by a man and a woman in love. Leah stroked and absorbed into herself the convulsive jolt of power from his muscle. He loved her, too. He'd told her once before. Now the knowledge filled her with voluptuous strength.

"Wait," he breathed, "wait, my love."

He faced her, his chest heaving, and Leah almost stepped backward, impaled by the intense light in his eyes. Slowly, he bent his head, and their mouths met, grazing tantalizingly back and forth. He braced his hands on the tile above her head, keeping inches between their bodies, until Leah unconsciously strained toward him, brushing erect nipples against wet chest hair.

Guy urgently thrust his hips into her belly, and they came together in a frenzied embrace that rocked her soul. His kisses inflamed her mind and her senses. She threaded her fingers into his hair and stilled his face, making him wait as she carefully ran a trail around his lips with her tongue before delving deep into his mouth.

"You're driving me mad," he muttered when she released his head and swept her hands to knead his hips. "And, little friend, the water's getting cold."

She burrowed against his chest, clinging, while they laughed. "Turn it off."

Guy held her away, his smile fading. "I want to make love to you, slowly, in my own bed." He cupped her breasts, his gaze flickering down to the softly swelling flesh beneath his hands. For seconds, he teased her nipples, watch them peak, then carefully tongued and took each one between his teeth.

Hot flashes of sensation coursed through her body. The nuzzling action of his cheek and the pressure of his mouth drove her against the cool wall of the shower. His hand went to her stomach, then swept down between her legs, and Leah had to clutch his shoulders as her knees turned rubbery.

By the time her mind gradually cleared, the water was icy. Guy held her tightly in one arm and reached to turn off the shower. His face grew darkly impassioned, and her renewed arousal was instant in flesh that still throbbed.

He carried her to the bed, pausing barely long enough to pull the covers partially back before they fell, wet, onto the sheet.

"I guess we can forget slow," he said against her mouth.

Leah urged her fevered lover's damp body over hers, gloried in his weight, received him, surrounded and fused with him. Their union, new again, as her brain acknowledged it would always be between them, created a heated place where skin and muscle, bone, breath and pumping blood, the life of two, became one. With Leah, Guy moved as part of her, faster, higher, the sounds of their lovemaking small and garbled. Then came the final, triumphant call at their climax, the tangle of suddenly leaden limbs and the sweet whisper of mingled breath over warm faces.

"My love, my love." Guy's voice broke. "You're everything to me. I never thought I'd get so lucky. It scares me."

Leah slid an arm around his neck and pulled his head against her breast. "Don't be scared—ever. Just keep on loving me and saying you do."

They nestled in a languid embrace until Guy began again to do as Leah asked. Hours passed before they fell into an exhausted sleep.

When Leah awoke, the room was dark. Blinking and yawning, she rolled beneath the weight of Guy's heavy arm. She squinted. A muted gleam from a bedside radio's dial sent a faint shimmer over his tousled blond hair.

Memories of their lovemaking flooded back in vivid cameos. Guy murmured indistinctly, and his fingers tightened around her ribs. Leah smiled, trying unsuccessfully to make out his features.

What were they going to do? The persistent question wormed its way into the center of her happiness, spreading its gray pall steadily outward. Leah pushed back her hair and chewed the inside of her lip. Something bigger than either of them, or certainly her, was going to have to sort this one out.

She slipped from the bed and went into the bathroom. With face freshly scrubbed, her teeth cleaned with a new brush she found in a drawer and her hair arranged into some semblance of order, she returned to slide into bed.

"Hi, lady," Guy said from the darkness beside her.

Leah started and turned into his outstretched arm. "Hi. Thought you were out cold for the night. I almost wrote a note and snuck out of here, but you and this delectable bed lured me back."

"Mmm." Guy's breath tickled her ear. "You'd better not sneak out. This is where you belong, and I don't intend to let you get away again."

She frowned. "I don't want to get away, Guy. But we both know I can't be here all night."

"Too dangerous for you?" he teased. "I'll behave whenever you ask me to."

He couldn't be as wide awake as he sounded. "You know what I mean."

For several seconds he stroked her hair and face. "Leah—" he kissed her lips softly "—we have to talk."

Hope made her heart bound. "I want to," she said. "I've wanted to for a long time."

"Would you consider marrying me next week?"

Leah's mind blanked. She must have imagined he just asked her to marry him. He wasn't even divorced.

Guy leaned away to flip on a small lamp, then propped his head and stared down into her face. "You do want to marry me, don't you?" He watched intently for her reaction.

Her body didn't seem to want to move. Her hand was a dead weight when she raised it wonderingly to the stubble along his jaw. "I want to be your wife, Guy. That can't be a surprise to you. But...yes, I'll marry you. As soon as it's possible. In the meantime, I can't stay here with you. I'll suffer every minute of the waiting, but we have to make sure we do everything right from here on out. I'm beginning to care almost as much about this place of yours as you do—and these people. Even the ones I shouldn't give a damn for. They'll be the biggest challenge."

His unwavering glance became disconcerting. Leah made herself keep her eyes on his.

"We don't have to wait, sweetheart. We can get married just as soon as we get the formalities out of the way."

Leah dropped her hand to his shoulder and let it slide down his arm. "I don't understand."

"My divorce is final." His nostrils flared. "I...Susan divorced me, and now I'm free."

"I see." But she didn't see, not quite. "Guy, do you mean that you've heard something from Susan and she's going to start a divorce?"

He shook his head. "No. Look, I intended to tell you this before. I'd planned to say it on Friday night, but I thought you'd get the wrong idea after the bombshell I got from the parish."

Leah evaded the hand that tried to restrain her and sat up, pulling the sheet around her breasts. "Let me get this straight, please. You found out on Friday that you were going to be divorced but decided to wait until now to tell me? Is that the way it went?" A sickening knot grew in her stomach.

"Does it matter how it went?" He pushed fingers agitatedly into his hair. "We can be married. We *need* each other, and we don't have to wait."

Cold calm steadily replaced confusion in Leah. "Do you mind telling me when you found out Susan was divorcing you? I guess I'm a bit obtuse, but you've caught me off guard."

Guy sat up and wrapped his arms around his knees. "Yup. I guess this must seem pretty bizarre coming all at once. But it's not so difficult." He looked at her over his shoulder and smiled. "Several months ago I got notification from Susan's lawyers that she was starting divorce proceedings. Then I heard the thing had gone through. So you see, there's nothing standing in our way anymore."

The sick sensation in Leah's stomach rose to her throat. He couldn't possibly believe she'd accept what he said and fall into his plan for marriage simply because he'd finally decided to tell her the truth about what had been happening in his life for months. She stared at him, shutting her mouth deliberately when she realized it had fallen open. The full reality of what he'd said was seeping through her, leaving ugly disappointment in its wake. He hadn't lied to her, merely done what he'd done so many times before—failed to admit the complete truth.

"Say something, sweetheart." His skin looked stretched over the bones, his eyes dark and troubled. "It's all right, isn't it?"

Begging. He was begging her to ignore how he'd punished her out of his lack of trust. "Did you know you were divorced the first time we made love?" She could hardly hear her own voice.

Guy scrubbed at his face with both hands. When he looked at her, anxiety had etched white lines from his nose to the corners of his mouth. "I found out the day before."

"Then you made love to me and let me feel guilty for making you compromise your principles?"

"It wasn't supposed to be like that—"

"But it *was* like that. And afterward you drew away from me and made me wonder why you were so cool. I accepted your behavior. I thought you were still fighting your conscience and you'd come around if I gave you more time."

"Please—"

Leah, scooting from the bed, cut him off. She grabbed her slacks and shirt, then remembered that her underwear was in the bathroom and disappeared into the smaller room, closing the door quietly but firmly.

Her fingers rebelled, fumbling with each hook and button, with the buckle on the belt of her slacks. By the time she reopened the door, she was shaking with hurt and self-disgust—and stinging anger.

Guy, wearing jeans he must have grabbed from the closet, grasped her arms as she emerged. "Listen to me," he implored. "You don't understand. And you won't if you refuse to let me explain."

She willed her heart to slow down and her voice to be steady. Neither plea was answered. "You lied to me. Oh, you didn't actually tell me things that weren't true, but you didn't let me inside your wonderful, private life. You made love to me in Sedona because you'd gotten word of the divorce. Don't ask me why you pulled back again afterward. Then—"

"Leah," he interrupted, trying to embrace her rigid body.

She shook free, backing away and holding out her hands as if to ward him off. "No! No more, Guy. There was never meant to be anything between us. It's as much my fault as yours. I was the one who came chasing after you—and the one who made the first advances. Don't feel bad; just let me go and forget me. Please!" The high, shaky note of her last word horrified her.

"I won't. You're going to listen." He stood between Leah and the door to the study. "I didn't do things right, and I'm sorry. I made a mistake. Give me another chance and I can explain."

Anger had already turned to panic. She *had* to get away. Dodging around him, she headed for the sliding door, clicked up the lock and slid the heavy glass wide.

"Damn it, Leah. Don't do this." Guy was behind her when she stepped onto the patio.

Rain was falling in diagonal sheets, slashing at her face, instantly soaking her clothes. For a second she was disoriented, unsure which way to run to reach the front of the house.

"I won't let you go like this," Guy shouted. His arm went around her waist, and she couldn't move.

In the glow from the bedroom, she registered his torso, naked and wet, his drenched jeans, the way his tousled hair curled in the downpour. Her own hair was plastered to her head and neck.

"Come back inside," Guy insisted, but she stood her ground.

"Why did you do it?" she cried. "How could you when you knew how I felt and how I was suffering." The silk blouse adhered to her skin now, and rain dashed in rivulets down her neck and dripped from her hair to her face.

Guy laid his face on her shoulder, but she made no move to hold him. "I thought I was doing the right thing," he said hoarsely. "If you'll let me, I can make you see it my way."

A bubble of blackness exploded in Leah's mind. *See it your way.* "I don't think so, Guy," she said. She was intensely aware of his proximity, the scent, the feel of him. Her every emotion urged her to hold him, but her mind argued, and it won. "You listen. Then maybe one day you'll know how to give yourself completely to...someone." She narrowed her eyes as she said "someone." The rain would hide her tears, but she didn't intend to cry yet.

He dropped his arms to his sides and stood there, tall, muscles gleaming wetly. "I'm listening."

Her breath jammed in her larynx. "You felt you could make love to me that first time because you weren't married any longer. Then, for some reason, you had a smattering of remorse, so you backed off. But you didn't expect the congregation to come up with their dirty little indictment. That triggered a whole different set of circumstances. They changed the rules on you.

"I don't believe you intended to tell me about the divorce on Friday or that you wanted to marry me at that point. How can I believe that? What have you really been afraid of with me, Guy? Commitment? If you'd told me the truth, would you also have had the guts to say you don't want to be permanently attached to one woman again? Back in Sedona. What stopped you from telling me then? Were you terrified I'd demand too much from you?'' She was exhausted and weak. The scratching quality of her voice had to give away her tears.

Guy held out his hands, and she saw agony in his face. He was beaten, in pain. But only because he'd hurt her, and regardless of how wrong he'd been, hurting people was the last thing he'd ever plan or live with easily.

"Leah," he said. "My love. Don't go away from me now like this. I didn't do things right, but we all make mistakes."

The muscles in her face contracted. "And how long before you do the same thing again?" Her breath came in little gasps. "Isn't this what happened with Susan? Different in some ways but the same. You shut her out, Guy, like you shut me out. I don't know if I'm wrong, but I think deep down you know you could do to me what you did to her, and that's what frightened you away from coming clean or risking another marriage."

"Leah, please—"

But she'd started to run, sobs jarring her teeth together. The sound of his bare feet, slapping concrete awash with water, speeded her steps.

He caught her before she reached the grass and swung her around. "I love you," he rasped. "Damn it, Leah. I do love you."

"You didn't care enough to let go of yourself and let me share all of your life. You manipulated me, and no one's going to do that to me again."

"I *love* you, Leah."

She wrenched her arm from his fingers and backed away, sobbing, doubling over to grasp her aching diaphragm. Every breath was torn from the bottom of her lungs.

"Not enough."

Chapter Sixteen

Guy walked unseeingly past clusters of people outside the church. Only Providence had pulled him out of an exhausted doze in time to make it to the ten o'clock funeral rites for one of the parish's founding members.

"Nice eulogy, Guy."

He absently met the speaker's eyes. "Thanks, Wally," he murmured. What had he said about an ancient woman he'd hardly known? He didn't remember. Blessedly, there had been no call for music. He'd had difficulty concentrating on anything but Leah's bright splashes of floral color and the repetitive snatches of her accusations that bored relentlessly into his brain.

The sandy turf was still damp from last night's downpour, but he set out between the palms, avoiding the pathways along which parishioners always congregated to talk after services. They liked to shake his hand and chat. Guy didn't want to chat or touch, unless he could touch Leah. He should feel guilty about that, but he didn't. Since last night he'd been going through the motions of living, avoiding the decisions he must make. Now there could be no more avoidance.

"Hey, Guy!" Dan caught up with him, puffing slightly. "Boy, you were out of there like a jackrabbit from a trap."

Surprised at the boy's unexpected-appearance, Guy frowned, slowly comprehending that Dan had been in church. He tried to rally enough reserve to do and say the right things. Holding on would be everything in the next few hours and days, for everyone concerned. At this moment, he had to forget himself and hold on for Dan.

"Man with a mission," he said with a brightness that threatened to crack his face. "Got a letter to write." Dan didn't need to know the letter would be Guy's resignation, addressed to his superior.

"We were going to talk, remember? I've been resting up since yesterday like you told me. Now I guess I'm about ready for that battle you've been planning for me."

Dan's blue eyes smiled into his, and Guy's stomach turned over. Before he left Phoenix, he must face the responsibility of completing some important projects he'd started. There could be no question of deserting the Ingallses. He rested a broad hand on the boy's shoulder. "I haven't forgotten, Dan. Can we get to it a bit later—say, late this afternoon?" He tried not to notice the disappointment that edged around the youth's smile.

"Sure," Dan said. "I'll come back about five on my way from work. Will that be okay?"

"Terrific. Five."

Guy had watched Dan sprint for his old bicycle and pedal away before he realized he hadn't given any positive reinforcement. Plainly, Connie had mentioned this morning's service, and Dan had ridden all the way from Indian School Road to attend, hoping to please Guy and to see him afterward. And Guy had hardly reacted; he'd allowed the boy to ride to work on the other side of town with the prospect of having to come all the way back again later.

Head down, Guy continued toward the house. He ought to put in an appearance at the reception being held in the social hall. But the prospect of smiling and nodding, exchanging banalities with strangers, his declared adversaries, or even friends, was unbearable. A mixture of all elements had been present in force this morning.

I need you, Leah. The phrase had repeated and repeated in his head since she had run away. He'd blown it, made all the wrong assumptions and decisions, and now they would both pay unless his last-ditch effort worked. Guy didn't trust his own efforts anymore.

Not looking into her empty office as he passed took superhuman restraint. The whole house felt hollow, and he didn't want to be there anymore.

He'd spent the night's waning hours in one of the guest rooms, unable to face the bed he'd shared with Leah. After she'd gone, he had sunk into a chair by the pool and turned his face up to the beating rain, willing it to wash away the anguish that threatened to burst his skull. He didn't know how much later he'd found the courage to go inside, stepping over the tangle of sheets on the floor as he went.

The morning had brought no relief, only more wrenching questions about himself and the conviction that Guy Hamilton didn't know what was true about him, or best for him, let alone anyone else. He had no right to stay here, guiding, when he was lost.

"Guy! Wait up, will you, man?"

He'd left the front door open, and Wally was hurrying along the hallway.

"What is it with you?" Wally asked. "Deaf or something? I bin calling after you since Dan left."

"Sorry," Guy muttered. He wished the old man would go away.

Wally pushed his hat to the back of his head, then hastily pulled it off. "Got something to tell you." A smile sent creases across his cheeks, but his eyes remained solemn as he studied Guy. "You okay?" He tapped Guy's upper arm.

Leaving this man would be hard, one of the toughest things Guy had ever done. "I could be better, Wally. But I think you know that. What's new?"

Wally took his elbow. "Where can we talk?"

Guy sighed. "I...do we have to do this now? There're some things I ought to get to right away." He felt sick.

"Won't take but a minute."

Defeated, Guy said, "In my study, then," and led the way. "I don't like putting you off, but I'm going through a rough time and..." His words fizzled away. He'd actually admitted everything wasn't coming up roses for him. He almost laughed in self-derision. *A bit late for mending fences, buddy.*

The door to his bedroom had been deliberately closed before he left. Showering in the same shower where he'd been together with Leah, dressing in a room that still held her fragrance, had left him shaky with longing. He had almost run from the memories, wishing he need never go back.

He slumped on the edge of his cluttered desk. "Shoot," he told Wally.

Ignoring his ungracious host's lack of manners, Wally lowered his rangy frame into a chair and leaned back. "You don't have a thing to worry about," he announced complacently. "Everything's taken care of."

Guy narrowed his eyes. "What's been taken care of?"

"McCleods, Culvers, Jenkins—the whole lot of them. They decided they didn't have so much they wanted to talk to your head honcho about. In fact, they decided they didn't have a thing they wanted to discuss, with anyone."

Wally's expressionless gaze met Guy's uncomprehending stare. "*They* decided, Wally?" Guy asked softly. "What does that mean, you old goat? What did you do—hire the mob to strong-arm them?"

"In a manner of speaking." The tips of Wally's fingernails suddenly enthralled him. "There isn't one of those turkeys who doesn't have some goody tucked away in a closet." He looked sharply at Guy. "The kind of goodies people like to keep hidden, if you know what I mean?"

"Oh, I know what you mean," Guy said slowly, massaging his jaw. "You cagey devil. All these years you've been mooching around here, quiet, not involved in anyone's business. But you never missed a thing, and now you've put the thumbscrews on the poor devils."

Wally's grin was smug. "A fellow can't help what he hears. People tell things to someone who's almost invisible, someone who doesn't talk. And I don't talk, Guy. Still haven't and don't intend to. But it didn't hurt to remind a few people of a few things."

Guy couldn't help smiling. "I don't want to know what these things are, Wally. You wouldn't tell me, anyway. And, of course, I disapprove of your methods. But thanks. At least that's one less thing to worry about." Not that it mattered now.

"Yeah." Wally nodded his grizzled head emphatically. "And our Leah won't have to be putting up with any more nonsense around here. I couldn't have taken much more of that."

"No." Guy stood and moved around the desk. His chest tightened unbearably. "Leah won't be putting up with any more... not now. Thanks, Wally, for everything. You're the best, I—I'm sorry I sounded off at you on Friday. There's no excuse except I lost it there for a while." If he didn't shut up, he'd probably cry and embarrass them both.

He held out his hand, and Wally shook it. At the door, he shot Guy a penetrating glance. *He knows,* Guy thought, gathering his forces to respond to whatever questions might come. But Wally silently inclined his head before the sound of his boots clipped steadily away.

So, his faithful flock had decided not to put him through the hoop. Not because they'd changed their minds about him but because they were afraid some probably innocuous snippet of gossip about each of them might be aired if they did. He fished around in a desk drawer for a fresh sheet of letterhead and started to write.

The words came slowly, and he tossed one piece of paper after another into the garbage. What he had to say was simple. He'd examined his conscience and found it lacking. He wasn't fit to do his job and wished to be released as soon as a replacement minister for St. Mark's could be found. He was asking for an open-ended leave of absence to decide on his career course.

Eventually, the sentences got his message across, and he slid the folded sheet into an envelope.

Could he do what he'd planned? Could he go to Leah one more time, as a plain man, unfettered by his calling, and ask her to take a chance on a future with him?

Exhaustion blurred his thoughts. If he went to her now, he'd botch whatever he said. Best wait, at least until he'd had some sleep.

He slammed a fist on the desk and buried his face in his hands. If he were confident of Leah's reaction, he'd already be on his way to her. A man who couldn't believe in himself couldn't expect anyone else to believe in him. Maybe she'd be better off with someone else.

He heard a muffled noise but didn't raise his head. What did he have to offer her? Not even total security until he knew where he was headed.

A tentative brushing against his sleeve startled him, and he straightened. Dan Ingalls stood at his shoulder, one hand still on Guy's arm. The youth's face was streaked with what looked suspiciously like the result of tears mixed with dust.

Guy ran his tongue over dry lips. "I thought we said five." He checked his watch and was amazed it read a few minutes after one. "Shouldn't you be at work?"

Dan sniffed. "Don't you care?" His voice held a tremulous wobble.

Without knowing why, Guy felt his heart pump harder. "I don't know what you mean, Dan. Care? About you? Of course I care about you."

"I don't give a—I don't give a damn if you care about me. You know what I'm talking about."

The kid looked ill. "Did you lose your job?" Guy stood and tried to push Dan into his own chair. The youth wouldn't budge. He was angry—with him? "Did they fire you?"

Dan curled his hands into bony fists. "You son of a bitch. You don't care. I hate you. I hate you." One craggy set of knuckles glanced off Guy's jaw before he could react. A second blow connected squarely with his nose, and he felt a trickle of warm blood run into his mouth.

Guy saw Dan's right fist coming again and grabbed the wrist, twisting just enough to flop his weaker opponent into the chair. "Stop it," he ground out, wiping blood from his lips. "Stop it, you little idiot. Calm down and make sense before I knock some into you." He tried to pin Dan's hands together in one of his own, but the boy was too strong. It took surprising effort to subdue Dan's furious writhing and hold him until he sank back, head lolling, his breath coming in staccato bursts.

"She's worth ten of you," Dan gasped between gulps of air, and he began to cry, tears slipping from wide-open eyes. "She trusted you, and you've done something to make her go away. I knew everything had gone wrong from the way you avoided me earlier. When I couldn't find Leah in her office, I went over to her place to find out what was up."

Guy slackened his grasp on Dan's wrists. "What did she tell you?" The adrenaline that had pumped briefly through his body evaporated.

"Your lip is bleeding all over." Dan scrabbled in his jeans pocket and produced a grimy handkerchief. "I shouldn't have done that, but I believed in you."

Half-formed conclusions whirled in Guy's head. "I asked you what she said." He took the handkerchief and blotted at his face. His upper lip was swelling, and his head thudded sickeningly.

"Nothing!" Dan almost shouted. "You know her well enough. She wouldn't say anything against anyone. Least of all you. She even smiled and said she just reckoned it was time to make a change—to move on, get a new job and meet new people. But I'm not a little kid who can't figure out when someone's covering up. Leah loves you. I thought you loved her, too. But if you did and everything was okay, she'd be down there in that office where she wants to be most. Near you. I can't stand it if she goes away like this." Dan's crying became audible. He bent over, rocking. "She doesn't have anyone, anywhere. Why'd you do it?"

Guy's brain cleared. Unwillingly, he absorbed the message in Dan's disjointed accusations. "Listen to me," he demanded. "Look at me and listen." He waited until Dan met his glare. "Are you telling me Leah's getting ready to leave Phoenix?"

"Isn't that what you wanted?" Dan continued to rock.

"No!" Guy roared, thrusting the bloodstained handkerchief back into the boy's hands. "It's the last thing I want unless I'm with her. Go and lie down somewhere. Use one of the guest rooms and get some sleep before you collapse. I'll be back."

FOOTSTEPS CLATTERING up the metal steps to her apartment made Leah pause before stacking another saucepan in a cardboard box. It must be Dan coming back. She hadn't handled him well.

"Come in!" she called before he could ring the bell or knock. "It's unlocked."

The door opened behind her; then she heard it quietly close again. Dan was confused, wounded by what he saw as her defection. Leah couldn't bring herself to look at him.

"Glad you came back," she said. "I could use a strong pair of arms to help me with all this stuff. I think it grew since I got here, although I don't remember buying a thing—except plants."

He didn't answer. Her throat burned. She wanted desperately to make him feel better, but her own hurt was more than she'd be able to contain much longer.

"Dan." She turned around slowly. "I'll always...
Guy!" Her mouth became dry at the sight of him.
"Wh-what are you doing here?"

He leaned on the back of the couch, his head averted.
"You'll always what? What were you going to say if I'd
been Dan?"

She swallowed. "That I'll always keep in touch with
him and let him know where I am."

"And me?" He jerked to face her. "Will you always
let *me* know where you are? Or are you planning to
disappear out of my life forever?"

"Oh, my God. What's happened to you?" She
crossed the distance between them in a rush. Dried
blood smeared his swollen upper lip and clung to the
corner of his mouth. A reddened knot stood out along
his jaw. "Guy, sit down. Did you crash into something?"

His mirthless laugh frightened her. "I always said you
were bright. You got it right in one shot. I crashed into
something. Or, to be more exact, it crashed into me."

She didn't know what to do first. "Shouldn't we get
you to a hospital for X rays?"

"This sounds like a replay of something I remember," he said. "Stop wringing your hands. I'm not
going to die. Not from this, anyway."

"Where's the jeep? Was anyone else hurt? Sit down
and I'll clean up your face."

Guy dropped onto the couch and closed his eyes.
"The jeep is in its usual mint condition. No one but me
is hurt. And I don't want you to play Florence Night-
ingale for me. I want you to love me—as I am—for
whatever I am. I just want you to love me."

Leah opened her mouth, but no sound would come.
Yes, she loved him. She loved him more than she loved

her life, but for a marriage to work, there had to be more than one totally committed partner.

She tore her gaze from his bruised face and went to the kitchen sink. What had she done with the bowls? Sun, glancing off stainless steel, broke into blinding fragments, and she covered her eyes.

Guy's arm, circling her shoulders, jolted her. He pulled her back against his chest. "I'm sorry," he murmured into her hair. "I never meant to hurt you, Leah. Please believe that."

Hyperventilation must feel like this, she thought. She drew in a deep, slow breath. "I do believe it."

"Then will you give me a chance to spill all the crazy notions that led up to what I did?" He was trembling. "Let me talk for as long as it takes to get it out. Then, if you still feel the same way about me, I'll get out of your life. For good."

Leah rested her chin on his tanned forearm, registering for the first time that he wore his black shirt. She gently clasped his wrist and faced him. Blood stained the stiff white band at his throat. "How *did* this happen to you, Guy?" She touched his jaw lightly as he winced.

"Someone who cares almost as much about you as I do decided to wake me up. He seems to think I've done something to make you want to run away from Phoenix. I'm lucky he isn't better fed. He'd have killed me."

"Dan?" Leah's eyes widened. "Oh, Dan, Dan. That's got to be one of the sweetest kids around. We both know he is. And he hit you. He didn't mean it, Guy. He's just confused."

Guy gave a wry grimace. "I know. But for a sweet kid he packs quite a punch."

"And you let him do it. He's lucky he didn't pick on someone who'd hit back."

"What makes you think I didn't flatten him?" Guy tilted his head. He was very close.

Leah's nostrils flared. Her eyes prickled now. "I know you too well. You wouldn't even think of hitting him." She pressed her lips together. It would feel so good to feel Guy's arms around her.

"Right." Guy sighed. "You know me well enough to be sure I wouldn't hit Dan—even while he was destroying my face. Why don't you know all the other things that go on in my head? Like whatever I've done about us—however badly I've loused up—I always intended to do what was right. I'm only human, remember?"

Her legs quivered inside. What was she supposed to do, to say? She turned on the faucet and grabbed a wad of tissues from a box on the counter. "This has to be cleaned." The jerky pressure she applied to his upper lip brought Guy's swift intake of breath. "Plain old warm water will do for a start. Then I'll hunt for some antiseptic." She needed time to think.

Guy, removing the sodden tissues from her hand, cut off her mental flight. "I've had a little nosebleed," he rasped. "Not a car wreck resulting in multiple contusions. I don't need antiseptic. I need you—listening to me. And giving me a chance—giving *us* a chance."

He led her to the couch, and she settled wordlessly into a corner. Guy sat at the other end, leaning forward, his elbows on his knees.

"By the time you arrived here, I knew Susan was starting divorce proceedings," he said dully. "There was no reason to blurt that out unless I had solid evidence that you might be as interested in me as I was in you."

Leah tucked her feet beneath her and rested a cheek on the back of the couch.

"Then there was that night when I kissed you—"

"When I forced myself on you, you mean," Leah interrupted.

"No." Guy swiveled toward her. "It's impossible to force yourself on a man who's done nothing but dream of making love to you since the first moment he laid eyes on you. And it was that way with me, Leah."

"Guy—"

"Please let me get this all out. I kept trying to figure out what was best for you. That's where I went wrong from the word go. I fell in love with you when you were still another man's wife. I even detested him for having you. Seeing him with you made me feel pure hate for the first time in my life." Sweat gleamed on his forehead. "Then, when you came to me, I was determined that if you were going to really be mine, I wasn't going to make the mistakes Charles made."

Leah sat upright. "Charles was good to me."

"I know, I know." Guy reached for her hand and held it fast between both of his. "But he made you dependent. When I saw you there in that—that gilded cage he'd made for you, I felt helpless. And cheated. Even then I sensed what you *could* be if you had a chance to grow. Oh, I didn't know what your strengths were, but I knew you had them and weren't using them. And..." His gaze bored into her. "And I wanted you for myself, because you were also the most beautiful, desirable woman I'd ever seen. I went away from you with a hole where my heart used to be. Every night I went to sleep seeing those incredible blue eyes of yours and trying not to imagine how soft you'd feel if you were beside me. Leah, I made love to you in my mind, over and over, from the night we met. When we were finally together, it was the realization of a dream I'd lived."

The small voice that said, "I thought about you, too," didn't sound like her own.

"I'm going to say the rest of this fast, so listen closely." He stood with enough force to bounce Leah on the couch. "If I miss something, you can tell me when I've finished. I should have told you the divorce was in progress. I should have told you when it was final. A hundred times I intended to, but I was scared. I was terrified that you'd quit school and turn into my shadow, the way you were Charles's shadow. Having you do nothing but center your existence around me wouldn't exactly be hard to take, but it wouldn't be right. And I would never have felt right about it. I wanted you to be all you could be and still be mine.

"But I was wrong for not letting you make your own decisions. I kept telling myself I was helping you to be free when in fact I was controlling every move you made like a human puppeteer. I pulled your strings, sweetheart. And I don't blame you for being mad."

Leah dug her nails into the side seams on her jeans and waited. She'd know when it was time to say something.

He stopped pacing. "Last night you said I was afraid of permanent commitment. By this morning, I was so shaken up, I'd almost decided you were right. You weren't. I'm more than ready to commit myself wholly to you. And we would have a successful marriage, because I wouldn't make the mistakes I made when I was a kid infatuated with his own importance.

"Finally, I didn't ask you to marry me because I wanted to cut off parish gossip. I asked you because it's what I really want—have wanted—for months. And, in case you still have doubts about that, the parish doesn't figure in this anymore.''

Leah's head snapped up. ''The parish is always going to figure in what we . . . in what *you* do.''

He turned the corners of his mouth down. ''Wrong. I quit.''

For several seconds, only the steady whirl of the air conditioner broke the silence. Leah slowly lowered her feet to the floor and stood. ''Quit?'' she said softly. ''You quit. Guy, you resigned, officially?''

''I'm going to,'' he said firmly. ''The letter's written. It would have been mailed if Dan hadn't decided to come for a chat. But I'm going to mail it, and if you'll have me, we'll get married, I'll start a new career, and you can carry on with your schooling. I thought—''

''You didn't think,'' Leah squeaked. ''As usual, you made a snap decision on what was best for me, only this time you included you. You're getting worse, not better.''

Guy's mouth fell open; then he sniffed and passed a hand across his face. A trace of fresh blood appeared beside his mouth. ''You mean you won't marry me.'' It was a flat statement, and she saw him blanch. ''There's nothing I can do to change your mind?''

''Oh, Guy. You dear, wonderful man. Lie down before you fall down.'' She pushed him onto the couch and maneuvered him into a supine position with a cushion beneath his head. Carefully, she lifted his lip and peered underneath. ''There's a cut in here, too. That Dan may have missed his calling. We'll turn him into a professional boxer.''

''I'll turn him into mincemeat when I get my hands on him again,'' Guy spat out.

"Shh," she ordered. "My turn. You aren't sending that letter."

"Why?" He frowned. "Because you're turning me down? I can't stay here without you either, Leah. I don't think I'd be any good to those people after all that's happened. I need someone to guide *me* for a change."

Leah sank down beside Guy, scooting him over to make room. "When two people get married, aren't they supposed to do that for each other? Be guides, I mean?" She didn't wait for his answer. "Well, they are. So you're going to have a guide."

He sat up and grabbed her. "We're going to get married?"

"Unless you want me to sue for breach of promise. You asked last night, remember? And I accepted." She worked the gold band of intertwined hands from her finger and held it up. "We already have the ring. The only wedding ring I could ever want. You even bought it to fit on my left hand."

"Oh, thank God. And I've got an engagement ring I've been blubbering over for days." He tugged the box from his pocket and slipped the sapphire band onto her unresisting finger.

Leah stared at pinpoints of light in dark blue. "It's beautiful, Guy. I'm going to cry again. But nothing would mean as much if we can't stay here. This place is my home now."

He looked away. "You want me to stay at St. Mark's?" he asked, rubbing a hand over his eyes.

"Yes. I'll just have to remember to make sure I grab your attention every time you start getting too preoccupied." Leah bent to brush her lips across his temple. "And do you think I could give up Dan now or Wally or good old Elsie? Everyone needs a challenge."

Guy wrapped her tightly in his arms. "I want to kiss you so badly. This damn mouth..." He held her away, a tender glow in his green eyes. "What kind of things will you do to me if I get preoccupied?"

Leah smiled and kissed the undamaged side of his jaw. "I'll reorganize your study," she said, laughing. "But first, can you arrange for us to be married in St. Mark's?"

He buried his fingers in her hair. "St. Mark's it'll be. My good people wouldn't accept anything less."